Also by Dawn Clifton Tripp

Moon Tide

The Season of
Open Water

The Season of
Open Water

A NOVEL

Dawn Clifton Tripp

RANDOM HOUSE NEW YORK

Library of Congress Cataloging-in-Publication Data

Tripp, Dawn Clifton.
The season of open water: a novel /
Dawn Tripp.— 1st ed.
p.   cm.
ISBN 1-4000-6187-3 (alk. paper)
1. Young women—Fiction. 2. World War,
1914–1918—Veterans—Fiction. 3. Westport
(Mass.: Town)—Fiction. 4. Grandparent
and child—Fiction. 5. Brothers and
sisters—Fiction. I. Title.
PS3620.R57S53 2005
813'.6—dc22   2004059323

Printed in the United States of America on
acid-free paper

www.atrandom.com

2 4 6 8 9 7 5 3

Book design by Dana Leigh Blanchette

for my mother and father

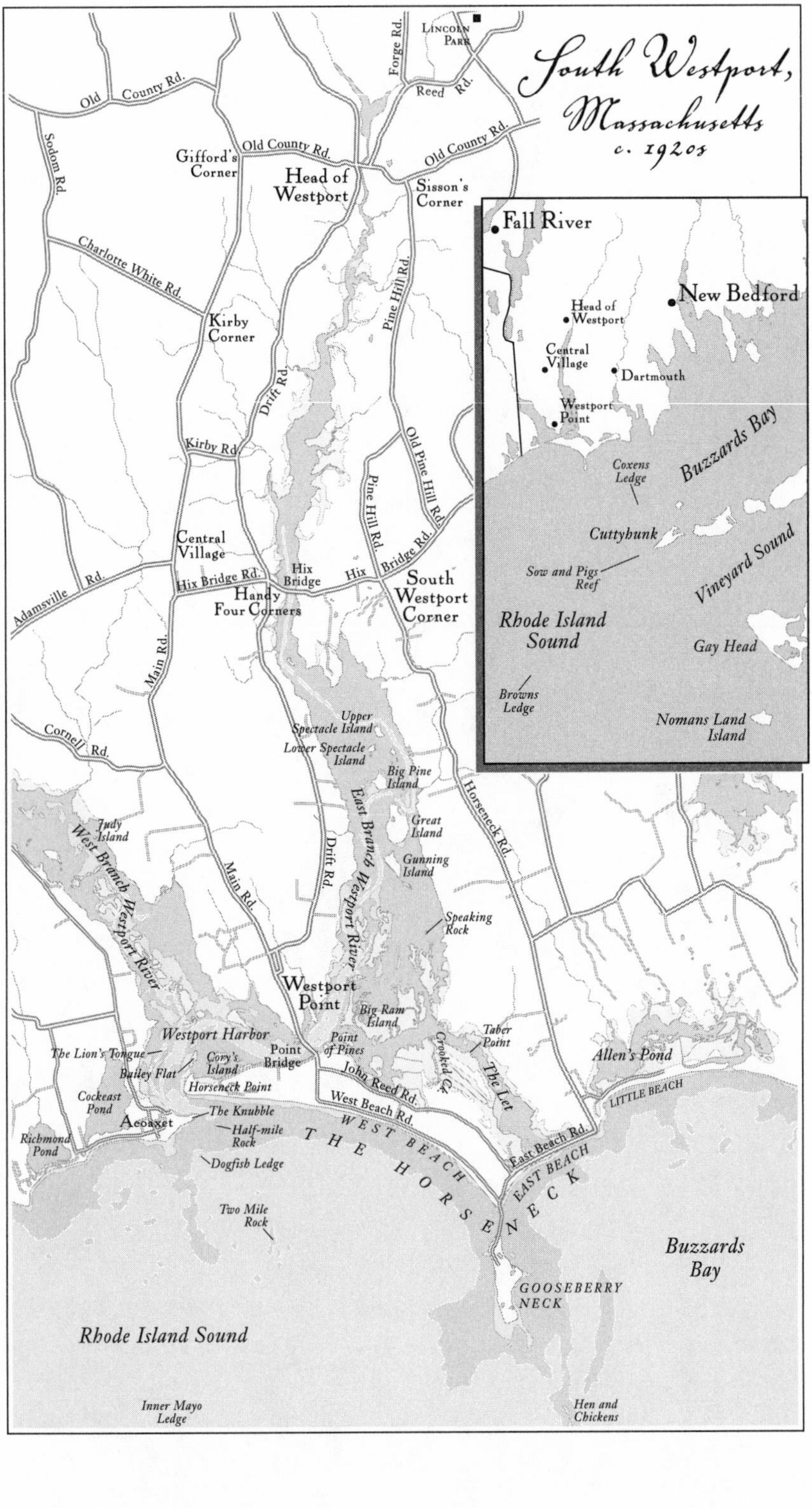
South Westport, Massachusetts
c. 1920s
Lincoln Park
Forge Rd.
Reed Rd.
Old County Rd.
Old County Rd.
Old County Rd.
Sodom Rd.
Gifford's Corner
Head of Westport
Sisson's Corner
Charlotte White Rd.
Kirby Corner
Drift Rd.
Pine Hill Rd.
Old Pine Hill Rd.
Kirby Rd.
Pine Hill Rd.
Central Village
Hix Bridge Rd.
Hix Bridge
Hix Bridge Rd.
Handy Four Corners
South Westport Corner
Adamsville Rd.
Main Rd.
Cornell Rd.
Upper Spectacle Island
Lower Spectacle Island
Big Pine Island
Great Island
Gunning Island
East Branch Westport River
Horseneck Rd.
Judy Island
West Branch Westport River
Main Rd.
Drift Rd.
Speaking Rock
Westport Point
Big Ram Island
Westport Harbor
Taber Point
The Lion's Tongue
Cory's Island
Point Bridge
Point of Pines
Crooked Cr.
The Let
Allen's Pond
Bailey Flat
John Reed Rd.
Horseneck Point
Cockeast Pond
Acoaxet
The Knubble
West Beach Rd.
Little Beach
Richmond Pond
Half-mile Rock
West Beach
East Beach Rd.
East Beach
Dogfish Ledge
The Horseneck
Two Mile Rock
Buzzards Bay
Gooseberry Neck
Rhode Island Sound
Inner Mayo Ledge
Hen and Chickens
Fall River
New Bedford
Head of Westport
Central Village
Dartmouth
Westport Point
Buzzards Bay
Coxens Ledge
Cuttyhunk
Sow and Pigs Reef
Vineyard Sound
Rhode Island Sound
Gay Head
Browns Ledge
Nomans Land Island

The Season of
Open Water

Noel remembers it this way:

It was the season of open water, of breeding, spawning, rooting, of thaw—a season brief, sudden, extravagant.

They had rounded the Cape, climbed halfway up the Pacific, then heaved to at Lahaina. They restocked the slops: casks of salt pork, fresh fruit, water, flour. They breamed the bottom of the hull, added another layer of oak sheathing to the bow, and continued north, in search of whales.

They spotted two early on, took them both, then had no luck for over a month. They scoured the North Pacific Grounds and shied into the fringes of the Arctic: through Seventy-two Pass, the Bering Strait, and up along that uncertain coast toward Icy Point.

It was 1868. Noel was seventeen. He had the strength of lions in his hands. With the other ship's carpenter, he stripped the resin pitch off the whaleboats and repainted the hulls white so they would seam into the ice. As he worked, he kept one eye skinned to the horizon, and still the ship pressed on, adrift for weeks through the endless daylight, the moon like an unfinished thumbprint lasting through the sky.

The season of whaling in the Arctic was brief: the ice melting, the water opening. The earth began to ripen: flowers busting up out of the tundra earth, blue spiked lupine, wild crocus, yellow poppy. The pack ice split to floes, and the trout ran thick through the hard fast streams; caribou, ptarmigan, lemmings, jaegers, terns. The sunlight blinding off the glaciers made their eyes ache, and still they cruised, as the leads widened, the snow softened out, and the water rushed over the ice.

They sailed west in the morning, east in the afternoon, tacking back and forth through the floes, waiting for some sign of the whale they had come to hunt, waiting for a slick or a spout, a fin or a blow. They listened for her call, that low and telling sound—a slow bellow. They waited for the black warp of her back to break out of a drift.

Once, as they came upon a flat meadow of ice, the whiteness exploded up and took itself to wing—not ice at all, but a raft of snow geese. The birds pulled together into shoals. Their wings hammered through the sky above the ship. Every man of the crew stopped his work and watched them, their barking cries shattering the stillness.

When he thinks back on it now, Noel remembers that he had loved the tedium, the haunting vacancy of days, the queer, indifferent light, the slow drift among the rotting bergs. But that same tedium made the other men restless. It needled them—they knew they had little time to do what they had come to do. The Arctic was a ruthless place, a treacherous and godforsaken place. Its lull was fragile: the wind could seize up, a gale blow in; on an instant, the ice could freeze and lock behind them. The waiting made the men edgy, feverish and cruel. They picked at one another, broke out in fights. They did not shave. They did not stop work on Sundays. Then they spied the walrus pod, the mothers breaching with their young. They set upon them.

They killed four hundred in two days—an unthinkable number. They slaughtered them. The cows screamed, clutching their pups under their flippers as they died and were hoisted on deck. They yielded little, but the men strained the meat for what oil could be rendered. They worked them through until the entire pod was taken and the water turned black and red, their carcasses drifting like a city of the dead through all the seas around them.

Now, more than half a lifetime since, and still every night, Noel dreams of the sea. But not of this. He does not dream of this.

Part I

October 1927

Bridge

Bridge first meets Henry Vonniker at the gathering after her cousin Asa's funeral. She does not see him right away. She does not notice when he comes into the room. She sits on a chair against the wall, a plate of food resting on her knees. She wears a white blouse, a wool skirt, and hard black shoes. The yellow glow of the kerosene light plays across the top edge of her plate, and she slides her knife through a boiled potato, splitting it in half. Steam rises from the flesh.

It is early evening, after candlelight. The room is crowded. The dead man's mother and his sister cry quietly in one corner. Two men, dairy farmers from Blossom Road, stand in front of Bridge, their backs turned toward her. They talk about Asa—how he had made quite a name for himself in the rum-running trade, then double-crossed the wrong man.

"Went all the way to Texas to get out of trouble," one remarks. "And trouble followed him all the way out there." The man speaking is a big man, a gray wool jacket tight across his shoulders.

"Did Asa find work out in Texas?"

"Yeah. Hauling water to the roughnecks at the oil wells. Talk was, someone wanted the job and killed him for it. Hard to believe—the guy slips out of the booze here, slips out by the skin of his teeth, then gets knocked off selling water."

The other man, black-haired and smaller, in a pinstripe suit, doesn't answer. He digs one hand into his pocket and glances over his shoulder. He notices Bridge sitting behind them. His eye trails down her leg. Then he catches her eye on him. His face flushes and he looks away, ashamed. He draws his handkerchief from his trouser pocket. A folded ten-dollar bill falls to the floor. He does not notice it.

Bridge stays with her knife and fork poised, staring at the dropped bill that lies less than six inches from her shoe. The two farmers go on talking about the dead man, one saying how he remembers when Asa was a boy, his uncle took him to the first World Series in 1903, the year the Boston Pilgrims beat the Pittsburgh Pirates. When slugger Buck Freeman popped one high into the crowd, Asa—nine years old—reached up and caught that ball with his bare hands.

"He caught a ball alright—small shiny bullet kind between the eyes. Black luck runs through that whole brood."

Bridge bites her lip as the smaller, dark-haired man clears his throat and jerks a slight nod over his shoulder at her. The big man turns and takes her in. He smiles. She smiles back and goes on cutting up her food.

"Just saying the way I see it, Leo," the man says, turning back around. He pauses, then remarks, "Pete Lowry came in earlier. Did you see that? He's short on brains to show up here."

Bridge slices off a piece of turkey and spears it with her fork. Without looking down, she slides her right foot across the floor and covers the ten-dollar bill with her shoe.

"Who's the natty dresser over there?"

"Where?"

"In the corner. Standing with Millie."

"Oh that's Vonniker. Forget the first name. He's Millie's boss at the mill."

"Never seen him before."

"Lives down on West Beach. The big house near the causeway. Was a doctor once. War ate him up."

"War'll do that."

"To some."

They fall silent for a moment, looking toward the corner of the room. Without taking her shoe off the bill on the floor, Bridge leans slightly forward in her chair and follows their gaze.

Across the room next to Asa's mother stands a man in a dark suit. Bridge has never seen him before. He wears glasses. The bones of his face are strong, and he is tall, a few inches taller than Bridge's brother, Luce. As Bridge watches, the man sits down in the empty chair next to Millie Sisson. He says something to her and takes her hand, and Bridge can sense a sadness flow between them. Millie begins to weep again, her old eyes swollen, and the man does not bend closer; he does not try to say or do anything to mute her grief; he just sits there with her, quietly, holding her hand.

Bridge sits back in her chair. She does not think of them again. She is thinking of the ten-dollar bill under her shoe. She cuts up another potato and eats it, killing time as the two farmers talk. After a while, they move outside for a smoke, and when they do, she lays her plate on the small table next to her, bends down, and with her napkin, pretends to rub at a smudge on the side of her shoe. She lifts her foot, slips the bill into her hand, then into the pocket of her skirt.

She straightens up again and looks around the room. The crowd has begun to thin. Millie Sisson is still in her corner, more composed now, her hands folded in her lap. The chair beside her is empty. Against the wall by the doorway that leads into the kitchen stands Bridge's grandfather, Noel, yarning with his old shipmate Rui. Her eyes soften as she watches them. They will be grumbling about the scallop season, she guesses, how the catch has been skinny so far—the fault of a too wet summer. Rui might mention the busted gunwale on his skiff. He will try to talk Noel into fixing it. Her grandfather holds a mug of coffee, his broad weathered fingers wrapped around it. Beyond them, in the kitchen, Bridge's mother, Cora, is washing dishes in the soapstone sink. White crockery heaps, rinsed and glowing, on the wooden counter next to her.

Bridge stands up and walks outside onto the back porch.

The night air is damp and cool on her legs. A knot of men stand around a fire in the yard, her brother, Luce, among them. They feed the burn from a pile of scrap—boards and shingles, chunks of punk wood. They laugh and talk and pass around two canning jars of homemade gin. The heat wrinkles the air. Bridge watches Luce's face, flushed and wavering in the flames and smoke. He has loosened the collar of his shirt. She walks over to him. He smells of the drink and the fire.

"Tell Ma I'm going home," she says.

"Had enough?"

She nods.

"You gonna walk?"

"Yeah."

"Smells like rain."

"I'll be fine."

"Wait a bit. I'll get Billy to drive us."

"When?"

"Half hour or so."

"Alright then. I'm going to take a walk down to the pond."

He grins and bends toward her, his breath near her ear. "Watch out for Asa."

She walks away from him across the sloped yard.

"Little sister's looking fine, Luce," she hears someone say behind her.

"Put a bung in it, Mills," Luce snaps.

Bridge climbs up onto the dirt path that borders the millpond and walks toward the woods. The grass is tall and wet. The smell of the fire fades out behind her, replaced by the sharp clean scent of trees. There are rings around the moon, glowing yellow and blue in the fog. The moon is heavy on the surface of the millpond. The water seems to bend under the weight of the light.

She hears voices ahead of her on the path—men's voices, angry. She sees a flash of white behind the old pump house. She slips into the trees and strains her eyes—shadows moving—a white shirt— two men, no, three. She continues walking toward them, slowly, quietly. She keeps behind the trees.

She recognizes two of Asa's older brothers, Mike and Jude Sisson, and a third man, blond and thin, who she knows by sight as Peter Lowry from the north part of town. Jude is holding Lowry by the arms, and Mike, a good six inches shorter than Lowry but wide as a bait barrel, is right up close to him, his finger in the other man's face.

"Telling you, Mikey, Asa was my friend," Lowry says, his voice slurred.

"Hell of a friend," says Mike. "You show up just to be sure we put him in the ground. Show up in the bag to boot."

"Telling you, Mikey, it wasn't me who snitched—"

Mike hits him hard in the gut. Lowry crumples, but Jude holds him up, and Mike hits him again. Lowry gags.

"Shit, he puked on my shoes." Mike takes a step back and drags his feet through the grass. He runs his other hand over his knuckles. "He's a bony one, Jude." He steps back in again toward Lowry. "No room for blue jays in this town."

"It wasn't me—"

And Mike begins to work him over, the punches thrown slowly, evenly paced, intentional, his fist sinking into the other man's body. Bridge watches them from behind a tree. She does not take her eyes off them. What they are doing does not feel wrong to her. It does not make her feel anything. It is an act of reliable violence, clear-cut and justified. The order of things. Mike deals Lowry one swift, stunning punch to the head, and Lowry's face snaps sideways, his chin falls forward toward his chest, a small sound whining out of him, then silence. Mike steps back. He nods. Jude lets go. Lowry drops to the ground.

Mike wipes off his hands on his trousers. He takes out a cigarette. "You got a match, Jude?"

"Nope."

"I got a box somewhere." Mike fishes through his pockets.

"He'll sleep it off, you think?" Jude asks.

"Well, he's not close to dead."

"Won't be as pretty for a while."

Mike has found his matches. He strikes one against the box. The flame illuminates his face as he draws in on the cigarette. He throws the spent match at Lowry. "He will get dead by somebody one of these days. He's marked for it. But that somebody won't be me."

Jude gives Lowry a small kick in the thigh. He doesn't move. The two men start back toward the house. They pass close by Bridge without seeing her, and continue on the path around the millpond. Their smells drift back to her, sweat and fresh smoke. She breathes softly in the shadow of the tree. She watches them until they have passed down the knoll and she can see them crossing up the yard toward the fire. They fold in among the other men. Behind them, the house glows—smooth yellow light through the windows, the curtains curved inside them. Her heart beats strongly in her chest. Her hands are damp. She looks toward the man lying on the ground. His hair is thick and fair, and there is mud in it. He stirs, groans. He tries to push himself up, and she goes to move toward him, to help him. She catches herself, stops. He folds his arm under his head and slumps back down again. She looks away, toward the millpond. The beauty of it startles her. The water, the light wind scattering across it, the woods deep, untouched, and still—all of it so serene, it takes her breath, and for a moment she feels that the hardness of her world has softened. A sadness sweeps through her, for Millie, for Jude and Mike, for Asa. He was young to die—just a few years older than her brother, Luce—too young and it had happened. He had fled the earth or got kicked off the edge of it. Either way, it didn't matter. It was done.

She walks slowly back toward the house to look for Luce. But he is not outside by the fire. She sees Mike and Jude Sisson, and they stare, seeing her walk out of the woods, knowing, perhaps fearing, what she saw. She stares back at them. Mike gives her a weak smile. She nods at him. He looks away.

She walks into the house and scans the room, but there is no sign of Luce, no sign of her grandfather Noel, or her mother. She sees Millie, still sitting in her corner, her hands still folded on her lap, eyes closed, as if she has resigned herself to that chair. But apart from Millie, the room seems full of strangers, people she might have known an hour ago, they all seem distant to her now. Again she feels a slight wrench in her heart, and she turns to leave the room, the house, to get back outside into the cool and open air. She notices him then—the man Vonniker—standing alone. On the wall behind him is a crude sketch of a ship drying sail. Without intending to she stops, her eyes on his face. He is close to her, looking away, across the room, but close enough that she can see the smooth planes of light across his cheekbones, the fractured lines at the corners of his eyes. Her hand goes to the pocket of her skirt, the folded edges of the stolen ten-dollar bill, crisp and dry against her skin. He glances at her suddenly, and for a moment—it only takes a moment—his eyes touch hers.

He smiles. She feels her face flush. She turns on her heel, walks out the door and runs straight into Luce.

"I was looking for you, Bridge."

"Then let's go."

"You look queer."

"I'm fine."

"See a ghost down there by the pond?"

"I saw nothing. Come on, let's go."

Noel

The cold morning air bristles his skin as he sits up in bed. The pain in his left thigh stabs when he lands his weight on the floor—it is an old wound, an ancient break, only sometimes healed.

He pulls on his underclothes. He passes the closed door to his granddaughter Bridge's room and takes the narrow steps down into the kitchen.

"Still letting that girl of yours bang nails in the shop?" his old friend Rui had asked him the night before. "I know you don't want to hear it, but what kind of life you think that's going to be for her when you're gone?"

Rui was right. Noel saw it clearly. Bridge was eighteen now, and he had no idea what kind of future he could build for her. The worry of it fell like a weight on his shoulders and left him feeling empty.

In the kitchen, the woodstove is already lit. His daughter, Cora, has set out his trousers and boots to warm beside it. Through the worn cracks in the kitchen floor, he can see her shape moving through the cellar, mixing a fresh batch of soap for her washing. He can smell the lye.

He pours himself a coffee. There is a plate on the counter with a wedge of cake and some lemon squares left over from the gathering after Asa Sisson's funeral.

He takes a piece of the cake and sits down on a chair. The suit he wore to Asa's, his only suit, his funeral suit, is hanging in the doorway. Cora will brush it out before she puts it away in the cedar chest. He sips his coffee and thinks of the day, a few years ago, when he saw Asa outside of Shorrock's store talking to Honey Lyons. He knew even then that, for Asa, it would all come down to trouble. It wasn't that he couldn't understand the draw of the rum-work for a bold local kid—the lure of the money, the adventure. It could seem like an easy ticket, perhaps the only ticket, to a better life. It was one thing, though, to do the simple jobs for the local rummies—to drive a wagonload of liquor or keep a lookout in exchange for a whack of cash when times were tight. But to get tangled up in more than that, as Asa had, was to risk too much for too little. You'd wind up fast with the wrong crew, then wearing your suit for that last time.

Noel sets his cup in the sink, ties on his boots, and steps outside into the fog.

The damp cold works into him as he walks to the privy. He stubs open the door with the toe of his boot. There is a pail of corncobs and Sears catalogues on the floor by the seat. He can hear the holler of the crows through the slatted pine walls. He tears out a page from one of the catalogues. A cool wind brushes up between his legs.

He crosses the yard to the barn. Cora has let the hens out of the shed. They scratch at the dirt. He throws them another handful of meal. Then, he hitches the mare to the wagon, loads the mucking rake, a pitchfork, and two buckets into the bed, and hauls himself up onto the wide plank seat.

He heads south into the fog. The world swirls in around him, and his mind begins to leak and stretch and give—gusts of fog like the breath of some great god bank each side of the road—and in the whiteness of his own breath mixing with the cold dense air, he can see the things that used to be: his boyhood on Nomans Land, the stiff green light lying offshore, his mother's black hair, and the frowning colored cliffs of Gay Head across the shoal. He can see the lapstrake boats his father and the other men worked out of, tied three-deep in the ladder shale off Stony Point. In the fall and spring, they would handline for cod and spread the catch out to cure in the sun. They would lay down the dead fish, gutted and dressed, on the round clean stones. At times, the whole rocky end of the island, all five acres, was covered with that white blanched flesh.

It is the fog that warps time. It is the fog that allows his life to extend behind him, ahead of him, the narrow of the road pulled under the wagon, with the known steady rhythm of Magdalyn's hooves as they beat against the oiled dirt. In the fog, the world loses its borders, its abrasiveness, its contour. There are no loose boards of remembering for him to trip on. No land to put off from or row toward. Driving through the fog is the closest he comes now to being at sea, and it was living at sea that had taught him there was nothing on land a man could hold on to, and when they died—his mother, his father, his wife—he let them drop like pins behind him.

As he drives, thoughts come to him, on the wind, on the fog. Thoughts about his grandchildren, Luce and Bridge, his hopes for them, his wondering what turns their lives might take. Luce at least, he feels, is somewhat settled. He has good work at the icehouse. Decent work and steady. Bridge is the one Noel worries after. He knows well enough she's not the kind of girl who will end up teaching school, folding a man's shirts or polishing his shoes. She loves to work in the shop, the dirt and the dust. She loves to plow out the garden and dig quahogs off the flats. She's a different sort of creature, a little fierce and free, and it makes Noel smile to think on it. At the same time, it troubles him.

Noel had been strong as a boy, hard as a young man. On ship, he had lived for months on salt horse, hardtack, foul pork—they called it walking food—so full of maggots and those small mites that grow in fetid air. He had crunched their spines in his teeth.

His body is an old hull now, barnacle-crusted, planks rotted out at the seams. A weight in sore need of heaving down. One eye has grown slouched in his cheek and is no good for seeing. Now, two years shy of eighty, years of living heaped on his shoulders, the doings of the world have ceased to frighten or amaze him, and when his mind grows unruly, he will rope it in and tie it down the way he would serve a piece of rigging, square it off and pull it taut so the sheet will catch some wind but not too much, and they will sail together then, that way, the old man and his mind.

He continues on the road. A motorcar comes up behind him. He takes the reins to the mare's neck to guide her to the side. He lets the car pass. As he heads south, the fog begins to thin. The wind airs up. It drives through the trees and the panic grass that sprouts along the dirt shoulder of the road.

He reaches the top of the hill. The last farm is on his right, the heavy roll of fields down to the river. The fog hangs low. To the east, out over the ocean, the morning sky is clear. He can see down to the point that divides East Beach from Little Beach, a silver wetness brushed over the rocks, the road ahead of him slick with light.

The wind shovels out of the southwest and fills his ears. He passes Ben Soule's house on the knoll, the last house before the turn. He veers right onto East Beach Road.

It is after-season, and the road is quiet. The summer people have gone back to their cities, the cottages boarded up, the village shut down except for the post office store and the Gallows Pavilion with the bowling lanes in the cellar. All along the beach, dank piles of sea muck heap like the carcasses of walrus in the white light.

It is always this way. The mounds of sea muck in the fall always remind him of the round humped bodies of the walrus. They always remind him that he never told Hannah about how they had killed so many in those few days, early in the season of 1868. Three years before he met her. Hannah. His confessor. His lover. His witness. His wife. He had met her halfway across the world, then brought her home, and they had lived out their life together in the house on Pine Hill Road. This was the secret he had kept. The ache of it now is double fold. He could not have put it into words for her. Not then. Perhaps not even now. He could not have explained how the violence of those few days had changed him. He could not have explained that the crime of it was not the act itself—whatever kind of carnage that might have been. No, the crime of it was that they had taken them in that fertile season, the season of open water, in the midst of all that life.

He passes the post office and the Surfside Hotel. He takes the turn onto West Beach Road. The Model T runabout is parked in the driveway of the third cottage. Noel guides his wagon two houses farther down and parks at the edge of the road. He takes the rake and pails and walks through a wide opening in the box-hedge. He crosses the garden down to the low sand.

Spud Mason has driven his pigs down to the beach. They run squealing up from the tide line. They root through the muck and the rockweed, digging into the dank rich smell for fish parts, dead crabs, bugs. Their waste mixes in with the seawater. Noel chuckles to himself as he watches the pigs wander over the wide-flung lawns of the vacant summer houses. They loll in the grass. They root through the gardens, dig up the bulbs and munch them down.

Yesterday's storm has pulled the sea muck into steep packed cliffs, matted together with channels dug between them by the tide. Noel uses the rake to comb it loose. He pulls it apart and rakes it into smaller piles. He finds other sludge washed up—lobsters with their backs cracked, trash fish, broken glass. He finds a burlap sack with two bottles of bootleg liquor. With a tine of the rake he nudges open the cloth, and he can see the whiskey shot through with sun, the color of amber, a dilute gold. He slips a bottle into each deep pocket of his coat.

When he has raked out six piles, he goes back up for the wagon. As he is driving it down onto the beach, he glances up at the sea and, with his good eye, at the end of the bay he can just glimpse the darker outline of a boat breaking up—a bend in the light—an odd double shape—what is it? A boat and its reflection? No. He stands up, caps one hand over his eye. He squints, and his seeing sharpens. It is one boat towing a smaller boat. Stem to stern, they seem to be heading toward the harbor mouth.

Somebody had a bad night last night, he thinks to himself. Some black ship got nabbed oiled up with a full load. He touches his coat pockets—the harder heavy shapes of the bottles of whiskey. It was a dangerous business now. What had started out as a good-natured game of cat and mouse between the locals and the Feds turned cutthroat when the big-city syndicates started putting their fingers into every small-town pie. More and more money thrown around. More violence. More graft and crooked stuff. Everyone wanted a payoff or a cut. Half the town was in on it, while the other half looked the other way. Boys went out in boats to meet the mother ships anchored in Rum Row, and from time to time one wouldn't come back. Water was an easy place to lose a man.

Noel slips the bottles from his coat and tucks them under the seat of the wagon. Again he trains his eye on the two boats heading in. They have passed the bell. He can see that the larger boat is one of the new 75's—a Coast Guard cutter. As they come up on Half-mile Rock, he recognizes the black by her lines. It is Frank Mac-Donald's boat, the *Anna Louise*, named after his two daughters. A forty-six-foot lobster boat that pulled no traps. Frank had never been much of a fisherman, not much of a captain for sure. He'd been moving cases since '24. He was arrested once on land by the constable, dragged off to Fall River court, and fined two hundred dollars.

Three nights later, he was back at it. But now they had his ship in tow. Must have caught him with a full cargo this time. Must have caught him good.

"Fool to get caught, Frank, with all that ocean out there," Noel murmurs. He climbs down from the wagon, takes the pitchfork, and digs the tines into the piles of sea muck he has made. He tosses it up onto the wagon bed. With Bridge, he will shovel it against the base of the house. They will bank it up all the way around, to keep out the winter weather.

By half past seven, the wind has stiffened, pushing off the last of the fog, blue sky hollowed out behind it.

Noel breaks for a smoke. He sits down on a bench in someone's front yard. To the southeast he can see Cuttyhunk, the island in the shape of a woman lying on her side. He closes his eyes. He knows that there are certain types of love a man can lose himself to, other types that hammer down his insides until he is like beaten metal. Hannah grew more beautiful as she grew old. The life peeled away from her like husk, and her skin had thinned to the softest wrinkled silk before she died. They did not speak on that last day, but he held her hand until he felt the life slip out of his fingers. He sat with her body awhile longer, and he could feel her soul nibbling around, trying to find its way back in.

When he and Hannah were young, it had never occurred to him that one day she'd be gone and he'd be wobbling around without her. Now when he thinks of her, he thinks of their daughter, Cora, and of Cora's children: Luce, Bridge.

He opens his eyes and looks down at his hands: the gnarled fingers, the veins tough and raised under the skin. They are old hands.

He knows his life is a long coiled line inside him, and he knows it is unwinding.

He looks up as the young man comes out onto the porch of the third cottage. Henry Vonniker. Noel had been surprised to see him the night before at the Sisson house. He had never seen him out anywhere around town except here, down at the beach, or once in a while, driving up Horseneck Road. Every morning, in fair weather, it is the same—this young man steps out onto this same porch. He is somewhere in his early thirties, Noel would guess, always alone, thin glasses, brown hair cropped short in the back, the front ends longer with a slight unruly curl that skims his eyes. He wears pajamas and a flannel shirt. He holds a teacup. His hands are square, his fingers long. He wipes off a small table, sets the cup down, then sits in one of the wooden chairs. He looks out across the water. The bone along his jaw is strong-cut, distinct.

Noel has heard he was a doctor in the war. There is talk he saw too much there, and it broke him up. Noel can see this. He can see too that Henry Vonniker is the kind of man who didn't have the armor for what he saw. And now here they are, both down on the beach, each on his own, protecting his own solitude.

Noel looks west toward the harbor mouth. The 75 and the boat in tow have reached the Knubble Rock. They pass through the break in the coastline and disappear around the point.

Noel lights his pipe again and leaves the match in the bowl of a mosquito torch. The wagon bed is piled high with sea muck. He loads the fork and rake into the back, takes one of the smaller pails and wanders along the tidal zone. The moon jellies have washed up on the low beach, saucered, incandescent shapes, their eyes caked with sand. He kicks over a dead skate—one thick with meat, but dead too long. He gathers up a mess of sea clams. He will bring them home to Bridge so she can make a chowder or a pie.

As he is setting the full pail of clams into the shade of the wagon seat, Noel notices that the young man on the porch of the third cottage is gone. He draws the wagon through the soft sand to the road and sets off through the quiet summer village of East Beach.

Just before the Surfside Hotel, he sees Dirk McAllister in his new Buick touring car with the sleek soft top headed toward him down the road. A year ago, Dirk McAllister worked as a warper in the Fall

River Mills, and when the mills made the pay-cut, he couldn't scrape up two spare cents. Like half the town, he pulled his shades at night, huddled his wife and children into the kitchen, while the other half of the town passed by with trucks and wagons loaded full of liquor. Then, nine months back, Dirk started showing up with new things: a radio, a red bicycle for his youngest girl. A new telephone with a private line. He paid off his grub bill at Shorrock's store. He had a ham at Easter. Midsummer, someone gave him that new car, which was rumored to be fitted with hidden compartments along the driveshaft that could hold up to twenty sacks of booze. The word was that Dirk had taken up with the Point gang. He was making big runs to the city gin mills for Swampy Davoll. No one judged him for it. Eight mouths to feed. How could you judge a man for that?

The Buick slows, sunlight glinting off the wiper blades. Noel draws the wagon to a halt. Dirk McAllister rolls his window down.

"Fine day, Noel, isn't it?"

Noel shrugs. "Reckon Frank MacDonald's luck ran out last night."

"How's that?"

"Coasties must've caught up with him out there. Saw them dragging him in by the nose." Noel sees the expression on the other man's face change—the troubled look.

Dirk shakes his head, a grim smile. "Thanks for the tip, Noel."

"Don't know what good it does you."

"I'll have a look. See you around then."

"See you around."

As the Buick continues on toward Gooseberry Neck, Noel gives a light slap to the reins. He heads north up Horseneck Road.

Half a mile past South Westport Corner, he spies the carcass at the side of the road. A young fox. Recent kill. Neck snapped. The pool of urine steams off the dirt. The pelt is perfect, worth twelve dollars at least. The thought flashes through his mind to take it. As a boy, he would have skinned it straight there in the road, thrown the guts in a bush and gone to sell the pelt even before going home. But he is an old man now, and he knows it takes some time for the soul to work its way out of the bones. He knows there is a cost for messing with the dead. And so he stands over the carcass for a good slice of time. He shoos away the crows as the scales tip back and forth inside him—those two familiar voices warring through his brain. Finally, he picks the body up and lays it down carefully under a chokecherry bush. He will leave it, he thinks, but as he is turning toward the wagon, a dart of sunlight nips the tail and sparks the long red fur. The light strokes through the pelt like flames. He turns back.

His hip aches as he climbs up onto the plank seat. He lays the fox on the floor by his feet next to the two bottles of bootleg whiskey he had found on the beach, and he drives the rest of the way home. As he bears left into the drive, he sees them waiting for him: Honey Lyons and three strangers dressed in dark suits, soft hats, a fat-cat car. He drives the wagon up to them and climbs out. He can see the reflected sky in the glinting new black polish of their shoes. He knows what they have come for.

Bridge

It was Luce who had taught her how to steal: sinkers, jigs and fishing lures, bayberry candles, and a box of the new blue-tip matches. They stole a galvanized pail from the wharf store at the Point, a pair of oilers, and two cans of Campbell's soup. At night, in a hardscrabble darkness, she would place one foot in his knitted hands and he would pitch her over the stone wall into Elinor Baughan's apple orchard. They would take what they could carry, their pockets loaded full. They siphoned gas from the two-ton tractor at the Tripp Farm. They crept into Haskell Ashley's henhouse and filched the eggs from underneath the hens. Once, when they stole honey from Rebecca Martin's hive, the bees came out and tailed them down the road as they ran home. The swarm covered Luce's arm, a black humming sheath, and stung him elbow to shoulder so his arm turned the color of a fresh bruise with the poison and swelled to twice its size.

They stole tins of sardines and jars of black pearl roe from the gourmet shop in New Bedford. They stole half-pints of tobacco and rolling papers from

Shorrock's store. They stole sacks of coffee, bullets, shells, packets of condensed milk, white sugar, saltines, nails and screws, jars of vinegar, small plugged tins of kerosene.

On a day she was alone, Bridge stole a ladies' tortoiseshell comb from Abigail Dean's hat shop. It was Luce who found her that afternoon setting it into her hair before the mirror. He came toward her, his eyes dark and inscrutable. He drew the comb from her hair, and when she demanded it back, he laughed and held it out of reach. She flew at him. Her young fists brushed against his face, and he threw her to the floor, pinned her down by the wrists and pressed his face right up close to hers. The sunlight poured in through the window and covered them there.

They stole horseshoes from the blacksmith shop and made a game of it in the field by the river. They invented their own rules. They stole a bottle of whiskey from Peleg Mason's stash buried under the floorboards in the old Yankee powderhouse, and they took it with their cigarettes through the pine wood to the river and wasted themselves there in the salt marsh hay.

And it was Luce who pulled her down into that tough and matted grass. Her fingers raked his hair, their young throats on fire with the liquor and the smoke, their breath stained the air, thin and bluish clouds, and they tumbled there together, laughing, through the smells of drowned earth, honeysuckle, the briny reek of soaked salt hay. The hollow stalks of the reeds nicked her back. Past his shoulder she could see the roaming sky above their heads, the smashed light of the stars.

And as they lay there, quiet at last, side by side with the bottle set between them, staring up into that smooth, untroubled night, it was Luce who told her there was no such thing as God or fate or law. The world turned on its ear by chance, and he wrapped his hands over her eyes so her mind was nothing more than darkness. He dragged in off the cigarette, put his mouth on hers and blew the smoke deep into her lungs.

Bridge wakes late that morning after Asa Sisson's funeral. Past seven. The wind splits between the window sash and the frame—a low whistle through the warped sill. On the table next to the bed is the folded ten-dollar bill. She stares at it, remembering the night before: the man, Vonniker, the stranger, how he had looked at her for that brief moment, and how she had felt something inside of her move.

She pushes off the thought. He has no business, after all, in her thoughts.

She slips out of bed, pulls her clothes on quickly—the flannel shirt and overalls, the heavy wool socks she will strip off later when the sun has risen high enough to warm the day. She puts the ten-dollar bill under a book in the night-table drawer and closes it. She creeps through the narrow tunnel that runs under the eaves to the room where her brother lies asleep. The coarse wool wraps his body like bark. She crawls into the bed with him, the ritual of childhood. She can smell last night's drunkenness still on him. She knows he will wake up with his head in his feet and a sick raw taste in his throat from where the drink burned through.

She looks at his chest, his arms, the roughness of his hands. She finds traces of yesterday's work, traces of the hours he is away, a skid of grease on his wrist, dirt settled in the deep long lines that wrap his palm. She can smell the soil and the muck, the rotted hay from the icehouse, the baked dusty mud off the wagon paths he drives, delivering ice. She can smell the places he roams through, the casual detours he takes off his route when he grows annoyed or bored: the sassafras wood, the pine grove, the eelgrass of the marsh. She loves him this way most, when he is deep asleep, beyond waking, when she can dig through his roughness and find him for what she knows he is—tender as blackskin, easily scraped down by a fingernail.

He stirs, and his body turns to curve around her. She will give herself a quarter of an hour to lie this way. She will listen to the wind hack against the roof as it breaks up the last of the fog. She will listen for the slighter sound of the mouse scurrying back and forth on small tough claws between the plaster and the beams as the sun climbs and marks her time.

He shifts in his sleep. Out the window, the trees seem to be growing down from the sky. Their roots hook deep into the soil. She hears the sound of a car in the drive, an unfamiliar sound, the steady low coil of the engine and the push of wheels over the marl. The car stops below the window. She hears a short hard rap on the kitchen door, her mother's voice, and another voice, a man's voice. Gently, she lifts Luce's arm and slides out from underneath.

When she comes downstairs, the kitchen is empty. Through the window, she can see four men, three strangers and Honey Lyons, standing around a newly waxed black Model S Mercedes parked in the drive. Her mother, Cora, is crossing the yard, her arms full of the wet wash. She walks around the men, a wide circle, her eyes cast down to the left, her feet holding tight to some invisible curve on the ground, with that strange and skirting way she has had since her oldest child, Rose, fell through an eel hole axed out in the ice and was taken by the current underneath that foot-deep frozen surface all the way to the river mouth.

As Bridge stirs a cup of water into the white-cornmeal batter, she takes in the three strangers, their dark suits, polished shoes, gray soft-hats, Honey Lyons in his coarse leather jacket and khaki trousers, a stain at the knee. His face is ruddy, shaved too often, skin full of a light red rash. He glances up at the window, catches her watching them and shifts the ball of tobacco from one side of his mouth to the other. He grins, his teeth long and yellow, one chipped close to the gum. He walks over to the side of the car, leans to the window and says something to the man in the driver's seat. He walks with a slight limp, left over from a jump he took once off the Point

Bridge at low tide. He struck hard bottom, and his anklebone shattered like milkweed.

Cora comes back inside.

"Who are those men with him?" Bridge asks.

"Don't know."

"What do they want?"

"They're waiting on Noel."

"What for?"

"Didn't ask."

"You didn't ask?"

"No."

Her mother takes an armful of white shirts and puts them to soak in the first tub. She shaves in a handful of soap.

"Mary Milliken wants these shirts by afternoon," she says.

"Why didn't you ask them what they want from Noel?"

Cora shakes her head. "I'm not sure today's wind'll turn warm enough to dry them by afternoon."

Bridge sighs. She fries up the johnnycakes, eats one and wraps three for Luce to take with him to work. Then she tells Cora she is going up to Shorrock's store at the Head for a sack of flour.

"How be ya, Bridge?" says Honey Lyons as she steps off the porch. He touches his cap.

She nods at him, says nothing. She doesn't look at the other men. She walks past the boat shop into the woods toward the river.

She passes by the path that leads up to the old burial ground on Indian Hill. When she was a child, Noel took her there. He led her through the trees and showed her where they were put down—the seven crude and unmarked stones.

The moon is the home of the dead, he has told her. They come down to earth on its light. They travel in boats and tie up in the trees. They crawl under bark and live among the leaves. They sprout and grow and turn, holding fast to their branches through the winds and summer storms. He has told her that when a leaf falls, there is a cry not easily heard. And as she walks the rut path along the river toward the Head, she listens for that sound. She treads lightly on their thin and brittle shapes, corpses rustling under her feet.

Abiel Tripp is sitting out by the mail-stop, a sack of letters dropped off by the mail truck next to his chair on the porch. He bites down the stem of his pipe the way she has noticed that all blue-water men do, as if the years at sea had set a certain tremor in the jaw, a kind of restlessness that might have come from months of gnawing on hard bread, months of waiting, drifting through a nothing sea. It was a habit of Noel's. The stem of his pipe would always give out before the bowl. Abiel jerks his head at her as she walks by. He takes in her boots, her brown arms. She is scrawny as an oar. She wears her brother's cast-off overalls and an old cap. She is hand to mouth, he knows this. The family has been since the father died. But the girl wears it differently. There is no shame about her. No apology. Her boots are crusted with mud from walking the damp river ground. She takes the two steps up to the shade porch of Shorrock's store and slips through the door. She lays it closed without a sound on the jamb behind her.

Henry

The beauty of the world, he knows, is a dream, a trick, a sleight of hand.

The shots wake him at dawn. He comes downstairs, cracks the front door. The fog has begun to loosen. He can smell slick pools of water on the rolled dirt road from the rain of the night before. He checks, then rechecks the lock on the screen; it is his habit, it has no purpose, he knows this. There is no one to keep in, no one to keep out, but he does it every morning this same way, and why should this morning be any different?

He takes a sharp breath and draws in the rough smell of the sea, and for a moment he remembers the girl, the dark-haired girl he had seen at Millie Sisson's house the night before. He had been standing against the wall, feeling out of place, and he had looked up and seen her. She seemed to be observing him—her eyes luminous and steady—then she had turned abruptly and walked out the door.

He goes into the kitchen, measures out two cups of water, sets the pot to boil on the stove. He measures out the loose tea into the bob. His measuring is—has been since he returned from France—exact. He marks his watch. He will let the tea steep for four and a half minutes. No milk. A mite of sugar. He steps out onto the back porch.

Sheets of fog press low against the water. The swallows flock in small droves over the cottage. They clutch their wings into themselves, dive into a trench of wind, and then rise up again.

Henry sets his tea down on the side table, takes a clean rag from his toolbox, and sponges the salt and dampness from the seat of the chair.

There is a volley of shots from the neck. Seafowl—eiders, skunk ducks—heading out toward the sea to feed. The men come down early—local men. They leak out of the fog with their shotguns, cross the bar to the neck, and crouch behind the rocks and in the scrub. They pass-shoot into the flocks as the birds fly overhead.

It is a Thursday morning, October 1927—his fourth year living out the fall and winter in the cottage at the beach, his fourth year as a boss at one of the city mills. The summer people have left. Henry had watched them leave—a sudden exodus of touring cars stuffed with sun-umbrellas, trunks, clothes, paraphernalia, children, dogs hanging from the open car windows. The houses are empty. The beach is quiet. He settles back into the chair, a thick woolen blanket draped over his knees. He can feel the bones of the wood through the cushion. From the porch, he watches the seabirds as they wheel through the white and glaring light—crooked shadows, screeching cries.

This is his morning. Morning after morning. Day after day. This is his life.

He clings to his everyday order of waking, wash, shave. His everyday drive up Horseneck Road, then along the trolley route to the mill, where he will burrow for eight hours into a dark and stifling heat, the rhythmic strike and shutter of the looms. In the afternoons, he leaves at five, to retrace his morning route on the return trip home. He comes back to his chair on the porch and if the weather is fine, he will spend the rest of the daylight hours there, with a book on his lap, transfixed by the changing of the light, the changing of the water and the sky. And as the chair rocks back and forth, he will move outside that very careful, well-swept room he has built at his center. He will slide the lock, slip through, leave the door ajar behind him. He will move beyond himself, far beyond his own edges. At times he does not even know he has been gone until he finds himself returning, marked by the journey—grit in his eyes, wind-matted hair—the evidence of distances, the evidence of speed.

At night he reads. Plato, Aristotle, Epicurus. Theories of geometry and light. Theories of physics and evolution, war, culture, medicine, class. Laws of gravity. Laws of matter. Laws of planetary motion and celestial mechanics, electromagnetic charge. Laws are a solace. His books, a solace. Reading strips the body from the mind. He takes a small pleasure, an occasional pleasure, in music and in art. The work of de Chirico, the work of Picasso—the refraction of the world into blue-grief, cubes.

He sips his tea. It is cooling now. A tea leaf in the crude shape of a bird hits the rim of the cup. He picks it off.

From the porch, he watches the pigs rooting through Elizabeth Hawthorne's hydrangeas. He watches the old man farther down the beach. He has loaded his wagon full of sea muck, and now he walks along the tide line, gathering clams. Henry has seen him before. They have never spoken. Never exchanged greetings, words, names. The man's skin is tarnished, deeply lined. He always wears the same woolen coat. Today the sun is behind him and he is cut to shadow. Henry cannot see his features. He cannot see the mountains in his face. But he recognizes the lopsided gait, the steady and deliberate way he works. He can tell from the limp, from how the old man bears his weight on his right leg, that perhaps when he was in his midthirties, Henry's age, his left femur was broken, high, close to the hip. If it was splinted (and Henry doubts that it was), the position of the limb was deranged and so the break never properly set, never properly healed. But he is a tough old spider. This particular man. He comes down every day in every type of weather to work up what the tide hauls in.

Henry was born in Boston, 1895, the only son of a cotton broker. He went to Harvard, then to medical school, then to France in early 1917 with a corps of students under Harvey Cushing. He started at the *ambulance* in Paris, then moved in soggy weather to the triage hospital close to the front, north of Armentières. He saw torn throats, wrecked faces, bleeding vessels that could not be secured, lungs shrunk to the size of a nickel by the gas. He sopped and shaved and cleansed maggot-crusted limbs. He stood on a plain above a chestnut grove under a clear and perfect sky, and when the sky exploded, they flattened themselves and hugged the earth.

Once, as he was crossing from the operating tent to the tree for a smoke, a shell burst overhead and he saw a man twenty yards away split at the waist, his top half blown to nothing, his legs kept on walking several paces before they crumpled at the knees.

After a while, Henry noticed that the horrors were not horrors. His mind had grown elastic to accommodate even the worst of what he saw.

He stayed on for six months after the war with the residual men at the military hospital near the tumbled wreck of Reims. He arrived home in the spring of 1921 with the luster of a hero and a career in full swing. He secured a lecturing position at the medical school, met the daughter of financier John P. Harkness and married her. The failing happened slowly. He began to lose his capacity to diagnose. Then a tingling that began in his right foot spread up his leg, hobbled him as he walked. Nerve-related. He knew that. But they could not locate the source. The trembling spread through his chest and down his right arm. He could not hold a scalpel without a tremor in his hand. He could not make a stitch across the simplest of cuts.

He left his practice, his marriage, the city. Without a look back, he came down to his father's cottage on the beach one week one summer and did not leave.

He took a job as a manager at the Narragansett Mill in New Bedford. He folded himself quietly into the factory world and felt his mind sink away into the dank air thick with cotton dust. He noticed that, after the first several months, his lungs began to grow heavy, his breathing shallow, his brain dull, his thoughts more soft. He liked the simplicity of the work, the simplicity of the language, the habits of the workers. He tuned himself to the whir and the slap of the belts. He took a particular comfort in the swift decisive motion of the shuttle running the weft through the warp, and gradually the sounds of the mill and the sultry air washed down the stutter from his limbs, so he moved again like an everyday man, through the long, high-ceilinged rooms, the albatross machinery, the rows of sloped, gray shoulders, faceless, slumped dark shapes—the cloth-splitters, the cutters, the slashers, the tenders clearing the waste off the scavenger rolls. After a while, he found he could think back on the war, and it was as if he were flipping through a book he had pulled at random from the shelves of someone else's life. He chewed what he remembered slowly, and the memories lost their edges and their taste.

Ten minutes past eight. The wind has picked up. It shoulders off the rest of the fog. The sky behind is clear, the color of Delft china, and still that white and aching light that makes skeletons of every form.

He hears the rush of wings. The swallows sweep past. They rise and fall. Their bodies cut like daggers through the sky.

Every year around this time, they gather. They come down to the beach to feed on the last of the bayberry. Then they flock up, skim the earth, pass on.

The old man, walking with his pail full of sea clams, pauses for a moment to watch them. One alights on a washed-up log near him. Two more dash through tidal pools. Pointed narrow wings, small weak feet. He takes a step, and they shy off, darting back into the flock still flooding in a stream above his head. He watches them go, and Henry watches from the porch, both men staring after that long black winding shoal of birds pressed between the channels of the wind. Then they are gone. The sky falls still.

Henry drinks off the last of his tea and goes inside. He puts the cup in the sink, walks upstairs, and pulls on his clothes, his boots, a light coat. He picks up his keys, his wallet in one pocket, his watch in the other. He unlocks the screen door, walks outside, and locks it again behind him. He takes the front steps and crosses the lawn to his car.

It is an old flivvy, a 1921 Model T runabout. It shakes when he drives at high speed. One wiper sticks, and the wheel is temperamental, sluggish at times to turn. When the engine coughs or the gears don't shift, Henry tinkers around with things as best as he can to get the car running somewhat smoothly again. Although money is not an issue, he is reluctant to replace it.

Driving north on Horseneck Road, he catches up to the old man from the beach, traveling by one-hitch wagon—a simple wide plank of wood set across for a seat, a middle-aged mare, a worn bridle and reins, the leather frayed. As the car approaches, the old man draws the wagon to the side of the road. Henry passes by, tips his hat. The man glances at him, gives a slight nod.

Half a mile past South Westport Corner, a flash of orange breaks out of the brush—a thick tail, sharp nose, a fox, it freezes in the road, eyes glued on the car bearing toward it, Henry jerks the wheel hard to the left, the car swerves, he will miss it, barely miss it, the sun glints off the hood, the fox bolts, Henry feels the soft thud under the wheels. He pulls over, stops the car, gets out. He walks back.

It lies still—jet eyes aslant and open, one ear bent, steam rising from its snout, and something of it, something perhaps in how it lies, reminds Henry of a boy he saw once, a beautiful creature, brought into an elephant shelter by the ridge. The boy had been shot through the open mouth, the bullet lodged in his cervical spine. He had been in the same clothes for perhaps a month and they had to scrape them in places to get them off his skin. The belt was caked with dried clay from the trenches. Clots of earth had rusted out in the buckle groove and it refused to move. They had washed his body, turning him slowly. One of the orderlies held a sponge above him, squeezed the water from it, and it ran like mountain rain through his young skin. Henry checked the wound, then the pulse on the wrist, and when he could not find it, he pressed two fingers against the boy's chest, and there, through the hard young weave of the bones, he could sense the faint and distant stammer of the heart, and it struck him then, in that far-off fading sound, that there was no logic of who was taken and who was left. There was no order to explain or justify what any one of them was doing in that place.

It is a quick memory. A stunning thought. By the time he grasps the fox by the tail, the thought is buried deep again inside him.

He drags it to the side of the road, leaves it and walks back to his car. He cranks the engine. It sticks twice, unwilling to start, then kicks back, jerking out of his hand. He finally gets it running. He climbs back into the driver's seat and sits there for a moment, quiet, in the cool air, the car humming underneath him, his breath hanging in a fog above the wheel. He takes off his hat, sets it on the seat beside him. He presses the clutch pedal down until he hears the catch. He releases the lever, gently. The car begins to roll, and he sets off again through the midmorning October light.

As he reaches Sisson's Corner at the end of Pine Hill Road, he realizes that he left his cigarettes on the side table in the front hall. He can see them there, the soft pack beside the crystal bowl. And so instead of a right, he takes a left. He drives down the hill, past the church, and pulls up in front of Shorrock's store.

The chimes ring as he walks in. Alyssia Borden is at the counter bending Shorrock's ear about a new breed of jasmine seedlings she has just received by mail.

"London," she is saying, "a new order-by-mail company. They send direct by boat. So much more competent than those companies out of the Midwest." She glances over her shoulder and takes Henry in. Her face lights. Her voice slows. "You would not believe," she says, still speaking to Shorrock, but looking at Henry, "every seedling so fresh, you would not believe how fresh."

"Fine morning, Alyssia," Henry says. She is the wife of one of his smoking room friends. They had a blunt and brief affair two years ago. He tries not to think about it.

"Hello, darling. What brings you to this humble end of town?"

"Cigarettes."

"Nothing more thrilling than that?"

"I'm afraid not."

She smiles, her teeth radiant, her mouth lined in red.

"Excuse me," Henry says, stepping toward the aisles.

"Running late?"

"Yes, I am actually."

"So unlike you."

"Is it?"

"Cigarettes are up front," Shorrock says.

"Right. Sure. A pack of Chesterfields. I'll just see if there's anything else I need." He steps away, around a display of Forhans toothpaste and white naphtha soap, toward the back of the store. He ducks into the last aisle and notices a girl at the other end, lifting a tin off the shelf, the smooth clean swipe of the tin into her overall pocket. Henry stops, and the girl glances up, catches him watching her. Her eyes flare, blue, stark. And he recognizes her as the girl he had seen at Millie Sisson's house the night before. She stares at him.

"We missed you at Lady Judith's party, Henry," Alyssia calls from the counter. "Last Saturday. It was a capital time."

Henry doesn't answer. The girl at the end of the aisle withdraws her hand from her pocket. She begins to walk toward him, without taking her eyes off his face. She brushes past him and walks to the counter. Alyssia steps back. The girl sets down a small paper sack.

"Flour?" Shorrock asks.

"A pound."

"That all for you, Bridge?"

She nods.

"On your grub bill then?"

She shakes her head, sets down a few coins, takes the sack of flour, and turns to leave.

Henry steps toward the door and she stops. He is almost in front of her, almost blocking her way. She looks up at him, her eyes cool and fierce and bold. "I'm going out," she says, and she raises one eyebrow as if she is asking for his permission and at the same time, daring him to give it. Her mouth wrinkles and then she smiles, a reluctant smile, her face melts down, and she is beautiful.

"Henry," Alyssia says sharply.

Henry takes a step back, away from the door. The girl walks past him, outside. The chimes ring as the door closes, and she is gone. Gone.

He moves quickly then. He drops a quarter on the counter for the cigarettes, doesn't wait for the change. "Excuse me," he murmurs toward Alyssia. He walks out.

From the front steps, he looks after the girl as she walks along the stone keeping wall that borders the river canal. She does not look back, but he watches her—the unevenly cropped black hair, her thin neck—he watches her until she has disappeared around the bend.

He climbs into his car and drops the cigarettes by his hat on the passenger seat. There is a bit of dust in his eye. He rubs the corner of the lid to work it out. He turns the car around and heads back down the old road toward the city. Dead leaves strike his wind-shield, and he sets on the wiper blades from time to time to brush them away.

Late that afternoon at the mill, an hour before the time bell, as he walks past the drawing-in room on his way down to the office, he sees an older woman seated at a harness in the far corner below the window. He stops for a moment in the doorway. She is old for the work. Hooked nose, thin arms, the veins rise out of her pale skin. He watches the fluid precision of her hands as she enters the yarn into the reed and threads it through the dropwire, and he thinks of the girl, as he has perhaps a hundred times since he saw her earlier that morning, standing in the dim light of Shorrock's store. He wonders who she is, what she stole, what would be worth stealing. And what was it about her—some slightly wild beauty—that is haunting him now? He wonders why one path should cross another. If there is some outlying reason that cannot be explained by natural or philosophic law—a twist of a fate, a fluke, something so mundane, so benign and accidental, a forgotten pack of cigarettes left on a side table in a downstairs hall.

The woman drawing-in has not noticed him. She is intent on her work. The sun streams through the window and rests on her shoulders. Her fingers, deft and quick, slip through the yarn.

Bridge

She could feel his eyes on her as she walked away, a light warmth like the sun on her neck. She does not look back. She does not turn around. She keeps walking until she is around the bend and out of sight. Then she stops. She stands still in the broken shadows at the edge of the woods, clutching the sack of flour. She looks down at her feet, at the sunlight flung in irregular patterns across the ground. She can feel her heart beating, and it is as if her body is hollow and she is only her heart.

In her left overall pocket, she can feel the tin of oysters that she stole, its slight weight against her thigh. In the store, she had recognized him right away, of course. But it took her a moment to realize she had been caught—she had never been caught— it had taken her another moment to realize he would say nothing. He simply stood there, at the other end of the aisle, looking at her, and the way he looked at her washed through her like cool water, strange and intimate and unfamiliar.

She tries not to think about it. She fingers the tin in her pocket. She feels young and ridiculous, ashamed that he had seen her take it, annoyed with herself, annoyed with him. She tries in her mind not to see it at all, not to see his face, not to be moved one way or another by their encounter or the odd chance of meeting him twice in twelve hours.

She cuts down to the river. There are skiffs tied up against the wall of the canal. She steps onto one and lies down across the wooden thwart. The sun is warm on her face. She caps her hand over her eyes to shield out the light and looks toward the Head. She tells herself that she is not looking for him. She knows it is a lie. But he is gone. His car is gone. The village has begun to stir to life, bodies milling in the clear, midmorning light. Abigail Dean is opening up her hat shop, hanging a set of copper chimes on a hook above the door, sweeping off the front steps. Harold Steele draws open the window shutters of the tea room and sets small iron tables on the walk outside. On the front porch of the mail-stop, Abiel Tripp hauls himself out of his chair. He readjusts his suspenders, then takes a turn to the other end of the porch and back, his worn body ambling with a rickety grace.

Cars and trucks flow back and forth across the bridge and up Old County Road. Bridge watches them from the boat. The thwart is hard against the back of her head. The sun is smooth on her face, the river rocking gently underneath her. Her mind is loose, and it occurs to her that she is thinking of him, still, Vonniker, without thinking of him. She is waiting for him, perhaps, without waiting for him. She smiles to herself. It is late—close to ten. She stands up and picks up her sack of flour. She steps off the skiff onto the wall of the canal and walks home.

Cora

Cora sits in the kitchen between two of the galvanized tubs—one filled with bluing water for the
whites, one for the rinse. She knows they are here,
and she does not want to think about them—Honey
Lyons and the three strangers he has brought with
him. They are waiting on her father. She wants them
to be gone.

She has known Honey Lyons since she was a girl.
She does not want him in her yard. He is a slippery
nail of a man, a damaged wolf. Once she saw him
twist the neck of a goose for no other reason than to
do it. She has heard he is up to his chin in the rum-
running trade, that he works for the Syndicate, and
these men in their dark suits he has brought with
him, she knows they are no good. When Bridge
walked by them earlier on her way to Shorrock's
store, two of the men had looked her up and down
with that slick and hungry way some men have.
Bridge had shrugged them off, paid them no mind.

When Cora was her daughter's age, eighteen, she
was already married. On the eve of her wedding to
Russell Weld, who would become the father of her

three children, Cora gnawed at the skin around her nails until it bled. She wore gloves for the ceremony. Calfskin. White. They were not new, and there was a tea stain on the inside of the right wrist where the second button closed. Her mother, Hannah, in a rare act of domesticity, had baked the wedding cake—sweet and rich, a buttery lightness, so full of hope—it fluttered up like wings in Cora's mouth.

That night there was a meteor shower. She and Russell stood outside, still in their wedding clothes, her feet chilled against the doorstone. He held her tightly, their faces upturned toward the heavens as those thin green lights sliced open the sky all around them. They stood there for over an hour, gripping one another, in that strange and silent storm of dying stars.

Cora had expected that when she woke up the next morning, she would find herself changed. She had expected that to be a wife would add some weight to her, some root. And as her husband lay sleeping on the bed behind her, his naked chest rinsed in the early morning light, she had stared into the mirror above the washbasin. She scoured every inch of herself, looking for some altered feature, some sign. Her face was still her face—more peaked than usual perhaps from lack of sleep—stiff dark pockets around her eyes. She bit her teeth into her lip to flood it with color, and lingered awhile longer before the mirror, but there was nothing different, nothing changed. She dressed, gathered up their wedding clothes from the pile on the floor, and went downstairs, and it was only as she stepped outside onto the back porch that she realized that the world itself was different—everything around her, everything familiar—trees, yard, sky—all of it suffused with a new and deeper hue.

And then there were babies—one, two, three—two daughters, a son—and the world was full. Then one was lost, under the ice, and Russell was lost, in the swine flu—so much lost, so suddenly, so soon, her mind divided like a sheet of glass—and boxes and boxes of grief. They piled up and there was no room for her, so she removed

herself, and it happened then: the mystery of the wind in the curtains, the mystery of light shed through the leaves—all of it died to
her then.

It was the wash work that she clung to. She soaked and scrubbed
and rinsed and wrung and starched. She hung nightshirts, linens,
trousers, socks. She set clothes out on the line in every type of
weather. She pulled and washed the sheets until there was no bed
left to strip, then she went down the road to the houses of their
neighbors and begged for their soiled clothes. The money she
brought in from the work was slight, but steady, enough to caulk the
gaps.

Each morning, she sets out the tubs. Boils the water to fill them.
One for the dark wash. One for the whites. Two for the rinse. She
cuts out a fresh bar of soap with a warm bread knife. Then, with a
finer blade, she slices off thin chips and flakes them into the hot
water. She stirs the clothes as they soak, battling out the dirt, she
opens up the creases, the folds, so the soap can work its way through.
The water scalds her hands. The most stubborn dirt is always in her
daughter Bridge's clothes. (For her stubbornness, Cora thinks.) Each
piece rinsed, battled, rinsed again.

It is in the water that all possibility lives. And this morning, as she
sits in the kitchen with Mary Milliken's white nightshifts billow-
ing up through the sudsy water, she notices that the men are still
there—the men in the dark suits and Honey Lyons. Her father has
come home from the beach and they are speaking with him. She
can hear their voices through the moving surface diced with light
as if the voices live under the water, as if they live in that trembling,
fractured image of her face. She does not listen hard enough to make
out the words. She does not want to. But she can sense the seesaw of

the exchange, the back and forth, the tug and push and pull. She can tell her father doesn't like them. His voice seizes up once, just once, then relents, softens down again. There are chinks in her father now that weren't there before. He is awkward with anger. He does not have the knack for it he used to have. For years, she dreamed his rage. She dreamed it damp and lovely, something tangible, a blanket or the wind she could wrap herself into.

The harsh smell of lye sticks in her nose.

Her son, Luce, is still asleep upstairs—she remembers this suddenly. She has not heard a sound, not a step or a creak of the bedsprings, and she says a quick prayer to the water, *Let him sleep, Let him be late for work, Let him not wake up until those men outside are gone.* She does not want his path to cross with theirs. She does not want any dark little part of him to be tempted. Cora knows him well, so well it is a splinter in her heart.

When she thinks of her children, they are close to her, they are almost in her skin or she is in theirs—she can feel them wince and kick and breathe—but when she thinks of herself, it is always from a distance, as if she were observing some separate creature passing beyond the reach of her own will. It happens most often when the white clothes are soaking in their bluing water, and her hands stir through the surface—pale and thin, the webs between the fingers nearly translucent in the water with a queer and greenish cast, like the hands of a sea-maid from out of the myths.

She thinks of it this way: she was a woman once free—she was exiled by grief to some lost pocket of herself, and she waits there in that dark corner, crouched and listening, waiting for the sky to open up again and take her.

Noel

Bridge comes back from Shorrock's at quarter past ten. The day has warmed. Noel shows her the fox.

"Found it in the road," he says.

"What a beauty." She turns the pelt in her hands. "Don't let Luce get hold of it. Did he ever get off this morning?"

"Left half an hour ago," he answers. She nods and lays the fox on the porch.

"What about those men Honey Lyons brought around?"

He looks at her squarely, his eyes cool. "They came and went."

She smiles at him and, for the moment, lets it go.

Together they unload the sea muck off the wagon bed and shovel it into low banks around the foundation of the house. Then they go into the shop to start work on the overturned hull of Duff Barton's skiff.

As they are stripping the gooseclams and the barnacles off the bottom of the boat with a wire brush and a putty knife, Bridge asks again about the men—

Honey Lyons and the three strangers. She asks what they came looking for.

"Wanted some work done."

"Rum work?"

"Boat work."

She laughs. "I know who they are."

Noel shakes his head. "Doesn't matter. I didn't take it."

"How much did they offer?"

"A bit."

"What's a bit?"

"A bit more than you'd expect."

"You're an old crow."

"It's a no-good job. No-good men."

She shrugs and sets back to work on her side of the hull.

Noel doesn't tell her that although he didn't take the job, he didn't refuse it either. He told Honey Lyons he would need a night or so to think it through. Everyone knew that Honey Lyons was in tight with the Syndicate, and had no allegiance to any of the local rum-running gangs. He'd work shoulder to shoulder with each of them, any of them, if there was a season for it, but he was a double-bladed knife. They all knew it.

"This one here's rotted out," Bridge says, prying up one of the planks. "This one too. Most of them are nailsick." Noel comes around to see. He fingers the hole where the nail has been reset so many times the wood around it has worn out. "They won't hold again," Bridge says. "Does he want the nailsick ones replaced?"

"That's what he said."

"Alright then."

Noel thinks of the money. What Honey Lyons has offered him for this one job is more than he'll turn in a year. He grips for the stool behind him and leans against it. He watches his granddaughter as she works. She pushes her hair from her eyes, her face oiled by sweat, lacquered in the dusty light cast through the windows, and he remembers back to the first time he held her, the day she was born, he remembers her soft ridged skull in the palm of his hand, and even then, he had had the sense it was the whole of his life he was holding, not in pieces or fractured notions, but all of it, in her all of it, and he had felt a stunning joy, and at the same time, a sober, chilling sense of his own age.

She is grown now, and he loves her the way he used to love the sea. His life is measured by her. Sometimes as he watches her work over a busted hull in one corner of the shop, he will remember the places he has been, and his heart will ache for the wandering. He yarns with her as they work. Every so often, he will glance up and see her face, as fragile and rare as those objects he brought back with him from his voyages: the pelican feet and the ivory mussel shells, the fishing line strung out of mother-of-pearl.

He has taught her all the knots: the clove hitch and the monkey's fist, the shroud knot and the Turk's head. From the time she could walk she has helped him in the shop. He has taught her how to use beeswax to bind frayed strands of thread, to caulk a seam and wield an adze. He has taught her how to push her weight just enough into the saw to make a clean, swift cut, how to force a broadax to shape timbers, how to steam oak ribs and soak wood in water until it bends.

Before the causeway was built across the tidal flat between Gooseberry Neck and the mainland, he took her seafowling on the bar, and they would wait there together, the old man and the child, crouched in the rocks, their shadows crouched behind them, their boots dug to the shins in cold wet sand.

He has taught her how to bait a hook and grease a trap, how to stalk and hunt and kill, how to clean, oil, load, cock, point, and shoot a gun. He could tell from the first time he took her down to practice shoot in the gravel pit that she had a knack for cold metal. She had that certain kind of ruthlessness it takes to pull the trigger

over and over again, without emotion, without rage or cruelty, desire or greed. She was not like her brother, Luce. She did not have
his hotheadedness. From the time she was a mite, she seemed to understand that killing, in its purest form, is an empty-eyed passion-
less art.

When she was still young, Noel bought a small gun for her off
Samuel Browne, a single-shot .410. Once, when she had left a splinter of air between her shoulder and the butt, the recoil hit back into
her chest and chipped off a bit of her collarbone. Another time, she
held up the gun, and as she fired, the comb slapped hard against her
cheek and bruised the bone. When she was older and he was teaching her on his gun—a double-barreled twelve gauge—she pulled
both triggers and the shock of the blast sent her ass-over-teakettle
into a pile of shale. She got up again, brushed herself off, and said
nothing of it. That was just her way.

Once, he had believed that what he taught her, what he had to
give, would be enough.

He knows that the world is changing. Bridge reads him snips
from the newspapers, and he has heard stories of men who have cut
their fortunes overnight. His old friend Rui has made a small but
tidy bundle for himself trading in the stock market. A little money
is a little means. A little freedom.

Money is reason enough to take this work, he tells himself. It is
only one job. To refit a boat. To strip out her insides and rebuild her
lighter, faster, more silent. And if the work had been offered by anyone else, he would have snapped it up, no hesitation, no questions
asked.

He looks up again at Bridge. She has stripped off the dead bottom boards and stacked them in a heap on the floor. She is setting
down new ones, the heart side of the wood facing out, and he notices then that, as she works, there is a thin forked line between her
brows. It is slight but so unlike her, a small frown, it puzzles him,
and he watches her more closely.

She can feel his eyes on her. She bites her lip. She isn't working well, he must notice it, he must have begun to wonder why. Her hands are clumsy, and she is annoyed with herself. It is simple work she is doing, but now again, for the fourth time already, she pinches her finger setting one board against another. She swears under her breath, shakes her hand loose. It is only a nip, the pain sharp, no blood, no broken skin, but everything feels upside down, her head upside down. The planks don't seem to line up. She is thinking about the morning, it is all the fault of the morning, and that man, Henry Vonniker, seeing him last night at Asa's, then seeing him again at the store, stealing the oysters and having him catch her do it, and the way he had looked at her, astonishment and frank desire, she had seen it, felt it. It had made her feel alive.

Why should that happen? What should it matter? Why was she even asking herself when she knew very well it couldn't mean anything? And thinking about it now makes her restless, impatient, a little bit angry that the thought of it, the thought of him, is taking up room in her head. When she works, she likes her head clear, like calm water, so she can see through to the bottom of things. That is what she wants. That is the way she likes it, and the only thing now that she feels a little bit grateful for is that Luce was gone by the time she got home so she didn't have to banter with him, because she wasn't in the mood. He might have sensed something was off, and if he had, he would have bugged after her about it, because that was just the way he was. Luce couldn't let things go.

She takes a breath in, but doesn't look up. She still feels her grandfather watching her. She keeps lining up the planks, setting the nails, slamming them in with the hammer. It is a sound she loves— that clear, square hit of a hammer on the head of a nail that drives it clean through the plank into the frame. And usually it is a motion she can do without thinking. Her grandfather is not saying anything. She can hear the sound of his teeth grinding on the stem of his pipe, but he is not working, he is sitting still, very still, his eyes on her. Finally she puts down the hammer and straightens up, one hand on her hip. She looks at him and says, "So you're not going to be much use today, are you?"

He bursts out laughing. She blushes and smiles. He looks at her carefully. "I'm just watching over you."

"You don't need to do that."

"Just want to make sure you don't get sloppy."

"Why should I get sloppy?"

"You'll have to tell me."

She looks down at her hands and notices a thread on the cuff of her sleeve coming loose. She gives it a tug, and it quickly unravels. She breaks it off with her teeth.

"I don't really think it's me," she says slowly, her voice controlled. "After all, I'm not the one sitting around, idle hands, thinking about the men who came by this morning and what they might have offered me."

He doesn't answer right away. She watches his face. But there is no change in his expression, no twitch, no shift, nothing in his eyes, nothing she can see. He is good at hiding things. She knows this. He shifts his pipe to the other side of his mouth. "Maybe I'm thinking about that fox," he says.

"It was a beauty of a thing," she admits.

"Well, that's what it is. I can't stop thinking about that fox."

She laughs and brushes some dust off a seam between two of the planks. "That might be a lie," she says, "but I can let it be that, if that's what you want."

She is more composed now. She feels lighter, happy even. Her world seems to have turned right again. Her world is her world. She picks up the next plank and sets it down. "So you're just going to sit there?" she asks him, rummaging through the box of nails.

"I'm thinking I might."

"Well, why don't you draw me a sketch on the panbone?"

"I can do that."

"Cut me a whale," she says. She picks up the hammer. "Gallied. Big flukes sweeping eye to eye."

"You want an iron in her?"

"As long as she scuttles the boat of the man who threw it."

Noel chuckles as he goes to the wall by the steam-box and picks up the panbone—a huge flat piece from the jaw of a sperm whale he hawked years ago from a shop near the Seamen's Bethel in the city. He carries it back to his stool and rests it over his knees. He finds an empty spot in the broad center and, with a pencil, draws a light sketch. Then with his needle, he begins to cut. Over the years he has carved into the panbone, filling in the lines with black and colored ink: sketches of the voyages he took, the rafts of birds, buckling seas, the postbox on the turtleshell rock south of the Galápagos where a sailor might find a letter sent three years before. He has sketched the angled noses of the atolls just north of the Sandwich Isles, the pod of devilfish they glimpsed, the suckers finning close against the cows; scenes of drifting north through the pack ice in the Arctic, glaciers, musky light, the sloped eyes of the Inuit women, their dark faces roped by fur. He has sketched scenes of Kauai—the island he came to and could not leave, the island where he first met Hannah—the green water off the reef clear as gin, palm trees, red clay roads, the sheer drop of the black cliffs into the surf, the folding hills where the tribes lived west of Hanalei. Sometimes as he cuts, he will tell Bridge stories of where he has gone, of what he has seen, bony tales worn through years of being retold. The stories of the island are the ones that seem to make her happy, and in her happiness, he finds the place comes alive for him again: the

fierce summer heat, the drenching tempers of the rain. On that island, he has told her, at every early dawn, there is an unthinkable
calm, so still, so silent, one can hear the mountains breathe.

He is spooked by the places he has been—the geographies he's
passed through—they gather around him in his shop—in the tins of
bolts and drifts, in the shavings at his feet, chips of cedar, oak, pine.
He sniffs in old smells with the sawdust through his nose—smells of
creosote, coconut, oil.

He cuts another line into the bone, the long straight end of a
second harpoon, fleshed deep into the whale. They jut like pins
from her huge body, breaking out of the sea. Another line.

"Damn!" says Bridge. "I muxed it."

He looks up. She is standing in the corner, holding the ripsaw
and a plank.

"You cut the wedge?" he asks.

"I sawed out the wrong side."

He smiles. "And see, there it is—why I need to still be watching
over you."

"What a waste," she says, staring in dismay at the board in her
hand.

"It's just a plank. Set it out to air and cut another."

She is clearly upset. It surprises him she would be upset over
something so trivial. She looks at him from across the room. Even
from that distance, he can see her eyes fill. "I am no use today, Papa.
I can't do a thing right today. No use at all."

He smiles at her gently, shaking his head. He won't ask what's on
her mind or try to coax it out of her.

"Some days are like that," he says simply. "I'm having that same
kind of day myself."

She manages a smile. She pushes her hair from her face with the
back of her sleeve.

"That's all it is," he says. "Just that kind of day. And that piece of wood in your hand is just a piece of wood. So go to the loft and get another and cut it again."

She nods and carries the plank out of the shop. He hears the thud as she leans it against the sidewall in the sun.

He looks again at the panbone on his lap—the bare sketch he has drawn so far, the whale and a small boat beside her, flung up against a wave. He tilts it toward the window to see the lines more clearly, to see what he has done and what is left to do.

Money is reason enough to take the work, he tells himself. It is a good reason, a solid reason. Money for the children. He could set aside a little pile for Bridge.

He knows better.

When Noel sailed on the *Sarah Mar*, his work was as ship's carpenter. But from time to time, the first mate would send him aloft. Noel had a gift for seeing. It was his mother's gift. He could stay for hours aloft, his body strapped to the crow's nest. He could mark a blow on the horizon when another sailor would see nothing but an empty, light-wrecked sea. At times, he could see a thing before it came.

The thought of taking the work makes him uneasy—the money itself makes him uneasy. It's not the lawlessness that bothers him. It's the prospect of tangling with a man like Honey Lyons. It's the deep grating sense he feels in his gut that if he takes this job, things might not turn out so fine in the end.

Bridge comes back in with a new board. He glances up.

"What?" she says.

He shakes his head.

"You still thinking about that fox, Papa?" She laughs.

"Guess I still am."

She looks at him a moment longer, then takes the new plank to the corner and picks up the ripsaw.

———

Luce comes home at half past four from the icehouse, with a blade of tall grass between his front teeth and news of how Frank MacDonald got shot up last night at sea by a 75.

"On his way in, and they got him. Took his boat and all its stuff. A hundred and fifty cases at least, I heard. And Frank got two slugs, one in each side of him."

"Is he dead?" Bridge asks.

"He's not, but Ruth Mason's terrier is. Got run over by a dump truck. Dog was flatter than piss on a platter." Luce's boots are covered with mud and soiled straw. He stamps them out on the porch and leaves them behind the garbage pail. In the kitchen, he peels off his socks, the heels full of darning. He puts them on the floor by the stove to dry, then sits back in the chair. His skin is dark from long hours outside, hair thick and black. He pushes his hands through it. Bridge has shucked out the clams, and she is chipping onions into the pot of boiling water, potatoes and meal.

"You up for tag?" he asks her.

"I'm busy."

He glances up, a sly cool look in his eye. "That's never stopped me before." And he chases her out the door, down the porch into the yard. He catches her halfway across the grass to the shop, and they tumble to the ground, laughing, underneath Cora's wash pinned to the line. The white sheets flap like heavy sailcloth in the breeze.

In the doorway of the shop, Noel takes a smoke. He watches them as they wrestle through the grass, and it is how they always are with one another—they shriek and growl and box and buck and fight until they are worn through and done. Then they fall quiet and lie close, with the linens drifting loose around them. They whisper together, hatching their schemes. He knows what they do. He finds the slumgullion scraps of their stealing—the broken hair comb, the empty tins of caviar.

He knows that there is only one pure love—young love, first love. The heart can only be broken once. Every other love that comes afterward has some restraint, some compromise. After that first, the heart can be winded, skinned, bent, betrayed, or bruised, but never broken.

His own heart was a door he had walked through long ago and left dangling on busted hinges behind him. He knew enough to leave it open so when the wind came, it blew clean through.

His leg aches and he sits down on a cask by the door of the shop. He tips his weight back and leans his head against the sidewall. The afternoon sun bathes his face. The warmth soaks into the warped places, the deeper lines. He can hear the wind bristle through the maple leaves.

The girl shrieks. He opens one eye. They are wrestling again. Luce has pinned her down by both hands but she kicks up. He lets go and she rolls out from under him.

She has grown beautiful, he thinks—grown up almost overnight, but she does not seem to know it yet. She cut her first two teeth at six months—he remembers this—they broke through the pearly surface of her gums. She did not cut the rest until she was past a year old, and she would squawk at him and gnaw on his thumb with those two teeth like a baby tautog.

They lie apart now—on either side of one of Cora's sheets. Only the girl's feet are visible, dirt ground into her anklebones, overalls rolled halfway up the shin. They are laughing together without seeing one another, the stark white vastness of the sheet dividing them. They talk and snicker, on either side of it, without touching: biting words, nonsense, scathing words that have no apparent context, no clear meaning. They tumble back into laughing.

Their closeness now concerns him. They have always been close, since they were children, but they are older now, and it doesn't sit right. Sometimes when he squints he imagines he can see slight pale threads that bind them.

He looks away from them across the yard to the blue spruce. It is dying, and its needles have begun to blanch out at the ends. There are patches of baldness on the lower branches.

He stands up and sets out across the yard. He passes the garden and takes the path down the hill into the white pine wood. He crosses the creek and cuts around the swamp, then climbs up to the old Indian ground. There is no fence. No gate to mark the site. The stones are rough. Unetched. They were here when he bought the butt of land. He wouldn't have known them for what they were but for the ritual pile of clamshells on a clear spot of ground by the small beach below. He notes the deer rub on the sassafras. He sits down on the cold earth.

The wind has fallen off, and the air is still. The clouds press down over the hills on the far side of the river, blue clouds like sea-pigs diving low. The sun, heavy-lidded in the west, settles until it is a glowing shiver on the earth, then disappears.

After supper, Cora pulls the shades on the windows that face the road, then goes back into the kitchen to mop the floor. Noel sits in the deep chair in the big room with his pipe, the back window cracked open behind him, while the children play cards on the cleared table. He does not feel the same love for his grandson that he feels for Bridge. Two years older, nearly twenty-one, Luce is slapdash, but not lazy. He works the ice route his father, Russell, used to work. He can handle a gun as well as his sister, but he does not have her cool eye or her patience. Noel has marked a streak in him—a restless greed, a devil nature that pokes its face up from time to time. But Luce knows the river. He has a feel for its channels, its holes and jogs. He can handle a boat up the narrow switch-back turns of Crooked Creek. He can run the rocks around Cory's Island, even at night, and make a skiff disappear between the mud-flats and the eelgrass at midtide. He knows every hidden beach and break and cove. He can run the river, from the head to the mouth, with his eyes closed.

They are playing pitch, and it is Bridge's turn to deal. Noel watches the swift relentless movements of her hands as she gathers the cards, breaks them apart, bends them back and lets the two halves fall. She slides the deck across the table to be cut.

The horsehair stuffing in the chair has begun to rot out. Noel can smell it through the cloth. His teeth grind into the stem of his pipe. He can hear the rub of the grinding in his ear. The outside darkness presses up against the curtains, and he realizes that in his heart he has already decided he will do it. He will take the work. He will build them their boat. He will build it to run fast and light. He will tell Lyons he is in for the one job, and the one job only. He will not let himself get yoked in. He will take the work for the daylight reason of the money. It is a good reason. It is why most men of his means and circumstance have stepped into the rum trade. It is an economic necessity—this kind of work—in a day and age when it is not enough to work the river and the land. He will take this one job for the money, and no one will judge him for it. They will look the other way. He packs away his doubts—the decision is made. He smiles quietly to himself—it will be a breath of the old life for him, a little piece of the adventure.

He looks up at Bridge. She holds her hand of cards close to her, the edges tilted in, her face impassive. She gives nothing away. It is dangerous, he knows, the way he loves her, when life, by nature, is as swift and fleeting as a change in weather—clouds, fog, mist— passing through an empty sky.

She sets her last card down. "I've won," she says, slamming the table.

"Play again," Luce says.

"No, two out of three already. I've won."

"We'll do three out of five."

"No good."

"Come on."

"No."

"Come on, Bridge."

"No!"

She shakes her head and stands, and Noel sees the ripe and wicked glance she throws back over her shoulder to Luce as she steps through the back door out onto the porch, the tension pulled tight as fresh rigging between them. Luce follows her. Noel watches them through the window that looks out onto the backyard, their shadows moving through the crisp night, as they chase the hens into the chicken shed and then stand for a while, a pair of black knives, looking up into the clear night sky.

He goes to bed early that night. Just before he sleeps, he has that old sense of someone walking soft across his eyelids. That night, he dreams he is young again, and out on open water. He dreams of the sharp salt wind, the stink of oil and blood baked into the deck wood by the sun, the flap of sails, the rip of water up against the hull. In his dream, he remembers how the hips of the sea thrust up underneath them and their keel ran deep into the gully of her spine.

Bridge

That night, waiting for Luce in the mud-thick darkness of her room, she lies on her bed, fully dressed, the stolen tin of oysters in the deep pocket of her coat. She hears the trucks pass: the low voices of the men, the tinkle of bottles in their crates, rockweed and salt hay stuffed around them to muffle the sound. Soon after, she hears the low swift knock on her bedroom door. They steal out. Luce carries the pail of baitfish and the poles, and she carries a small sack with two potatoes and the shank spade. They walk down Pine Hill Road in silence, past the houses with their shades pulled, the windows framed by yellow slits of light.

They walk through the village at the Head, past the closed store and the mail-stop, to Chape Clay's garage. Luce slides the flat mouth of the spade through the crack in the door. He pulls it down in one swift run and springs the lock. The door swings in on its hinges, and they can see the hulking gleam of the new-style Ford pickup in the dark.

Bridge slips into the cab, into the driver's seat, pulls the brake and sets the truck in neutral while

Luce pushes them out into the road. They roll over the bridge and turn left past the green. Luce gets in. "Come on," he says, "move over."

She shakes her head. "Let me drive." And he smiles and he lets her, she puts the truck in gear, pops the clutch, the engine starts, they drive without lights the rest of the way out of the village. She heads down Drift Road, past the orchards and the icehouse. They take the hill that runs past Howland's farm and the black rolling shadows of cows clustered in the darkness.

She turns left onto Hix Bridge Road.

"I thought we were going to the Point," Luce says.

"No, let's go around to the beach instead."

They pass the clambake pavilion and the teahouse. She lifts her foot off the pedal as they cross the bridge and pass over the river, thick bands of light flushing underneath them. They drive through the quiet village of South Westport, and she takes the sharp right turn onto Horseneck Road. The telephone poles set by the road seem to move alongside them, a small trail of staggering crosses through the night.

They come down onto East Beach and drive along the warped arm of the Let. She starts to tap her fingers on the wheel, then catches herself doing it. She holds her hand still. They pass the new church, the second pavilion, its windows boarded closed for the winter. Just before the causeway, she slows and looks down West Beach Road. All the cottages are dark except for one—the third cottage in. Henry Vonniker's house, she thinks. It must be his house. She feels a quiver in her stomach, a light flutter. There is a hedge out front, and above it, she can just see the top of his car in the driveway.

"What are you looking at?" Luce says.

"Who lives there, in that cottage, the one lit up?"

"How the hell should I know?"

And she smiles to herself. She keeps driving. They cross the causeway to Gooseberry Neck and park the truck at the end. They take the rods and the pail of baitfish and walk the footpath through the bittersweet and false heather, the sea-myrtle and the pepper-bush, the beach pea scrub gone by.

Once, as the path rises, Bridge glances behind them, across the water toward West Beach. On the bottom floor of the third cottage, she can see the glow of a lit window.

"Are you coming, or what?" Luce calls back to her. She follows him. They walk past the kettlepond and then cross down over the windrows of mussel shells that lie crushed, blue-black and iridescent in the moon. They leave their boots in the sand, roll their pants up past the knee, and walk through the shoal water pools between the narrow strip of beach and the rocks that lie like sleeping lions in the low tide.

Bridge can smell the reek of dead fish and rockweed, busted clams and cold wet sand. They cross the bar and walk through the rocks along the tip of the island, casting out into the shallows. Luce pulls in a fish on his first cast—a schoolie. He knifes it in the gills and hooks it to his belt. He rebaits his hook and, as they go on walking, he tells her, as he has told her a thousand times before, that someday he will make a good dollar, enough to leave this scab of a town. He will set miles, he says, between himself and this place. His voice is a cool whisper through the pull of water over the stones. He will take the train to California, then a ketch to the island, Noel's island, Kauai. Bridge smiles in the darkness. It is always the same ragged dream. She stops listening. She thinks of Henry Vonniker in his house. She wonders why he is awake—it must be close on midnight—she wonders if he always keeps late hours—if he is up reading or writing a letter. Did he hear the truck as they drove past? She wonders if he leaves a window open at night to let the sound of the wind on the water and the cold salt air from the outside world press in.

"So what do you think?" Luce is asking her now.

"Yes," she answers.

"You weren't listening."

"I was."

"What did I say?"

"You said you'd make off."

"Said more than that."

"A train to California—all the rest of it."

"I said I might go to Arizona first."

"That's a dumb place to go."

"Hell it is."

"Arizona's desert."

"You can buy a lot for nothing there."

"Nothing's nothing in a desert."

There is a pause. Luce casts out again into the deeper water off the bar. He draws the line in, and she can hear the slow rub of the leader through the metal eye.

"Besides," she says with a smile, "you'd never leave Ma."

He doesn't answer. He swings the rod back over his shoulder. A long and aching cast. She hears the bait slap the surface.

"You could come with me," he says.

"I could," she replies.

"Yeah, you could."

They fish in silence. Her feet are numb, the feeling below her ankles sucked down by the cold.

Once, her hook catches on a rock. She jerks the rod, the line breaks free and comes back to her, aloof and strange over the waves.

Luce is ahead, and he sees the signal first. The red light blinking off Little Beach at the break in the shore by Allen's Pond. The light blinks a homemade code, and he can tell by the glow around it that they have set the torch in a box so it cannot be seen from the land. Luce draws in his line without taking his eye off the light as Bridge comes up behind him.

"What is it?" she asks.

He grips her arm and points seaward to the black swift-moving shapes of two craft heading in. "Listen," he says underbreath, and she listens and she can hear it—that high-pitched, distant, unmistakable sound of engines running, finely tuned.

"They're heavy with a load," Luce says. "Do you see how they ride in the water? That second one there—do you see—how low she goes—watch, when she hits light—there!—do you see the crates in her bow?"

And she suddenly remembers that she has not told him.

"They came by today," she says.

"Thirty foot each, at least, they must be. How much do you think it's worth—that load they're bringing in? Came down from Newfoundland, I'd bet. Or all the way from France." Luce's eyes are fixed on the boats, his face taut, rigid with excitement, his cheeks slashed with moonlight, and for a moment it frightens her, the hunger she sees in his face. "That's what I should be doing, Bridge," he says. His voice is hushed.

"To wind up dead like Asa?" she says flatly.

"I'd do the job ten times better than Asa."

"Doesn't mean you wouldn't wind up dead."

But he does not take his eyes off the two boats heading in toward the red blinking signal light on shore.

"Honey Lyons came by today looking for Noel," she says.

"Yeah, what'd he come by for?"

"He brought three other men."

"What other men?"

"I've never seen them before. But they were top-dressed, spats, rake hats. Fancy car."

She sees it register then in his face, what she is saying. He looks at her sharply.

"You think they want him to run?"

"Might."

"He's too old."

"He knows the river well as anyone. Can handle a boat better than you."

Luce doesn't answer. He looks back toward the rum-running craft. They have reached the softer water of the bay. They cut off their engines and glide through the darkness on the tide, a strong clear line toward the beach and trucks waiting on shore.

Luce and Bridge leave the shallows. They climb back up to where they have left their things—the potatoes and the baitfish pail. They move to a higher point that faces east-northeast. They watch from there.

Distant black shapes moving against the sand, men working, unloading crates off the boats, crate after crate, passed down a chain, man to man, strung from the shallows to higher ground, and loaded into the trucks. As the boats speed off back out into the black water, the trucks back around, straight in a line. Luce and Bridge can see their headlamps filing up the dirt path around Allen's Pond toward Horseneck Road.

The baitfish pail is between them. Bridge crouches down. She puts her hand in and she can feel the shiners, their noses quick through her fingers. They cut, darts of silver through the pail. There is one in particular, smaller than the rest. She tries to follow it with her eyes as it pounds back and forth, a half-mad thing, small nose, small fins, into the sides of the pail.

Luce says something, but she does not hear him.

"What'd you say?" she asks.

"What's up with you tonight?"

"Nothing."

"Yes, there's something. Something's been gnawing at you all day."

"You're wrong."

"Since last night at Asa's."

Her head snaps up.

"That's it then," he laughs. "Dead cousin Asa's got you spooked."

"You don't know what you're talking about, Luce."

"Sure I do."

"I'm quite sure you don't."

He does it then, one swift jerk of his leg, his foot kicks the pail and it turns over on its side, a soft rush as the water empties out, the fish flush into the sand. And perhaps it is what she should have expected. Perhaps it is what she should have known he would do.

The cry of a nightbird hammers through the stillness.

"You didn't have to do that," she says.

Luce shrugs. "They're no use."

"That was cruel."

"But you forgive me."

She shakes her head. "No."

He digs a fire-pit in the sand, lines it with rocks, then slips into the brush to gather driftwood. He leaves her there, at the tip of the island, and still she watches them—the baitfish—small, wet-skinned, smooth, flipping slower now, breathless, caked with dirt.

She looks across the water back toward shore. She can see the hidden curve of Little Beach, quiet now, the empty sand rinsed by the moon.

She finds a smudge on her wrist. She rubs it out. She crosses her arms under her head and lies back, her thoughts grow liquid, moving dark wind, blue flax, sweet crushed fern, the smells of deep fall, the last smells, bayberry, wild grape, salt rose, pine. The darkness is cold. The stars pierce the sky, harsh white scraps of distant light.

She had felt the change in her grandfather that morning—he was more quiet, kept more to himself—and she knew it was about the money. Maybe he was kicking himself for not taking the job. He had told her, hadn't he?—it was a job he wouldn't take.

It was not the first time he'd been approached. She knew this. The first time was years back, when the rum trade was just starting up—back when they still used small boats—any craft that would float—catboats, dories, skiffs. It was clear and simple business then—

nearly legitimate business. The rum-zone was only three miles off-shore and supply ships like the *Arethusa*, with her captain Bill "the real" McCoy, would hang off Nomans Land for weeks. The small boats went out to meet the mother ships, took on their load, then sped back in.

In those early years, she knew, there was no hijacking, no piracy, no go-through men. It was before the big syndicates, before the mystery sinking of the *John Dwight* and the slaughter of her crew. Bridge was just twelve that afternoon when Rui, the Port-i-gee, came by. He wore an old monkey jacket. It was noontime. Luce was gone, on the ice route with their father. Cora was gone to the store. Noel had known Rui back on Nomans Land. They had shipped to-gether on the *Sarah Mar*. Rui was a salvageman now. He was a trap-per, and he hawked his skins and old scrimp and Sailor's Valentines down along the city wharves. Bridge had stayed in the shop, knock-ing off bungs with a wooden mallet, while the two men yarned out-side. She had overheard Rui telling Noel about the new business, the rum business, about how you could make fifty dollars for one night's work if you read the water right.

"Is that your taste, Christmas?" the Port-i-gee had asked.

"Not mine, Rui," Bridge heard her grandfather say, "but you're an old rascal, and I wish you well." He had laughed then, low, went into the house and came back with a bottle of brandy and a fruit-cake. He called to Bridge and told her to come outside, sit with them, have a bite of cake. When Rui said it was time for him to be getting on, Noel went down to the orchard to pick him a sack of fresh pears off the tree. Bridge and the Port-i-gee watched him to-gether, as he twisted the small pears from the ends of their branches, taking only the ones that were ripe and easy to pull.

"You know, girl," Rui had said, his face lopped in shadow under the brim of his hat, "I knew your pappy back on island." His voice was thick with accent. "Nomans Land. I knew him back when he was small as that wheelbarrow. Had no fear, your pappy, even as a young scrap, he'd swim out to the break off Stony Point, catch the waves out there on storm days, past where the rest of us would go. He's fish, your pappy is, gills in his throat you don't see."

Bridge had not answered him. She said nothing to him that day. She nibbled on the cake, her teeth digging in to find the chunks of sweet date. The sun was relentless and made chewing slow. With small bites, she took in what the Port-i-gee told her although it had no match for what she knew. She looked across the yard to her grandfather, the light on his shoulders, his careful, brutal hands still gathering pears. She could not imagine him small. He was a country to her.

By the time Luce comes back, his arms full of kindling, she is shivering. He gives her his coat, then kneels in the sand and builds the fire. He sits back on his heels as the flames catch and the light begins to grow. She has almost forgiven him for the baitfish. Sometimes she feels she doesn't have a choice. They have grown up close, tight for so long, their stalks indistinguishable, roots bound. It doesn't matter now, she tells herself. The baitfish or anything else. Nothing seems to matter now. The air is cold, and the fire is warm, and the light is gentle on his face, his skin burnished, his eyes softening as he looks across the fire to her and smiles. She takes the potatoes from the paper bag and sets them to roast. He guts out the fish and drapes it down whole. She draws out the tin of smoked oysters, twists the key off the bottom, and rolls back the lid. They eat them with their fingers. They talk and laugh, and their voices catch in the orange sparks crackling off the wood until the fire dies. He lies down beside her, and they watch the ashes smolder, the last blue glow in the heart of the black-charred wood.

Henry

He finds himself thinking of her, looking for her. Most often on his morning drive up Pine Hill Road toward the Head of Westport. He glances into yards and down dirt lanes, over the new snowdrifts and the shoveled walks. When the days grow short and he is driving home in the early evenings through the late November darkness, he looks into the lit windows of the houses as he passes by, hoping for a glimpse of her.

He knows her name is Bridge. Perhaps it was Bridget once, and the "t" got broken off somehow. He knows nothing else—who she is; where she lives; how she spends her days. From time to time, he might see something or someone that reminds him of her, and his mind will take a sudden, wild swerve. He will see her as clearly as if she is still standing there, the way she was in the store that day back in October, at the other end of the aisle. He will see the shadows on her face, her skin, her hair— that cool expression in her eyes as she stared back, then began to walk toward him.

He finds himself stopping in more frequently at Shorrock's. He buys something he needs or something he doesn't. When he steps back outside, his eyes smart with the cold, and he looks across the road toward the river and the path running along the stone wall where he had seen her walk away.

Sometimes he is impatient, annoyed with himself, and he turns his back on his thoughts of her. Other times, he allows himself to dwell on that single image of her face that has somehow woken him out of his dark sleep and set a new tilt to his consciousness.

One afternoon, as he is driving home on his usual route down Horseneck Road, he comes to the top of the last hill. The fields drop away underneath him, rolling down to the sea. The sky is wintry and gray but, out over the ocean, the sun breaks through one spot in the clouds, a handful of raw light thrown like diamonds across the still water, and it strikes him that the laws of probability are not on his side. He has lived in the town for four years, and he has seen her twice. It might be another four years before he sees her again.

He feels a sudden disgust with himself for being such a creature of habit, so locked into his routine, traveling through the world with blinders on. He never takes that occasional left. And he senses then that if he wants to see her again, he will have to do things differently.

He is still thinking about this the following morning when he stops in at the post office. He picks up his mail at the window, then turns back toward the door and, as he does, he sees the notice pinned to the wall.

AN EVENING OF POLITICS AND POETRY.

A HAM AND BEAN SUPPER AT THE CENTRAL VILLAGE

GRANGE HALL TO BENEFIT THE WESTPORT REPUBLICAN PARTY.

OPEN TO NON-MEMBERS.

DONATION TWO DOLLARS OR AS YOU CAN PAY.

He pauses for a moment, his fingers on the knob of the door. It is not likely that she will be there. But she might be. He opens the door, and the wind strikes his face. He has already made up his mind that he will go.

Noel

They bring the boat to him the first week of December, and he is paid a third up front. He rolls back the door of his shop and clears out the middle of the floor. He cuts new keel blocks and braces them down so he can work her right-side up. She is a thirty-six-footer, an old work boat—a good sea boat—and he thinks of how senseless it is, and a little heart-bitter, that he will take this strong-hulled fishing boat and he will pull the seablood out of her. He will strip down her wood, strip out her use, and refit her into something that has no true worth or place, and Honey Lyons and his gang will take her, they will run her hard, they will load her with weight beyond what she is made to carry, and when she is worn through, bullet-riddled, her planks bruised, slammed, stove, they'll junk her. If she's lucky, she'll have a year left on the water.

He unscrews her side rails, and begins to break up the planks. He will strip out the work-room aft, cut back the space of the wheelhouse, so she will be all deck and hold. The smell of salt and wear sticks in his nose. With the back of his sleeve, he wipes the grit off his face, out of his eyes. In the age of whaling, the work he did was noble work. He would take busted hulls and smashed ships, he would rebuild their crippled shapes and mend them back into repair.

And now it's come to this, he thinks to himself as he throws another plank into the pile on the floor. He has heard about the boat-builders over in Fairhaven who build rum-boats to look like yachts, all dickeyed up, their cabins finished off in mahogany, and he shakes his head to think how easily the wind shifts, the world tips, slides out from underneath you, and turns alien, new, utterly changed.

When Noel finally left Kauai and followed Hannah back to Old Dartmouth, he had been gone for over ten years. He was twenty-nine years old, and it was almost 1880. They luffed sail as they reached New Bedford harbor. He stood on deck. The view of the city staggered him, because it looked as if the world had stopped while he was gone. It was all the same—the skyline he had left—the millstacks and the church steeples. The masts of the whaleships berthed at the wharves pierced the sky. But there was something cockeyed in the scene, something vague and wrong that at first he could not put his finger on. He stood at the rail and squinted, and he could see small black creatures crawling on those whalers tied up three-deep at the piers. He stared at the ships as they approached, and it was not until they came near that he saw it: the fretted rigging, the sheathing ripped out from their sides, the grass grown up on the wharves, shin-deep, unscythed. Hundreds of barrels lay abandoned, their hoops rusted, black pools of oil leaking out around them. Long alleyways of weed sprouted thick and deep between the casks. And those small black creatures he had glimpsed as they crossed the bay—they were young boys—wharf rats. They rowed on rafts made out of old hatch covers. They swarmed over the decks, shimmied up the masts, and slid down the backstays.

On one bark, he saw a pair of white-bearded men a hundred feet aloft. They bent the sails and served the rigging on a ship that would never see open water again. They hung there, those old sea-men, strange and ancient monkeys, swinging off the spars.

He raised his eyes then from the ships and took in the city behind them. It was the millstacks that caught his eye. The long buildings. There were more of them, he realized. They had thickened in the time he was away, and now they were humming with new life, the city's life, the heart of its industry. Black plumes of smoke filled the sky.

He walked the waterfront streets with his sack thrown over his shoulder, and he had the sense that he was passing through a boneyard. The smithy shops were closed. One chandlery gutted. Another gone. The sail-loft at the corner of Johnny Cake Hill had been torched by fire and they had not bothered to rebuild, so the frame of the building wavered there, a black and soot-filled shell. The light shot down through the fallen beams, and he knew then, standing on the corner, that the age of whaling was a golden age gone by. Men like him would lose their work slowly.

And it happened that way. He had his Hannah, but dark years would follow. Years of barely making do. In the end, he would always manage to scare up some boat work or carpentry work, some use for his hands. In the few seasons when there were no proper jobs, there was always fishing, trapping, wooding, haying, picking the sea clams off the beach. There was always a way for him to make a man's store pay, but nothing close, nothing within a world's length of what he will make now, for this job, on this boat, in one fell swoop.

She will be a sorry creature when he is done with her. There will be no brass fittings, no porthole glass to catch the light. He will paint her out a flat dull gray. He will not shore out her kinks or putty-smooth over her rough places. He will leave some wear to her—a few knots, a few hammer dents to lend her the illusion of still being a work boat, a fishing boat, nothing to bother with, well used.

———

Four weeks, and she is finished. He refits her with the two new Liberty engines they bring to him, Maxim silencers installed so she will move through the water with barely a sound. Lyons has paid him and it is done. He can see they are pleased with his work, and so it does not entirely surprise him when Lyons comes around again ten days later.

It is the beginning of January, a Saturday. Cora and Bridge are in the kitchen, ironing out the linens for the ham and bean supper at the Grange. Luce is in the back of the yard wooding—splitting the logs and stacking the cords. Noel is at the stone well, fixing a hinge on the well cover. The light is scarce. Pale and milky blue. The pine needles grazed with frost.

Honey Lyons's old truck turns into the drive. Luce looks up, then goes back to his wooding. Noel invites Lyons into the shop. He stokes the fire, leaves the door open so the flames can draft.

"Have a cup?" He points to the pot of cider on the stove.

"No thanks," Lyons answers. He sits down in the armchair. "Not here on a social call."

"Something wrong with the boat?"

"No."

"What is it then?"

Honey Lyons doesn't answer right away. He stretches out his legs toward the open doorway. The light breaks on the scuffed toes of his boots. He ticks his thumbnail against the edge of the chair, a steady crisp sharp-paced sound.

"They need someone to run her," he says at last and looks up at Noel. "Someone who knows the river."

Honey Lyons's eye shifts away, and Noel gathers his reasons: he is too old—they must know this—to go gallivanting over the ocean in the dead of night. He is hardly spry. He has no heart for work with risk—it was the boat he wanted—the one job—he took it, did it, and now it is done. He might consider building another. It was, after all, the work with the wood that he loved, but to run it? No. He would be no use to them for that. His eyes are tired. They do all right in daylight, but at night they cannot tell one shadow from the next. He is about to say all of this. He is about to give Honey Lyons a list of reasons he will not be able to refute, and Noel is sure it will be enough to blunt any more asking. He opens his mouth to speak and suddenly realizes that Lyons is not looking for him—perhaps all along, since the first time they showed up in his yard with their black fat-cat car, perhaps even then, they had not come looking for him. He follows the other man's line of sight, through the open doorway and across the yard to where Luce is working down the kindling branches off the fresh-hewn logs.

Bridge

It is just past five that night, already dark, when they pull up in front of the Grange. The coal stoves are already running, and the upstairs room has begun to fill with the warmth and the smell of roasted hams rising from the kitchen ovens below.

Bridge and Cora had gotten a ride with Abe and Sarah Pelham. They had loaded the baskets of pressed linens into the back of the pickup. Cora had squeezed into the front cab next to Sarah, and Bridge rode with the linens on the bed. As they drove, Bridge rubbed her hands together to keep her fingers warm. She placed her palms over her cheeks. The cold wind burned her eyes.

At the Grange, they carry the baskets of linens inside, unfold the tablecloths, stretch them out to cover the long tables. Harold Manchester and Walter Sills are hanging a red, white, and blue bunting over the stage. Grace Mason is laying down greens. She has broken up Christmas wreaths, and she arranges princess pine and holly through the middle of each table as a centerpiece. As Sally Wilkes sets down the silver, Cora and Bridge fold the napkins and lay them out on the china plates at each setting. Then they carry the empty linen baskets downstairs into the kitchen.

Cora sits in a chair in the corner by the window as Bridge goes outside to talk to a few of the boys shoveling coal. Annie Deacon and Elizabeth Searle draw the pots of beans out of the oven and set them on the stove. The heat is thick in the room with the smell of molasses, brown sugar, and meat. When the door to the outside yard swings open, the wind strikes through, the fires hiss, and the cold stings Cora's face.

When her husband, Russell, was alive, they had always come to the Grange. Russell would do the ice for the summer events, and Cora did the linens. They would bring Luce and Bridge to the game suppers in the fall and spring, and to the Indian clambakes held out back in the summertime. They would come to the dances in the winters—Cora remembers the sound of the fiddle playing the "Devil's Dream," the room spinning, beeswax candles and soft red light, their shoes against the newly polished floor. Russell always held her tightly as they danced. He would laugh softly, hum along off-tune, whisper something in her ear, then spin her out away from him. She misses him. Sometimes desperately, and every smell and shadow of the Grange Hall reminds her of him. The memory is sweet and bitter, but she would not trade it.

Owen Wales comes in from outside. He is the Master of the Grange, and tonight he is dressed in stiff clothes. He owns the farm directly north of them on Pine Hill Road. He grew up with Russell, and he is a handsome man, still a bachelor. Cora has heard talk he keeps a woman in the city. He looks at Cora as he comes in. He has never spoken to her beyond a curt greeting, and he does not speak to her now. He asks Annie Deacon when the food will be ready. Then he straightens his jacket and goes upstairs.

Cora looks out through the window. Her daughter is leaning against a tree, her hands in her coat pockets. She is talking to two of the Manchester boys as they shovel coal into the wheelbarrow. She is flirting with one of them, the older one, and then she is laughing, the three of them laughing, and her hair is dark against the snow, her teeth straight and bright. Cora watches her. She watches how Bridge looks away from the boys across the road toward the woods. One of them says something to her, and whatever it is, she does not like it. She shoots him a look, her eyes cool, detached. She says something back. The boy's face reddens, and he bends again to his work. She has always had that coolness, Cora thinks. From the time Bridge was a child, she seemed to be able to pick through and choose what she felt when she wanted to feel it. She and her mother were at opposite ends of nature that way.

But when Russell was alive, there was a balance to the family. Each one of them had had their proper place. Father, mother, grandfather, daughter, son. Russell was the soft-spoken glue, the ballast in the keel. And when he was gone, that order shriveled. They became edgy, combustible. They scrapped among themselves. As Cora sees it, her father, Noel, and her son, Luce, are cut from the same brooding cloth. The things about Luce that her father despises are the things most true to his own nature. Bridge is their battleground, their tug-of-war. After Russell died, Luce and Bridge became inseparable. In small ways, Noel tries to break them up. But Bridge is wise to it, and strong-willed, and the more Noel does it, the more she clings to Luce.

Bridge comes back indoors, her face flushed with the work and the cold. Samuel Wilkes has begun to carve out the hams. He lays huge slices out onto the long platters. Annie Deacon hands Bridge another carving knife and the whetstone. Bridge goes to a chair, puts a few drops of vegetable oil on the stone, and runs the blade back and forth across it.

When Bridge carries the first tray of food upstairs, Cora follows her. She herself won't help serve. She did once, and on her first trip up, she dropped two meat pies on the stairs, then slipped on some loose filling and slid down the rest of the steps to the bottom.

She does the linens now and that's enough. She will strip them later when the tables have been cleared. She will take the soiled dinner napkins and tablecloths and she will soak them out tomorrow, wring them until they are clean. It is enough, she thinks, as she comes to the top of the stairs, it is enough to be here in this open room she loves with her sweet ghosts and the smells of fire and roasted meat and pine.

When Henry first walks into the Grange, he is not sure for a moment where he is. A large open room, broad ceilings, polished floors, white sheets laid out on long tables, women in white aprons, the glint of silver, the colors of the flag above the stage, and for a moment, it seems that he has just stepped into a room of the military hospital at Neuilly, and he teeters, one foot in the old world, one foot in the new, the silver on the cloth, the white sheets on the tables—he can feel a pressure in his chest—his body turning to wood—his heart begins to race, his mind split, broken up.

There is a small group of people to his right, men in trousers and wool jackets, a few in overalls, women in heavy dresses and sweaters. They were talking among themselves, but they have turned and they are looking at him now. One older woman with worn and lovely eyes, a red scarf around her neck, leans toward a broad-faced man beside her, and she whispers something to him, still looking at Henry. They don't know him, he thinks, his mind in pieces, strange warps to it. They can't know anything about him. He has never seen them before, never been here before.

The broad-faced man nods to the woman in the red scarf, and they step toward him together. Instinctively he goes to take a step back, then collects himself and forces a smile but his heart is in despair as he thinks to himself that this is exactly why he has sidestepped the world of the living for so long. He is not capable of functioning in it.

The broad-faced man is extending his hand. "Arthur Russell," he says, and smiles. "Cousin of the incumbent."

Henry nods, shaking his hand. "Henry Vonniker."

The man's grip is strong and his hand is rough.

"My wife, Alpha."

"A pleasure to meet you," Henry says.

The woman smiles at him. "Are you a new member?" she asks.

"Of the Grange? No, I am afraid not."

"But you live in town?"

Henry nods.

"Might I ask where?"

"At the beach."

"Oh," she says. "You live down there year-round?"

"Yes."

"I don't recall seeing you before."

"I work in the city."

"Oh?"

"In New Bedford, at one of the mills."

"I see."

"So will they strike or not?" Arthur Russell asks.

"I think it is likely they will."

And there is silence then among the three of them, and Henry can see that they are piecing it together. They will not ask if he is one of the bosses at the mill, they have already gathered that he is. He lives down at the beach in one of the cottages. Perhaps they are remembering talk they have heard. Oh yes, they are thinking, he is that cotton broker's son. The one who was in the war.

Alpha smiles, a bit embarrassed at the silence, and she takes Henry's arm and leads him over to the rest of their group. "You'll sit with us, of course," she says. "We're mostly farmers here. Well no, not all of us. This is George Small. His is the blacksmith shop near Sisson's Corner."

Henry lets her steer him through introductions and conversation. He follows her lead, and she smiles at him kindly from time to time. When the food is brought up from downstairs, she seats him at the table between herself and a bearded man.

He still feels unsettled, misplaced, but he does what he can. Heaping platters of ham are set down on the table among the pine boughs, bowls of beans, potato salad, plates of brown bread, and he answers their inquiries, he smiles and nods; when their focus shifts to the town meeting and the upcoming articles on the warrant, he admits apologetically that he has not followed recent town events as closely as he should.

He serves himself a small plate of food.

"Take more than that," Alpha says, prodding him gently. "You've next to no flesh on you."

He lets her lay another slab of ham down on his plate.

They are talking about streetlights down at Horseneck, the bearded man on his right and a younger red-haired man who sits across from him. They are talking about the expense of keeping them lit through the winter. Is it really necessary? They are talking about the money needed for a gasoline shovel, and other money needed to finish laying macadam on the new Cornell Road from where they left off the year before, down to Artingstall's Corner. But he is only half listening. He is only half there. His mind is at war. He is at war. And men are dying around him. They might not know it yet. But they are dying. So many have already died, and his body was wood then too. His hands were quick, but their insides spilled out. He could not save them. Alpha is touching his arm, asking him something. She is asking him if he knows much about farming. They'll have to burn the asparagus beds, she says, when the snow melts. There are thorns in them this year. They have a vegetable stand in the summer, and they are going to try to grow strawberries this spring. Fresh strawberries seem to be a favorite among the summer people. Sally Ivanheld grew them last year and sold out every weekend. Does he have a taste for strawberries? she asks and he nods. He mumbles something. Alpha turns to the dark-haired woman on her left. Henry looks up, and across the room he sees Bridge.

She has just come up the stairs, carrying a fresh plate of ham. The steam rises off the meat around her face. She looks directly at him, her eyes hook into his for a moment before she turns away and walks toward another table close to the stage at the opposite end of the room. He watches as she lays down the plate of food, and his mind is suddenly straightened, suddenly clear, his anxiety gone. He does not take his eyes off her. She crosses to a side table and picks up a china pitcher and refills the water glasses. Then with the empty pitcher she retraces her route along the edge of the room. She does not look at him again. She goes back down the stairs.

"Are you alright then?" Alpha is asking him.

Henry turns and looks at her. "I am in heaven," he says slowly.

She stares at him, concerned for a moment. The wrinkles deepen at the edges of her eyes. Then she giggles and points with the end of her knife to his plate and the food still untouched. "Eat up then. Ham's good to bring a young man back to earth."

Cora sits with the rest of the help at the table near the top of the stairs. They are the last to be served. The men and boys sit down at one end, some with coal still on their hands and on the cuffs of their sleeves. Cora sits at the other end with the women. Bridge walks around the table filling the water glasses. Annie Deacon and Lucy McIleer are talking about someone.

"He was in France, I heard," Lucy says. "A doctor in the big war."

"Pass those pickles, please, will you, Annie?" Norma Jakes says.

"Not much use after it," Lucy goes on. "So the talk is."

"Was he in Paris?"

"No, not those pickles. The sweet ones there by the butter."

"I don't think it was Paris."

"I heard it was."

"No."

"I'm quite sure."

"Why don't you ask him yourself then."

"I heard it was Paris."

Bridge sits down next to her mother. Her work is done, and she fills her plate. She picks up her knife and fork, and without a word begins to cut into a piece of ham. She seems nervous, Cora notices with some surprise, agitated, which is unlike her. Cora busies herself with her own food, then a sip of water. She finds a stain on the tablecloth. She studies its shape. Bridge eats quickly. She swabs the last of the beans off her plate with a piece of brown bread. She wipes her mouth with the edge of her napkin. Then her hand stops. Cora senses her pause. She glances up. Bridge is looking across the room, and Cora follows her gaze. It is a man she is looking at. A stranger. He is young, fair, well dressed. He is sitting beside Alpha Russell, his head bent toward her. The older woman is speaking to him, and he is listening. Then he looks up directly at Bridge, and Cora can sense something electric, something understood pass between them. Bridge's eyes snap around. She glares at her mother.

"What?" she says, her voice sharp.

"Nothing," Cora answers softly. She shakes her head and looks away. "Nothing."

Bridge breaks off another piece of bread. She finds her knife and cuts a slice of butter off the pound.

He has cleared his plate. He lets Alpha fill it for him again. The food is fresh and good, and he finds that he is hungry.

"Do you always eat so much in heaven?" she teases, dishing out another serving of beans. Her pale eyes sparkle. She has deep lines through her cheeks, and he notices how they gather when she smiles. "You remind me of my oldest boy," she says.

He could tell her that whatever she has seen in him tonight is not his everyday character. He could tell her that tonight, for the first time in years, he can feel something stirring in him, some old smooth river waking up.

"Do you know what sort of poetry they'll have later in the evening?" he asks her.

She shakes her head. "Arthur and I only come for the food."

He smiles and looks away again. His eyes search the room for Bridge. She is still at the table. She has turned toward the woman seated next to her. She says something, then glances at him across the room. When she sees he is watching her, she looks away sharply. He smiles to himself. He will find her when the meal is cleared. He will go up to her and introduce himself. He will say nothing about the incident at Shorrock's store. He will ask if she has an interest in poetry. He will ask if he might call on her sometime. He eats a bit more of the food, and then he is full. He lays his knife and fork down on his plate. He looks up again across the room to the table where Bridge was sitting, but she is gone.

She steps outside into the darkness. The cold is sharp. It burns her throat, and the burning soothes her. It had unnerved her, the way he was looking at her, all of it had unnerved her, him being there, watching her that way, he had no right to be there, in her world. And every time she had glanced at him—sometimes without intending to do it—but every time her eyes had strayed to his face he seemed to sense it, and he would look up and catch her watching him. She shivers and pulls her coat more tightly around her as she walks. She shovels her hands deep into the pockets of her coat. It will be a long walk home. She thinks of him often, more often than she would like, as she walks down the steep of Handy Hill toward Hix Bridge. She thinks of him less once she has crossed the river. She begins to climb the hill on the other side. Her breath is white in the moonlight. Her head aches with the cold. But when she hears the rough sound of the car engine behind her, far off, but growing nearer, she knows who it is. She does not turn around. The sound fades as the car dips over the first rise, then grows louder, approaching. Her first instinct is to disappear, behind a shed, into the trees, to let him drive by. But she keeps walking, her body suddenly flushed with heat, and she senses, without knowing for sure, that he has come looking for her. Her shoes sound loud against the oiled dirt. The headlamps play ahead of her, casting her shadow tall and long on the road. The car slows down.

Henry Vonniker leans over and unrolls the window. "Can I give you a ride?"

"Oh, no thanks," she answers, but she smiles, she tries not to, but she does. She keeps walking.

He lets the car run slowly alongside her. "It's freezing out. Let me drive you home."

She stops and looks in at him through the open window. "It's not on your way." His face is very pale in the darkness. His eyes sink into her.

"Please," he says.

She hesitates for a moment, then opens the door and climbs in. His gloves are on the seat between them.

"Do you need them?" he asks her.

"No, I'm fine."

"You have no mittens."

"I forgot them at the Grange."

He gives her the gloves. They are soft leather, flannel-lined. She slips them on. They are large on her hands. She has no feeling in the tips of her fingers from the cold. She rubs them through the gloves, bending them back and forth at the joint. "Thank you," she says. She can feel him looking at her, and she wants to look at him, and at the same time, she is afraid. They are too close. The closeness terrifies her.

"What is it?" she says quietly, looking down.

"I'm sorry." He looks away, out the front windshield.

"Shall we go?" she says.

"I don't know where you live."

She laughs, suddenly more at ease. "No, you don't, do you?"

"I don't."

"Take a left up ahead at the corner."

He puts the car into gear, and they drive. He takes the turn, and they head up Pine Hill, past the woods and the chicken farm. She notices that he does not drive quickly. He looks straight ahead at the road. Through the window the cold clear night winds past. She feels torn by the silence. She wants to ask him why he came looking for her, why he came to the Grange, if he came because of her, and at the same time, she doesn't want to know. The feeling is coming back into her fingers. His hands are on the wheel, his skin white as bone in the dim light. They come to the end of the road. He stops.

"Left again," she says.

He makes the turn. "Your name is Bridge."

"Yes." She smiles. She looks down at his gloves.

"I saw you for the first time at Asa Sisson's funeral. Do you remember?"

"Yes."

He does not say anything else, but she can feel that he wants to. She can sense the strange and fitful air between them, and she wants to touch him, his face, his hands. Every muscle in her body is tense.

"Here," she says quickly. "The next house on the left, but you can just pull up here on the side of the road. This is fine." She slips off the gloves and lays them on the seat. As the car rolls to a stop, she goes to pull the door latch.

"Wait," he says.

She looks up at him, her fingers on the handle, the metal is cold, like ice.

"Could I . . ."

She stares at him. He is looking at her intently, searching her face, and she can feel a slow and quiet trembling deep at the end of her.

"Thank you for the ride," she says. She pulls the handle and gets out of the car and closes the door behind her. She doesn't look back. She crosses the road into her yard and rounds the corner of the house. She stops there and waits in the darkness, until she hears the sound of his car pull away.

Over the next few days, she finds him sneaking around in her thoughts—a thin and solitary current that seems to have its own whim, its own restless mind. She thinks of him while she works in the shop with Noel or as she is doing chores around the house: dusting, cooking, feeding the stove. She sees his face as she sets the logs into the fire.

Later in the week, when she stops by Abigail Dean's hat shop to buy a few hairpins for her mother, she notices a dozen small blue bottles of perfume by the cashbox.

"Soir de Paris," says Abigail Dean, her voice glossy over the French words. "It's all the rage and very expensive."

Bridge nods. She fingers one of the brushed silver caps.

"Nice cap," she says, then shrugs. Her hand drops to her side. "I can't wear fancy perfumes myself."

"Why ever not? A young girl like you."

"They make me itch. Big red spots like the hives."

Abigail Dean's nose wrinkles. "That's quite awful."

"It is what it is, I suppose," Bridge answers. "But I'd like a small bag for those hairpins, if it wouldn't be too much trouble. I'd hate to lose one on my walk home."

"Oh yes, of course. I'll dig a bag out for you. Just a moment." Abigail steps into the back room of the shop.

Bridge picks up one of the small blue bottles of perfume. She turns it over in her hand, then slips it into her coat pocket. She leans back against the counter, and pretends to study the colored scarves, dyed wool and silk, hanging from pegs along the opposite wall.

Abigail Dean returns with a small paper bag. "It's well used, but there doesn't seem to be a hole in it."

"That'll do fine," Bridge says. "Thank you." She puts the hairpins into the bag and folds the open edge over tightly. She walks out the door into the snow.

At home in her bedroom, she opens the small blue bottle and puts a few drops onto her fingers. The oil is slick and cool. It smells of crushed flowers. She rubs some into her wrist, some into her neck, and she lies back on her bed. She looks toward the window. There is ice baked around the edge of it. The rough winter light sticks in the snowflakes frozen on the glass, and they glow. She closes her eyes and thinks of Henry, with the warm scent of the oil on her skin.

She hears the door slam downstairs, the sound of her brother's voice below in the kitchen. She sits up sharply and screws the cap back onto the bottle. She stuffs it into an old sock and buries it in one corner of a drawer.

Part II

Mooncussers

Luce

She is all bones to him. For as long as he can remember she has been—a soft bag of limbs in his arms. And it was only that fall—before the first frost set in on the leeks, before the last tomatoes had gone by, when the icehouse had been emptied nearly to the floor and he had to wade through two feet of rotted-out, soaked straw—it was only then that he noticed how her body had begun to change.

She is still thin, still a little wild. She has always been his. Trailing a slight distance behind him, the way any other young, not tame creature would. But it is only now that she has begun to put on a little flesh, only now that she has begun to grow into something more than simple bones, that it occurs to him that he could hurt her. That she could hurt him. The realization fills him with an odd sense of guilt, fear, and at the same time, a strange, complicated desire. He does not know what to do with this, but because of it, an unspoken, unspeakable line has begun to grow between them. It is not that he would cross it. He would risk losing her if he did. But the desire troubles him. He tries to duck it. He goes about his route selling ice—a quarter for a slab—a nickel for a poor-piece. After the first cold snap, he and Harry Spire walk down to check for skim ice on the ponds. And when Bridge comes to him in the early mornings through the short pitched tunnel that runs under the eaves, when she creeps into his bed, as she has done since they were little, and tucks herself like something small and warm under his arm, he tells himself that how they are together is nothing more than how they have always been.

He knows every breath of her—the yellow spot in her right iris, the slight discolored mark on the inside of her wrist. He knows how her hair grows from the root—a swirl around the back of her scalp. He knows her the way he knows the river. He feels he owns her the way he owns that kind of knowing.

They cut ice early that year. By mid-January the first crop is better than eight inches thick. For a week they go down to the ponds with the handsaws and the ice plow hitched up to a two-horse team. They set the horse saw, and Asa Vaughan leads them out across the ice, cutting the rafts five feet long, three feet wide. Luce and Harry Spire work behind with the double-barbed poles—they work the rafts of ice across the pond down toward the raise.

As they walk, the cold knifes into him. The snot freezes on his lip and he can feel the tightening of the skin. He cups one hand over his mouth and breathes out warm air to thaw it, then wipes his nose. The snot leaves a pearly skid down his sleeve.

With handsaws, they break the rafts into single cakes and haul them by pulley into the icehouse. The inside walls are sheathed with sawdust, and they stack the blocks of ice from floor to ceiling. Between each layer, they set down sawdust and hay.

Luce does the ice work because it was his father's work. The route he drives was his father's route before his father died in the swine flu. The ice work is good work. Steady work. But he knows it is work that won't last forever. He can see the writing on the wall. The newer summer homes, the homes of the rich—even some of the cottages down on the beach—they have the new ice chests that plug into the wall and need no ice to keep them cold. So when Honey Lyons stops by the ice pond that Thursday morning as they are hauling the last of the crop inside and asks Luce if he can have a short talk with him, Luce doesn't hesitate. He walks with Honey Lyons outside.

Just a small job. Lyons says. One job, there might be more if Luce takes to the work. He has heard Luce is good with a boat, and some men he knows need someone for a job the night after next. Dirk McAllister was on for it, but they can't seem to find him. The jimmy seems to have taken a cut that wasn't his and got himself gone.

They have walked away from the icehouse toward the edge of the pond. The frozen hay cracks under their boots. Luce glances up toward the pines, their branches shattered with snow.

"Tell me the job."

"You'll be told if you take it."

"I'll take it depending on what it is."

Honey Lyons grins, his face hard, and when he speaks, his voice seems to come from between his teeth. "What it is depends on if you'll take it."

Luce stubs his boot into a long blade of ice. He splits it with his toe.

"If this weather keeps," he says, "the sides of the river'll be frozen night after next, I'd bet, all but the channel."

Lyons doesn't answer.

"So the job's not in the river, I'd bet."

"I wouldn't bet one way or other if I were you."

"Is it mooncusser work?"

Lyons looks at him sharply. "You get this straight. Breaking up ships on rocks, salvaging someone else's load, all that pirate stuff is for the dirt poors. You accuse a businessman of that, you're only showing what you come from."

Luce feels his face flush. "You know what I meant," he says under his breath.

"I know what you said. You want the job or not?"

Luce doesn't answer right away. His eyes swing across the frozen water. The crows shriek through the trees. "I want a third more than what you're planning to offer," he says.

Honey Lyons laughs. "If you tell me that up front, I might offer you a third less."

Luce glances at him, then looks down at his hands chapped by the cold. "I can run the river at night better than anyone—you know that." He peels one bit of skin off the nail.

Honey Lyons studies him for a moment. He does not say anything. He offers nothing more.

They stand together on the edge of the frozen pond. The clouds mass above the trees. Luce watches them, aware of the other man standing beside him, waiting, as the clouds tumble like boulders down into the pines.

"I'll take it," Luce says. He does not look at Lyons.

"Once you're in, you're in."

Luce nods.

"Like I said, it's the night after next."

"Black-of-the-moon night."

Lyons nods. "You'll leave from the Point Wharf. You'll come back into the river to unload. The stone pier, two landings up from the Meadows."

Luce shakes his head. "No man with a drop of common sense would bring a boat upriver of the bridge this time of year, this kind of winter. You hit the wrong spot, ice'll slice her bow like a knife through cheese."

"Better not hit the wrong spot," Lyons says. Then he smiles, the gold stub of his tooth sharp in the light.

That first night out, Luce meets Honey Lyons down at the Point Wharf on the east side, the sheltered side, behind the bridge. When he sees the boat tied up, Luce smiles to himself. The old man's boat, he thinks. Lyons has a boy with him, Johnny Clyde. Just seventeen, Johnny comes from the Narrows in the north part of town. He is tall and skinny, black hair, pale skin, a soft apple face. He talks little.

"He'll be your other hand," Lyons says to Luce.

"Already got two of my own."

Lyons shoots him a look, and in the dim light spilling from the dock house behind them, Luce can see a hard, cruel glint in the other man's eyes. Then it is gone, and he gives Luce a sly, complicit smile. "You're captain," he says. "Johnny's your mate. As long as you're working for me, he'll be your mate."

From his coat pocket, Honey Lyons draws out a sealed package wrapped in brown paper.

"This is what you'll give them for your order." Luce reaches out to take the package, but Lyons's hand snaps back. "Don't even think about opening it, big boy. I'll know it if you do."

They leave on the ebb tide. The river is empty, frozen in patches. Luce steers them gently through the thin plates of skim ice. He gives the engine some gas once they pass Crack Rock, but then he cuts her back again as they come along the Lion's Tongue. They pass Charlton Wharf, out the harbor mouth.

The ocean is cold, the air slick, the water and the sky black ahead of them. They run without lights, speeding out toward the bell, and then past it. The land drops out of sight behind them. For a while, they can still see a faint brushed glow over the horizon, but that too fades, and they are left steering through the night, the sea black as pitch underneath them.

They head south-southwest. They pass the ledge. At 11:25 off the port side, Luce spots first one sail, then another. The ship rises up as if she were rising out of the darkness, out of the sea. She is a schooner, a beautiful fisherman, trim and knockabout-rigged. Her masts are tall and strong. Her lines slope down in long and graceful curves.

Several smaller boats are already pulled up along her starboard side: other customers loading up their decks. One of the crew waves them in, and Luce pulls the boat into a clear space alongside her. Johnny Clyde throws the truck tire fenders over the rail and ties off a line. They climb aboard. Luce notices how the men take the pair of them in, eye them warily. They are strangers. Each man of the crew has a heavy Colt strapped to his hip.

One comes up to him. "We've got it all from a drink to a barrel. What's your order?"

Luce hands him the package. The mate takes it up to the wheelhouse. As they wait, Luce takes a turn around the deck. He can see cases of liquor stacked and covered under canvases and tarps. There are huge barrels and smaller kegs pressed in tight pyramids aft. A man he takes to be the captain returns with the mate. He is tall, red-bearded. He extends his hand. Luce takes it, starts to introduce himself, but the captain cuts him off and shakes his head.

"Don't want your name," he says. "Don't know the names of some of my own men. Don't want to. Your boy'll stay here. You come with me."

He leads Luce down a steep ladder, belowdecks. The hold is divided into smaller walled-off compartments according to brand and price and kind. One berth holds nothing but champagne, another brandy, another gin. The whiskey room is twenty foot fore and aft, ten foot across, and crammed deck to overhead. The bottles are

stacked in crates and sewed up in gunnysacks. The captain takes
one, rips it open, and Luce can see five quart bottles of Cedar
Brook, 100 proof.

"Your order's for this. And twenty cases of Golden Wedding."

Luce nods.

"Bring your boy down and oil up." He takes out one of the bottles of Cedar Brook and holds it out to Luce. "Yours," he says. "On
me."

Luce nods. He does not smile. He takes it.

Although the wind is behind them on the return trip in, the boat
runs slower. She is sluggish, her hull sunk low in the water by the
weight. Luce keeps her out to full throttle, and they speed through
the brutal cold on the flat black sea. Spray strikes against his face.
The wind cuts his eyes. He can feel the hot burn of the whiskey in
his throat, the searing cold of the air in his lungs, and he feels brutally alive, cut free from his life, a part of something larger, something grand and beautiful and strange, a territory without borders
or names, a part of the cold and the burning and the speed and the
limitless night.

He cuts back on the throttle as they come up to the Knubble
Rock, through the mouth of the harbor, the engine running soft
under the silencer. Once, on the other side of Cory's Island, the bow
nudges up into a thicker pack of ice, and Luce can feel the grinding impact against the hull. He backs away and steers her left, into
the deeper channel.

They come in under the Point Bridge. He threads through the
open running water between the shore-fast ice. They put in at the
stone pier, upriver of Ship Rock. Luce can see that someone has
broken up the ice alongside the pier and left two new lines coiled on
hooks nailed into the piles. They tie up and unload the cases. They
work quietly in the cold still darkness. They do not speak. When

the boat is empty, they carry the cases up to the barn. The door is rolled back, and some distance away, up the drive, Luce notices two trucks waiting. A man gets out of one and comes toward them. Luce has never seen him before.

"It's our job from here," the man says. "Get scarce."

Luce and Johnny Clyde bring the boat back under the bridge. They tie up again at the wharf in the slip on the east side. Johnny Clyde gives Luce a lift in his pickup, a 1924 Ford that has one lean deep dent along the right tail side. He drops Luce at the end of Pine Hill Road.

"So we're in then?" Luce asks him just before he closes the door. Johnny looks uncomfortable for a moment, unsure.

"Guess so, I guess. We are, I suppose. Dunno, really." His eyes shift. He looks away and taps the steering wheel with his left hand.

"Sure then," Luce says. "See you around."

"Sure then," Johnny says. "See you."

The following week, Honey Lyons comes by the icehouse again, looking for Luce, and Luce walks away from his work that day and he does not go back. He runs the boat through that first winter, paired up with Johnny Clyde. They run twelve days a month on the dark of the moon. They run through mud-thick days and clear cold nights, stiff breeze, flat calm, heavy rolling seas. They run out to all types of ships anchored in Rum Row—tramp steamers and fine-rigged schooners, old sailing barks, the occasional tugboat, barge, or packet ship. Sometimes they will go out late, after the moon has set, and come back in through the fog just before dawn. They bring in crates of whiskey, bourbon, Double Eagle, Old Tom gin, Bene-dictine, cases of French wine and vintage champagne. They meet the shore crews and load crate after crate onto flatbeds and into the trunks of cars.

They follow each order Honey Lyons gives them. Once, when Luce hears news ahead of a patrol blockade gathering after midnight at the mouth, he dumps a load in deeper water among the rocks off Gooseberry Neck. He ties each case to a buoy and a block of salt that they keep in the hold. In three days, when the salt dissolves and the buoys float up to the surface, he and Johnny Clyde go back for them, on a full-of-the-moon night. They haul the cases up and run them into shore.

He notices that on the larger runs, money rarely changes hands. The deal is prearranged. Prepaid. Lyons will give him a note, a skinny package, an envelope, a coded message scribbled in black ink, and that is what Luce will take out to the rum-ship to exchange for the load. And he likes it that way. He likes having no money on him, nothing to tempt the thief in him, nothing to worry after, nothing to lose.

He takes to the work quickly. He learns the rules. He sees into the guts of the business, and he keeps his mouth shut, his ears open. Working out of the wharf, he begins to sense the unsettled tension between rival gangs. Swampy Davoll is the lead man of the Point crew. Luce knows him by sight, a tall, big-shouldered man with a thatch of white hair turned early, a wind-scarred face. He carves wood and is known through town as a good man. Tough as dried codfish, he'll turn if you cross him, but the talk was he kept many a family in food and heat through the winter. If a fellow was hard up for cash, Swampy would give him thirty bucks and tell him to forget about it.

At the Point, the wharves are crowded with boats—a few built only for the rum trade that have never had another use. Others are work boats, cats, swordfishing vessels, draggers, a few skiffs. The Coast Guard cutter, patrol boat 317, keeps a space in a berth on the middle dock, opposite the boat Wes Wilkes runs with Caleb Mason, the *Mary Jane*.

One blustery Sunday, mid-February, when Luce comes down to the wharf to check the engine, to make sure the cold has not seized her up, Swampy Davoll steps out of the Shuckers Club across the road from Blackwood's store. He lights up his pipe, takes a look around, and spots Luce down at the boat on the east pier. He walks over to him and asks him into the club for a game of cards. Luce goes. Three of them are already in there, at a table in one corner of the room past the slate pool table: North Kelly, one of the Masons, and Wes Wilkes, who is the youngest of Swampy's gang, a few years older than Luce. They offer him a drink and a smoke, and the liquor is good. Wes Wilkes deals out the cards and they play, and Luce can see that Swampy is sizing him up, seeing what kind of cat he is. They know who he works for. They don't like Honey Lyons, don't trust him. And it is in that card game, when Luce has lost two hands, but is betting high in the third with three queens in his hand, that Swampy remarks casually, quietly, tapping used ash from the bowl of his pipe, that he has heard talk that Johnny Clyde, the young fellow Luce works with, might be Honey Lyons's nephew, would Luce know anything about that? His voice is low, barely skims over the tinny sound of the radio set up on the ice chest. He matches Luce's bet in the pot, and the third man in, Mason, folds.

"I'm not saying I know for a fact that it's true," Swampy murmurs when Luce doesn't answer. "I'm just saying you might want to watch your back."

Luce will say nothing to Honey Lyons about that conversation, nothing about being invited into Swampy Davoll's place for a round of cards. He winds up winning that particular hand with his three queens that beat out Swampy's pair of aces. He says nothing to Johnny Clyde the next time he sees him, but he watches them both a little differently from then on.

When he is down at the wharf, working over the boat, scrubbing her deck, wiping down the salt spray caked on her pilothouse window, he listens. He hears all the talk outside the papers: of how they store the loads of liquor in horse barns, vegetable cellars, haylofts; how they run it to the city in school buses, hearses, pickups, and wagons, in new sedans and old Maxwell touring cars, their backseats pulled out, bottles hidden in every spare compartment. He hears the story of the man from Tiverton murdered and put in a barrel of cement because he talked too much, and that other one about Helmut Gifford, who took five slugs to the gut and survived. He hears behind-the-back-talk about the legends: the rumored sightings of Al Capone, the *Idle Hour,* the *Black Duck* and her captain, Charlie Travers, who works out of the Sakonnet and shows her heels to every patrol that tries to chase her down. He hears the tale of the old farmer's house over by Barney's Joy—a house that was gutted in 1921, then bought by a Syndicate man and rebuilt for the rum-running trade, with a cellar floor raised and lowered by hydraulic pumps, a second cellar hidden underneath. The house was known to be a haven for the rummies, and the Feds had searched it four times and never turned up a trace, never found the gin stored in the water tanks, gin running through the pipes, gin coming out the cold water faucet on the kitchen tap.

He hears lower talk, hushed talk, about mooncussing and the hijacks, the go-through men, the occasional double-crossing of one gang by another. He hears about the salvagers, local fishermen mostly, willing to take the risk, who scavenge drops made by the inshore crews. They will watch a chase from land and mark the crates of liquor dumped overboard; while the Feds and Coast Guard are busy chasing down the gangs, the fishermen will steal out with their dories and their skiffs. They will drag up the cases and the sacks

with homemade grappling gear—oyster tongs and corkscrew poles.
They will clear the load before the rummies have time to get back
to it. They move it to their own hiding places and sell it in the city
themselves.

Luce works through the weeks, the months, toward the first
thaw. He does his jobs for Honey Lyons, and he keeps his head
down. He learns who can be trusted and who to keep an eye out for.
He hears what kind of graft is going on, who can be bought with a
bribe, and who is tipping what. He stores away what he overhears,
and from time to time he has the sense that he is ordering these details for some future ambition, some future use.

Down at the pier one afternoon as Luce is straightening the kinks
out of the anchor chain, he overhears a row between Honey Lyons
and Swampy Davoll. They are sitting on the bench underneath the
Sinclair gasoline sign, and it is queer enough to see them sitting
there, two men who are known as enemies, as unmixable as oil and
water, to see them sitting there like an old bickering couple at opposite ends of the same bench. Watching from the corner of his eye,
Luce notices that when they speak, they do not look at one another,
they look straight ahead. The other men from Swampy's gang have
moved off the bench and given them room, a wide berth. They talk
low, but the wind is out of the northwest, behind them, and their
voices carry across the pier to Luce. They are talking about Dirk
McAllister, still gone missing.

"Coming up on three months now. I know you know something,
Lyons," Swampy Davoll is saying.

Honey Lyons shrugs. He palms his pack of cigarettes. "From
what I hear, your man Dirk was skimming off what wasn't his. Talk
is he made south with quite a piece of cash."

Swampy looks across the water toward the Point Bridge and beyond it, upriver toward Ship Rock. "Bullshit. Cuts no ice with me."

Honey Lyons lights a cigarette, throws down the match. It settles in the dirt at his feet. "I'm sure he'll turn up one of these days. Maybe toward spring."

Swampy gives him a long cold look. He is a good eight inches taller than Honey Lyons, and his hands are tremendous, but sitting that way, on the bench, they seem nearly equal size.

On the other side of the mud dock, Caleb Mason and Wes Wilkes push off, bound on the *Mary Jane*.

The young Coast Guard officer on the deck of patrol 317 waves them off. "Have a grand time out there tonight, Wes."

"Sure." Wilkes grins. "You, too."

"See you out there then?"

"Not if I can help it."

The *Mary Jane* circles away from the wharf, out into the channel, then heads toward the mouth. The Coast Guard patrol pushes off a few moments later. She backs around and trails them from a distance.

"You're off your hinges, Lyons," says Swampy Davoll. With his eyes, he follows the two boats as they head off down the river. "Someday they'll find your elbows under a pile of stones."

Lyons laughs. "Don't be so worried after your man Dirk McAllister. Like I say, I'd take a bet with you that sooner, more than later, he'll turn up."

Noel

Noel knows what his grandson does. He doesn't like it, but at the same time he knows it is not bad work for Luce. His grandson has always had a ken for danger, a nose for it. What surprises Noel is how Luce keeps his mouth shut. Over that first winter and into the spring, he doesn't talk about what he does or where he goes, not even to Bridge. He'll bring home small gifts for Cora, which she accepts without a word: trinkets, plum sweets, a jar of fancy southern marmalade. He buys a new pullover for Bridge, and a pair of oxford bag trousers and a trilby hat for himself. Apart from that, though, he seems to have his mind set on saving up his money.

Sometimes on a morning after he has been gone half the night, when Bridge and Noel are working in the shop or in the garden, they will break for a cup and a smoke, and Bridge will read from the news-paper aloud. She will read through the headline news about the mill strikes in New Bedford, the bread lines, the picket songs, and the rallies. She will skip ahead a page and find a smaller piece that reports on the exploits of the *Black Duck* or the *Eider*—a harrowing chase, an exchange of gunfire, an arrest or two, aliases given, and a wry line about some other men that slipped away. The silence will heave up between them as they both wonder without saying what part, if any, Luce had played—if he had been in the thick of it, or on the fringe. They wonder what it was he had done the night before that made him sleep so deep into the afternoon. Even when he wakes, groggy, ravenous, they can see the adventures still in his wrinkled clothes, dark things not yet shaken out of him.

"It's nothing you should think about being mixed up in," Noel says to Bridge one day. It is a warm afternoon, toward the end of March, and they are sitting outside in the sun. There are new buds on the swamp maples, and the world seems to tremble, on the verge of breaking out into spring. Bridge is bent over the newspaper, reading.

"Wherever he is," Noel goes on, "is no good place for you to be."

Bridge glances up at him, surprised. "I really don't think of him at all," she blurts out. Then she bites her lip, her face flushed, and he realizes that she has a secret.

"You don't think about who?"

"Nothing."

"Oh yes, there was something." He smiles.

"Luce," she says. "We were talking about Luce. Right?"

"I was. You weren't."

She shakes her head and begins to fold up the newspaper. She folds it carefully, tightly, along its creases, then folds it again and puts it away into the pocket of her coat. "Come on, then," she says, standing up. She brushes off her trousers. "Back to work. Don't get lazy on me."

He laughs and follows her into the shop. He sits back down at the worktable with a pencil and several sheets of draft paper. He is drawing out a set of plans for a new dory Howie Sherman has asked him to build. Bridge goes to the corner and starts to sort through a pile of wood. They work in silence for a while, then Noel asks, "You think there's hope for the Sultan of Swat this coming year? You think he'll break his own record?"

"I doubt it."

"You want to make a penny bet on it?"

"You're betting more than sixty home runs?"

"Yeah."

"I'll take that bet." But she doesn't look up. She keeps her head down, sawing out a length of wood. Her actions are quick and precise, her mouth in a thin stubborn line.

"What are you cutting all that wood out for anyhow?" he asks.

"I'm building you two new sawhorses," she says, still working the ripsaw. "I told you that before."

"You sure you're not just doing something to keep your mind off something else?"

She ignores him.

"Whatever happened to that fellow who gave you a ride home from the Grange a few months back?"

She freezes, but only for a moment. Then she puts down the ripsaw. There is sawdust on the sleeve of her shirt. "I don't have any idea what you're talking about."

"Can't lie to me, Bridge, you know that," he grins at her. He has guessed and she is furious, he can see it in her eyes.

"What are you digging for, Papa?"

"Is there anything worth digging for?"

"Absolutely nothing." But her face is flushed, and she fiddles with a raw edge on a piece of the wood she has cut.

"The night you went to the Grange, you got a ride home. I recognized the old engine on that car from the sound, not many of those around, and I knew whose it was. I was surprised when that car pulled up in front of our house, more surprised when I saw you get out of it."

"Oh," she says. "That car."

"You remember now?"

"I think so. But that was no one. Just a man I met at the Grange. We didn't really meet. I started walking home. He happened to drive by. He saw me walking and offered me a ride. It was a cold night. A ride home. Nothing more. That's all it was. I don't know why you're getting so worked up about it." She walks across the shop. From the shelf on the wall, she takes down a mallet, a few pieces of sandpaper, a tin can of pegs. "Is this all the sandpaper we've got?"

"He seems like a good man."

She is poking around in the tin can. "He might be. I have no idea. I don't know him at all. I don't think about him. I don't know why you think I do."

He smiles. "I didn't say you did."

She puts the can back on the shelf.

"All I'm saying, Bridge, is that you might do well to let a man like that into your thoughts now and then."

She turns to look at him. She stares. "That's enough, Papa. You have to stop talking about it, or I'll have to shut him out of my thoughts for good." She is gripping the mallet in her fist by her side. Her eyes are serious, and she is so obviously rattled and trying to keep herself in order that he bursts out laughing. She grabs a small chunk of wood and throws it at him. He ducks and it hits off the stovepipe. Now she is laughing too.

"Not another word about it," she says.

"Not a word."

She wipes her arm across her face. "It's hot in here, don't you think?"

"Don't feel hot to me."

She shoots him a look and he grins. She walks to the door and cracks it open. Cool air rushes in.

He knows her well enough to let it go. He does not bring it up again. But he notices small changes—how she files her nails, how she takes a little more care with her hair. That man has gotten under her skin, he thinks. That lucky man.

———

They plant peas and onions the first week of April. The herring are thick in the run. The days pass quickly, and the air is full of signs, as if the world has accelerated, new life swept into a small tight space and moving fast. Noel can feel it in the river, the brown water swelling up against the banks with the runoff from places higher north. He can smell it in the sweet tannic reek of rotten leaves.

Early May, schoolie bass come into the river. Noel and Bridge go down to the dock to ready the skiff. They throw burlap sacks down along the bottom and fill the hull with buckets of riverwater so the wood swells. For the first several hours, the water dribbles out between the seams. When the boat has drained, they fill it again and leave it there overnight. By morning, there are no leaks left at all. Noel bails the boat and takes it out to set his crab traps and his eel pots. He staggers them along the ledges and the rocks between Hix Bridge and Indian Hill.

By mid-June the summer people have begun to come back into town: window boards pried off the houses at the beach, rugs beaten and slung out to air over porch rails. The wind works through their fringes. Noel does not like summer. It brings the out-of-towners, their autos, their smells and sounds and crowds, their clambakes and surfbathing picnics on the beach, garden parties, lawn parties, men in white flannels and blue blazers, women in cloche hats and pongee silks. They alter the river and the light. The white sails of their teak boats dash like scraps of paper as they tack back and forth across the channel. They build angler stands in the mud off the islands in the East Branch. Their svelte new touring cars tail one another down the road, horns, shouts, brightly colored scarves waving. They clutter the space so the creatures of the off-season—the animals, the locals, and the dead—are not so free to move.

There is a loneliness Noel feels every year this season comes around, a loneliness in the long days of what they call "fine weather" and "fair skies." The sunlight pierces his eyes like nails, and still the heat builds, day after day, implacable and sultry, heat clinging to the earth.

It is in the summer months that he feels the longing most, a nibbling in his heart for the sea and his old life. He will miss the company he used to keep—his old friend Rui and the other blue-water men. He will remember the long days on the Pacific as the ship passed through the equator line. Their skins grew parched and eaten by the sun, dark as tarred rigging. He remembers how once, between islands, they ran low on fresh water. His tongue cleaved to the roof of his mouth. His lips cracked and bled. The sea stretched taut, light splitting off the surface like a blade.

It is in the summer months that his mind is occasionally troubled. Haunted by old thoughts, shadow things. Hannah. He never felt a deeper, more devastating desire than the desire he felt for Hannah. It was a desire that made him cross oceans. A desire that complicated, even compromised, his love for her.

Hannah was a naturalist. She had the mind and the eye of a naturalist. A piercing mind. A ruthless, scientific eye.

By the time their life together ended, she had turned open nearly every pocket inside him. She had picked every lock on every door he kept closed. She had pried open every sealed window and stood in every walled-off room, and there was a part of him that had resented her for how she would always insist on peering into those dark and unmarked places not meant to be seen. Now he walks alone through those same rooms. He draws down old things from their shelves—a dream he had once of building her a house by the ocean. He had imagined a sunken front room, just lower than sea level, and built so that, on a surge, the waves would strike up against the window glass. She had laughed when he told her. "Such an impractical house, Noel," she had chided him, "but then you are, of course, my most impractical fool." Her eyes were light as she spoke (he remembers this), and she was happy. He had held her and said nothing more about it. He buried into her body, smooth and bare and young against him, a swift soft summer darkness. It came and went so quickly. Throughout their life together he would go on dreaming of that house. He did not speak of it to her again but he carried the dream. He swore that someday he would build that house for her and she would love it.

There was only one point of true soreness between them, only one point of disagreement where they cut up against one another and left wounds, and that was over God. If Noel saw God at all (and he rarely did), he saw God in the river, God in the clouds or in a crow's eye. He had no patience for Hannah's God—the god of churches, the god of men. Secretly, he felt it was the one place where she faltered—where her mind, ordinarily so brilliant, grew a blunt edge. It was a difference between them they noted early on, when they were still young together. They shrugged it off, joked about it even. It was a fissure, a hairline crack, nothing more. But it widened as they aged. It came to matter. When Hannah first got sick, it was her God she turned to. It was her God she clung to. Noel hated her God for that.

In August, he takes another job for Honey Lyons, another boat to refit. This one is not a good fishing boat. It has already been revamped, already junked once, which makes it easier. He does not feel he is taking something beautiful apart. But even so he imagines he can hear her—Hannah—mocking him for taking the work at all, for being so easily seduced by the lure of the cash. He hears her voice in his head and sometimes on the wind, calling him a scoundrel or a fool, as she used to do—with that gorgeous derisive glint in her eye that made him angry, that made him want her.

He begins to look for signs of the change of season: blue cornflowers, the first turning of the Virginia creeper vines toward a brilliant autumn red, the ripening of the corn and wild blackberries to their full sweetness, the first monarch butterfly, the goldenrod and yarrow. The days grow shorter, and then one morning, he steps out and feels that first glint of coolness on the air.

The following Sunday, a storm breaks up the air, brings in the high surf, and a front of cooler weather. The tide washes all the way up to the edge of the front cottage gardens. The morning after the rains end, Noel goes down to the beach early. The fog is still thick. He wanders along the tidal edge, pailing up sea clams. At the corner where West Beach ends at the causeway, he finds a body floating facedown in the shallows, the flesh gone, the rib cage full of crabs. There is a knife hooked to the belt, "D. McAllister" engraved into the blade.

Bridge

Bridge can see the new turn in her brother's eyes, the quick new life. He begins to rub shoulders with the rich. Honey Lyons sets it up, hires him out. Luce gophers whiskey in to them, and in turn, he is invited to their parties. Lady Judith Martin's Dead of Winter party. Dick Wheeler's Spring Time Fling. In the summer, the parties become more frequent. He goes to lawn parties, supper dances, horseshoe matches and croquet. He will come home late, and the next morning he will tell Bridge the details of how he was introduced to one knot of them and then another. He laughs as he tells her how the women skirt him. He is a curiosity—a newly discovered, perhaps dangerous, token from the local underworld. They are careful at first, haughty, shy. They follow him with their eyes, then start to flirt, as women will. "Rakishly good-looking," one says to another in a tone just loud enough for him to overhear. He teases them, and they blush and laugh, a little nervous; they look at him with some fear as if he might be a predator, as if they are unsure of exactly who he is— not one of them of course—but still . . .

He laughs as he tells Bridge about it, and still the invitations roll in. Once in a while, he'll try to coax her into coming with him.

"Come on. It'll be a big night. We'll have a fine laugh, fine food, music. You can be my date."

She scoffs him off.

Halfway through the summer, he tells her that he has started up a small cottage operation of taking out the rich on his runs for a lark. "Idiot's work," he calls it. "Joy rides for the money guys." A few of them will book him for the night. He'll play the part and set the whole thing up like theater. He'll drive them out in the boat to Rum Row and the floating liquor stores. Occasionally he'll spice things up with a fake chase and scripted, preplanned danger. It is seasonal work. Summer work. He gets well paid.

One morning, the last week in August, he stops by the barn. Bridge is in the stable mucking out the stall. She has swept down the floor, raked the old bedding into the wheelbarrow, and dumped it outside in the manure pile. When Luce comes around, she is laying out the new hay with a pitchfork. He talks as she works. He leans against the doorway, his arms crossed, and tells her about a job he has coming up—on the last night of the month. He is taking out a few of the summer folk—Borden, you know him, don't you? He's got the knockabout beauty wife. Al Devereaux—the Frenchie—and another fellow, a friend of theirs, Vonn. Vonner. Some name like that.

Bridge stops for a moment, her hands gripping the fork, but Luce doesn't seem to notice. He is looking across the yard. "Sounds good enough," she says.

"Well it is. But I need an extra hand."

Bridge doesn't answer. She puts down the pitchfork and dumps a measure of oats into the trough. One of the stumped legs has broken off. She sets a block of wood under it to level the tray.

"It'll be a big night," Luce says.

"You're a 'tute."

His face reddens. "Hell I am. They pay a fine dime, Bridge."

"And that's exactly it."

"They're not all bad. Just rich, born into it. You can't hold it against them."

"Which is funny coming from you since, of anyone, you do seem to hold it against them."

He glares at her. "So that's a no, I take it."

"Are all of them going out with you in the boat?"

"That's the plan."

"I'll do it if I can go out too."

"Out to the ship?"

"Yeah."

"No, I need you on shore."

She picks up the pitchfork again and thins out a clump in the hay.

"Come on, Bridge."

"Let me go out."

"No."

"Why not?"

"I have things set up."

"That's not it at all," she teases. "You're worried a girl on the boat's going to wreck your reputation." She laughs.

He doesn't answer. The late summer light is weightless on his shoulders. His face is in shadow, and she cannot see his eyes. Behind him, in the tall oak, there is a flash of a yellow warbler through the leaves.

"Come on, Bridge," he says again.

Her thoughts shift again to Henry. Then she leans the fork against the barn wall and brushes her hands off on her overalls. "Fine," she says. "I'll do it."

They meet at Albert Devereaux's house, down a gated lane off Horseneck Road. A young woman, the housekeeper, opens the door.

She leads Bridge and Luce down a high-ceilinged hall, through a library and into a smoking room. Two men sit at a gaming table in blue plush gentleman's chairs. They are dressed in work clothes, dark jackets. There are caps and oilers in a pile on a chair. The work clothes sit oddly on them, and Bridge notices they are wearing dress shoes.

Albert Devereaux stands up as Luce and Bridge enter the room. "Hello there," he says. Bridge can see that he is nervous. "Here you are then. So we're ready. This is Borden. Will Borden."

Luce nods. "You have guns?"

"Guns?"

"Each man needs a gun."

"I didn't realize—"

"That's how it is," Luce says coolly as he walks around to the couch.

"I might have pistols," Albert says. "Would that be adequate?"

Luce smiles. "A gun's a gun."

"I didn't realize we would need—"

"Oh hell, Al," Will Borden breaks in. "Don't be such a chump. Go dig around and see what you have. Where did Henry get off to?"

"Here," says a voice from the doorway. Henry Vonniker comes into the room. He doesn't seem to see Bridge at first. He doesn't seem to register her presence. She stands by her brother, just behind Luce's shoulder, her face shadowed by the brim of her cap.

"Luce, this is Henry Vonniker," Will Borden says. " 'Our Henry,' as my wife Alyssia has named him. I suppose we all assume some ownership. Henry, may I introduce Luce Weld, our host for tonight's escapade."

Henry extends his hand. Luce takes it. Their eyes lock for a moment. Bridge can see that Luce is sizing him up.

"I'm not going tonight," Henry says quickly, withdrawing his hand. He offers an affable smile.

Luce shrugs. "Fine."

"I apologize. Just before you arrived, I was informed my friends gave you my name, signed me up as it were, but I can assure you I would be no use out there."

Luce takes a long look at him. "Are you the one who works in the mills?"

"Yes, that's correct."

"See much of the strike?"

"No," Henry says. "The mill where I work did not cut wages. We're still in operation."

"But you must see it. The strike, I mean. Driving through the city. I hear it's been bad."

"I don't actually know," says Henry. "That particular area of the city is not on my way to work, so in fact, I really haven't seen much of the strike at all." He doesn't mention that he has gone out of his way not to see it. He keeps himself removed. He avoids what he can to the extent that he can. He drives a roundabout route to the mill so he does not have to pass through the strike zone. The details that he does take in—either from the papers or from what he overhears—he notices only from a distance, from one corner of an eye, the way he might observe early light gathering at the edges of the marsh, spilling through the tall grass on an incoming tide.

"Henry works in Bowes's mill," Will Borden says.

"Oh right," says Luce. "Bowes. Isn't he the one stepping up production—making a profit all summer while everyone else's workers are out on their bread lines?"

"Where did Al get off to?" Henry asks Borden.

"He's gone to get guns."

Bridge, who has been watching Henry, sees him flinch.

"I hear you were in the war," Luce is saying now.

Henry nods. "I was."

"Where?"

"France."

"At the front?"

"For a time."

"Must have seen some big things over there."

Henry hesitates for a moment, and when he speaks his voice is measured, composed. He fingers a line of piping on the sofa. "War is like anything else," he says. "You see what you see. Do what you do. You adjust."

"Like anything else?" Luce asks wryly.

"Like anything else."

They are standing on either side of the sofa, facing each other. They are close to the same height, Henry a shade taller. Luce studies the other man's face, and Bridge can feel a small envy, a small hatred rippling off her brother. It is something no one else in the room might notice, but she can feel it. Her eyes shift again to Henry. There are dashes of light sweat at his temples.

"I hear you're a doctor," Luce goes on.

"I was a doctor."

"Ever work on a brain?"

Devereaux comes back into the room. "I could only find one—a pistol. Will that do?"

"We'll have to scare up one more," says Luce, still looking at Henry.

"You won't really need guns out there, will you?" Henry asks.

"Might. Never know what you might need in this business. Might need a doctor." Luce smiles. His teeth flash, rapid, white through his dark face.

"Anyone for a drink?" Borden says.

Luce turns away from Henry and sits down in one of the gentleman's chairs. He runs his hands down the upholstered arm, leans back, stretches out his legs.

"Look, Albert," Henry says, "I've got to get going."

"Oh, come on, Henry, stay for a drink," Will Borden says, pouring out whiskey into four tumblers. "A drink for your girl, Luce?"

"Sure, I suppose. She's a good girl."

And Henry looks at her then, takes her in for the first time. She sees the flash of recognition and something else she can't quite name.

"You sure you don't want to go with us, Doc?" Luce says to Henry, without looking up from the chair. But Henry doesn't answer. His eyes are on Bridge, and she can see then that he does not know who she is to Luce. He does not know she is his sister. He has made the first assumption, the easy assumption, that she is his girl, his companion, his wife.

"Good whiskey," Borden says. He drains his glass. "Is this your stuff, Luce?"

"Not mine. I just slob it in. I'm the nothing guy."

Albert and Will Borden laugh.

"How did you put it just then, Doc?" Luce goes on. "You see what you see—was that it? Well then, here's to what you don't see." He raises his glass. The two other men join him, still laughing. Henry is looking at Bridge, but Luce has not noticed. He is turned away, toward the low fire in the grate. Then his eyes play through the room, over the black iron fire tools, across the mantel, the gold-rimmed sea-clock with the jet face, the silver candlesticks, the inlaid mahogany card table, the Chinese lamp on the rat-foot pedestal, a blue and white china vase, a jade figurine, a Waterford crystal bowl. Bridge sees him do it. He is making his inventory, setting down a file of these objects in his brain. It is simply how he looks at the world—how he always has, perhaps how he always will—assessing the value of fine things, weighing their worth.

Luce drinks off his glass, stands, and straightens the collar on his coat. "We'll be off then. Don't want to miss the tide." He turns toward Henry. "So are you in, Doc?"

"No."

"Don't like boats?"

"Boats are fine."

"Don't like liquor?"

"Like I said, I'd be no use to you."

"Not even a fluty champagne?"

Henry doesn't answer him. "Are you going out with them?" he asks, addressing Bridge.

"No," she answers.

"Sure she's going out," Luce says sharply. "She's my mate. Why? Does that change your mind?"

Henry shakes his head. "I have no intention of going out."

"What is it? You don't like guns?"

"I don't like guns."

"Funny thing," Luce says, "you of anyone, a big guy in the big war."

"Exactly."

"You aren't any good with a gun, then?"

"Drop it, Luce," says Bridge.

She thinks of him on the ride out. It is a rough ride, a wind-chopped sea. The boat spanks the waves, and the damp night air stings her face. Just after midnight, they arrive at the ship, a Canadian bark, the *Dara Lee*. Bridge waits in the boat alongside as Luce and the other two men board. She watches the rum-ship crew. They are bunched together at first, but when they see her brother and recognize him, she notices that they begin to thin across the deck. She can see they don't quite trust him. Their beards are unruly, grown out over the long days at sea. She sees two men off to the side. One points to Albert Devereaux's dress shoes, bright, newly polished, poking out from under his oilers. They snicker, then catch her watching. They look away. The deck is piled with liquor, hundreds of cases and bursacks of whiskey, rum, gin. The rank, sharp smell of alcohol and the sweat of men is mixed in the cold salt air, and she notices suddenly that there is nothing in the scene that intrigues her. What she is witnessing is like any other trade of goods for cash. It is a business, like any other business, work like any other work. She smiles. She finds herself looking back toward land, thinking about Henry Vonniker. He is somewhere behind her in that darkness, beyond that paler skim of light that marks the shore.

She says his name quietly to herself and feels a small trip in her heart. He had left the house when they did. He had stood with Bridge in the drive as Luce and Will Borden checked to see that they had everything they needed in the truck. They were waiting on Albert who was still inside.

"You don't have to go with them, you know," Henry had said to her in a low voice. He was standing near her and she could smell his skin—a fresh clean scent. He avoided her gaze, looking straight ahead. The light off the truck's headlamps played over his face. She marked the deep forks at the corners of his eyes and she could sense a brokenness in him as the darkness spun around them and they stood together on the smooth dirt drive in a soft imperfect ring of light.

"Do you know that you don't have to go?" he asked.

Of course she knew. She also knew that now there was no way to explain to Luce why she might not want to go anymore, why she might have changed her mind.

"I'm going," she answered simply, then she walked to the truck and climbed in.

But now, standing in the wheelhouse of the boat, she feels a sadness. She feels, perhaps for the first time in her life, regret. She looks away from the shore back to the ship. She can hear her brother's voice, placing the order, issuing commands. He strides across the deck toward the first mate. The hem of his coat strikes out behind him. They are coming to the rail. Luce tells Devereaux and Borden to get back on the boat, and then Luce and a man from the *Dara Lee*'s crew pass the crates over the side. Luce boards and throws open the door to the false hold, and they load it until it is full. They push the few remaining cases to the stern, and Luce covers them with a tarp.

He comes back to the wheelhouse, revs the engine, and tells Will Borden to push them off. Bridge draws in the bowline, then comes to stand next to her brother, and they ride, the sea wind at their backs, the waves softer now underneath them. They speed through the cool black night toward shore.

Johnny Clyde meets them at Charlton Wharf just past the Knubble Rock at the end of Boathouse Row. Bridge says nothing, but she knows that on a regular night, on a real job, her brother would never have chosen that particular wharf. He would never be slack enough to unload in such a visible spot. He has grafted someone's help. Paid the Coast Guard off.

She will stay in the boat with him, and they will run it upriver. Devereaux and Borden squeeze into the cab of the truck with Johnny Clyde. He will bring them home with the booze.

The headlamps back out and swing around. The truck turns and heads down Boathouse Row. Luce keeps the boat on a soft idle as Bridge unties them off the cleat. She holds their port side tight against the pier until the truck's taillights have disappeared and the sound of the engine has eased into the night. She pushes them off. She coils the line four times around her arm and drops it on the deck of the boat. As Luce heads upriver on the flood tide, she comes to stand beside him at the wheel. He works the craft between Bailey Flat and Cory's Island, then swings back into the channel. They weave through the sailboats set at mooring in the harbor and press north toward the Point Bridge. She can see the new electric lamps set on the wharf, the dock house and the Shuckers Club, the Sinclair gasoline sign outside of Blackwood's store, the boats tied up at the town pier, the quiet dark shapes of trucks and cars. Farther up on the hill, by the pale spike of the Methodist Church steeple, she can see the windmill, its yellow arms lit like knives turning slowly through the moon.

They pass under the bridge, and Luce guns both engines. They speed through the steep black water. Bridge grips her brother's arm. He smells of the river. He smells of the salt and of the marsh. They press faster into the darkness up the open channel, the night soft and wet and cool around them, and she has the sense that they are moving away from what they have always known, hurtling forward toward some pitch black future, and this is the night that lies between. This night belongs to them, this end-of-the-summer darkness. This night is full of every moment of their past that they have spent together, and it is full of every possibility ahead. The wind rakes her hair and nips the corners of her eyes.

Luce veers around Ship Rock, a long deliberate right turn that circles them back behind the marsh islands. They pass the entrance to Crooked Creek, then Taber Point. The moon is ahead of them, a white deep line, whole and driven through the surface. Luce follows it, but driving slower now. Bridge leans over the side of the boat, her hand stretched out into the smooth warm riverwater. She can see the moon jellies, their startling green iridescence. They pass and break and spin out through her fingers.

As they come into the Let, Luce cuts off the engine and they drift. He draws a bottle of whiskey from one of the crates still left in the boat. He breaks the seal, hands it to her, and she drinks. It is good whiskey, strong. It burns her throat. It runs hot and fast to her brain. The river is full of stars. They drink and laugh about the night, the circus of it, the roguishness of it. They joke about the expression on Devereaux's face when Luce told them they would need guns—and about how Borden was nearly seasick by the time they came back in.

"More money than Heddy Green," she remarks. "But no sea legs."

Neither one of them mentions Henry.

They drink more, and she gets a little smart. She asks him how much he got paid for the night, and he tells her, and she threatens him with blackmail if he doesn't give her half.

"Come out with me again, and then I'll pay you."

"I want my money first."

"You have a taste for it, don't you?"

"For the money?"

"For the work."

She shakes her head. "It's dull."

"Nothing dull about this work, and you know it."

"Dull to me," she says, "but I suppose it's good enough to keep me out of trouble."

He laughs. "What kind of trouble you planning to get into?"

"Any kind that finds me on the road."

He looks at her carefully for a moment, sensing something, without knowing exactly what. "Come out with me again next week," he says. "I've got a good job."

"No. I'm on vacation."

"Come on, Bridge. I'm just breaking you in."

"Forget about it."

"I need you," he says.

She doesn't answer. She closes her eyes and leans her head against his shoulder. On the south wind that comes from over the dunes, she can hear the boneless sound of the surf.

Noel

When Noel goes out with Bridge the next morning to pull the potatoes, he can smell the liquor on her. He can smell it as clear as if someone had stuck his head in a piss-pot full of gin. He can smell it through the stink of perfume she has doused herself with to hide it. He can smell it through the reek of soap, through the sun-scrubbed scent of her clothes.

It is the first day of September. The potato vines have died back and turned brown. He works down the furrow ahead of her, pulling up the vines. He grips them close to the ground and the leaves droop around his hand. He picks off the baby potatoes stuck to the root and leaves the hill for her to work over with the fork. He is downwind of her, and the smell of the liquor leaking out of her young skin bristles in his nose. He says nothing. Asks her nothing. He listens to the scrape of the tines against the flesh of the potatoes. She moves slowly. From the corner of his eye, he glimpses her hands, tough with the dirt and strong. She wedges the fork down into the side of the hill, then levers it up, heavy with the weight of the potatoes. She shakes the earth loose and it falls away through the gaps between the tines. She lays the potatoes down beside the dug row to dry. She lays them down gently, the way he has taught her, with enough distance between them for the air to pass between their skins. He gets another whiff of the liquor.

This is not what he wants for her.

From the day she was born, she had awakened all of his old superstitions. Even in the first few months of her life, he had tried to keep a collar on her soul. When he put her down to sleep in her cradle, he would sneak a scrap of tin under her swaddling blanket. He placed it between the folds on her chest as a shield so that nothing evil in the night could take her. When she was older, the first time he took her out in the skiff, out onto open water, he smudged her face with ash so she would not be blown away.

Hannah told him once that Kauai and the other Sandwich Isles were born out of volcanoes. Each one had come from a crack under the sea and pushed its way up from those depths to grow thousands of feet above the surface. She told him that at one point every species of tree on Kauai had come from a seed blown at random across oceans on the trade winds; every species of bird had arrived there by mistake, having lost its way. She told him that before the first tribes arrived in their canoes, Kauai and the other islands had been home only to insects, birds, trees. There were no mammals—no rodents, no cattle or wild boar—until the first pigs were brought by man. Before then, those islands had been a veritable Eden, a territory of silence and beauty, untempered, untouched—as the Arctic must have been before the coming of the whaler—as his granddaughter was.

Now, as they work together down the garden row, digging up the potatoes, she falls a few paces behind. He can still smell the sullen reek of liquor off her skin. The sun warms the back of his neck, and he feels rage—a hotheaded burning rage toward Luce, for roping her in, for leading her down this tainted road. There is an

ache in his chest, and it weighs him down as he works along the furrow, dredging up the vines.

When Luce stops by the shop that afternoon, Noel is scrimping
with a needle into the panbone.

"Have you got some ten-inch nails, old man?"

"Should have."

"Where?"

Noel nods over toward the shelves above the ice chest. "Might
be there. Might be up top."

Luce rummages through some cans on the lower shelf, then on
the shelf above.

"Can I take this box here?"

"Sit for a talk."

"Don't have time."

"I talk short."

Luce laughs. "Alright then."

"Have yourself a cup."

"Not thirsty, thanks."

"Have one anyway." And it might be the edge in his grandfather's
voice, but Luce does what he says. He pours himself a mug of water
from the pail, drinks off the top, and sits down in the soft chair by
the saw. He drums his fingers against the arm.

"Heard talk of you going west," Noel says.

"Bridge tell you that?"

Noel nods. He goes on scrimping. "Never been out west, myself."

"A guy I know told me it's fine out there. Arizona, I was thinking. Land's cheap. Five dollars an acre in some parts."

"What guy told you that?"

"Just a guy."

"Can't remember?"

"Can't."

"Your fool cousin Asa maybe? Seeing as you're following his footsteps."

Luce shoots him a look, but doesn't answer. He takes a sip of water and wipes his mouth with the back of his sleeve.

"Out west," Noel goes on, "I hear they got crows the size of dogs."

"Never heard that."

Noel goes on cutting the needle into a small blank square on the panbone. "You know how those crows came to get so big?"

"No." Luce shakes his head.

"Got eyes for their bellies, kept eating up everything they'd see."

"That so?"

Noel looks up at him, straight in the face. "Sometime long back when, those crows—they came from here, just like you."

Luce stares at him. He puts down his mug and leans back in the chair, his face creased as he takes in his grandfather's meaning. Then his features smooth out again and he smiles, but his eyes are hard.

"What are you goading me for?"

"You go on doing what you're doing," Noel says, the needle ticking into the bone. "Hang your hat at whatever gin mill you want, oil up your boat heavy as you want, but you leave her out of it."

"So this is about Bridge."

"Seems it might be."

Luce leans forward in the chair. "You think I have her on a leash, old man?"

"You're thick in the head, Luce. Always have been. But you know, it's finest kind with me for you to go on and do your crooked work, your puddling work. Have your big nights. Make your big money. Go on and do what you do. But you leave her out of it."

Luce opens his mouth to speak, then he seems to catch himself, and slowly, deliberately, he grips the box of nails, and stands. "Bridge does what she wants," he says walking toward the door. "You'd know that better than anyone now, wouldn't you, old man? Bridge's always done exactly as she wants."

He steps through the door into the open sunlight, around the corner, and he is gone.

They move around each other carefully after that. Luce and Noel. They keep a proper distance.

There is trouble with the hens that September. On a morning early in the month, one sheds a drop of blood from the stretching as she lays, and at the scent, the others turn on her. By the time Noel comes in to check on them, they have picked her almost dead.

A few weeks on, he notices two hens seeming sluggish. As he sweeps down the hen yard, he finds worms in their droppings. Short white skittish threads. He treats them all. Moist mash mixed with a teaspoonful of gasoline. Once a week for two weeks, and every two weeks thereafter. They gain back their weight, they liven, but even after a month and no sign of the worms, they will still only pass an occasional egg.

The light cools. The leaves begin to turn. As the wind shifts around, and the blow comes out of the northwest, Noel finds himself thinking about Hannah, and it strikes him for the first time since she has been gone that perhaps she died because, in some small way, he slighted her. It is an absurd thought. He knows this. But it nags him nonetheless. That perhaps she died because he turned his back on her somehow, the life shriveled between them, and there was simply nowhere else for her to go.

He had not expected it. He finds he can admit this to himself at last. He could never have expected that she would be the one to leave.

Bridge

She is washing up the breakfast dishes that Saturday morning in September when Noel tells her she'll have to start work in the shop without him. He is taking the wagon down to the Point to collect the rest of the money Howie Sherman owes for the dory they built. He'll be back awhile later in the day.

"I'll go for you," she says quickly, setting the last mug on the rack beside the sink and wiping her hands on the dishtowel. She doesn't look at him as she pulls on her boots.

"I was looking forward to the ride," he says, curious to see if she'll pursue it.

"No, no. Let me go. I can take my bike. I'll be back before noon." He watches her tie her bootlaces precisely. She gives a last tug to check the knot and stands up. "How much does he owe?"

"You aren't planning any detour, are you?" he asks with a slight smile.

She ignores him. "What does he owe?"

"Thirty-two dollars."

"Alright. I'll be back. Try not to stew around too much while I'm gone." Then she is out the door and down the steps. She gets her bicycle from the barn and pedals off down the road.

She tells herself as she takes the turn at South Westport Corner that the thought of a detour might never have occurred to her if Noel hadn't slid in that last remark. But then she smiles, the wind pulling her hair away from her face, thinking about how she makes up these little lies, pretending to trick herself, when she already knows that she will take the long way home, she will ride by the beach, by Henry's house—he is not likely to be there, and she tells herself she is not even sure that she wants him to be there, although of course that is a little lie too. What is true is that since that night she left him behind at Al Devereaux's house, all she has really wanted was to see him again.

Within half an hour she has reached the Point. Howie Sherman's wife is outside, feeding the geese in the yard, and she goes into the house and gets the money for Bridge and invites her in for a piece of breakfast cake, but Bridge says, "No, thank you, we have a busy day in the shop today," and she takes the money and puts it deep in the pocket of her trousers, then pedals down past the wharf, over the Point Bridge. The clouds box in packs through the sky like great white fists. The sun squeezes through. She can feel a light sweat on the back of her neck under her hair and she is happy and the air is cool on her face. Yesterday's wind has stripped the sand off the dunes and it piles in small drifts on the beach road, and when it is too soft and deep, she has to get off her bicycle and push until she comes again to a clearer stretch.

Henry is out in the driveway under his car, changing the oil, when he hears the creak of bicycle wheels coming down the road from the dunes. There is little traffic this time of year, and on another day he might have been curious to see who it was, but he has been having some trouble with the drain plug on the oil pan. The thing had been jammed. With a box wrench, he finally loosened it, and it seemed to be moving more freely now, the way it should move, along its grooves. He unscrews the last few turns with his fingers, and with his other hand, he gropes for the tin tray that he will place under the hole to catch the oil. But the bicycle stops on the road in front of his house, and he looks over and sees her. He drops the drain plug. Oil shoots down over his shoulder. The plug rolls away from him. "Damn," he says, wedging his thumb into the hole to block it up again. The tin tray is out of his reach, the drain plug out of reach, and he is stuck now and he knows it.

She lays her bike down at the edge of his driveway and walks over to him. He has spread out the canvas, and on it, he has set down his tools in two neat and perfect rows, wrenches and screwdrivers, a ball-peen hammer. They are polished and they glint in the light. He has set out everything he will need: the funnel, four quart cans of oil, a few clean rags. She finds the drain plug on the ground. She picks it up and wipes off the sand, then squats down on the canvas near him and peers under the car.

"Do you need some help?" she asks.

"That's not very funny."

She laughs and slips the tin tray under the car to him. He places it under the hole in the oil pan, removes his thumb, and slides out. He sits up, pushing his clean hand through his hair. It is disheveled and his face is flushed, a streak of grease down one side of his cheek. She gives him a rag, and he wipes the oil off his hands and arm. He wipes off his glasses, then puts them back on. He looks at her. "Thank you."

She smiles. "You would have figured it out. You would have figured something out."

He laughs, then pauses. "It's good to see you."

She nods.

"Will you come in?"

"Not today," she says, but she sits down on the edge of the canvas near him. There is an empty teacup and saucer on the ground. He notices her looking at it.

"Can I get you something to drink?"

"No. Thanks. I was just on my way home. From the Point."

"Well, I'm glad you decided to come around this way."

She smiles and picks up one of the adjustable wrenches. "This is nice," she says, fingering the handle. "You don't use it much, do you?"

"I do in fact. I use it at least once every few months to make a fool of myself changing the oil in my car."

"Well, just don't do it in the driveway next time. Park in the dirt and dig a hole. Let the oil run into it."

"That would cut out one step, I suppose."

"Can you handle the rest?"

"I'm not sure."

"Do you do alright with the funnel?"

"Actually I would prefer if you would just come around again and do it for me."

She laughs, looking down at the wrench in her hands. She turns the screw, and closes the clamp on one of her fingers. She tightens it, then opens it again, and he can see the whiter indentations the clamp has left in her skin.

"Keep it," he says.

"The wrench?"

"I want you to have it."

"No."

"Please. It will be my first gift to you."

She shakes her head and puts the wrench down with the others on the canvas.

"You'd use it more than I do," he says.

"I don't doubt that." She smiles and looks away from him toward the hedge and her bicycle lying on the ground at the edge of the drive.

"Don't go yet."

She doesn't answer.

"Stay for a cup of tea."

"No, thank you."

"Coffee?"

"No." She giggles.

"Then let me make a pot. I'll have a cup and you can stay."

"You might drink very slowly."

"You might change your mind."

She looks at him then, the first time she has looked at him since she sat down, and her eyes are very pale in the sunlight, very blue. Then she looks away back toward the road.

"What's wrong?" he asks.

"Nothing."

"What are you thinking?"

She tries to find the words to explain it, but they don't come to her. They are words she has not needed until now. But when she sees him, when she is with him, she can feel things open inside her.

"I want to see you again," he says.

She doesn't answer.

"Is that alright?"

"I'm not sure."

"Why?"

She shakes her head.

"Is it because of your brother?"

"Luce?" She glances at him, surprised. "No."

"I worried about you that night you went out with him in the boat."

She nods.

"Why do you let him talk you into it?"

"Talk me into what?"

"Into doing that kind of work for him?"

It's a way of life, she could have told him, but she did not expect he would understand that. Any more than he would understand the childish faith she sometimes held that if she went with Luce, she could protect him. If she was with him, he would not fall into harm.

"That kind of work isn't safe," Henry says.

"Do you think," she replies slowly, still averting her eyes, speaking to the shed across the yard, "do you think it is safe—my being here with you?"

He pauses for a moment. He wants to touch her. He wants to take her face in his hands and draw it toward him. "That's not the point," he says.

"I think it might be."

"It's not."

"We're having our first quarrel," she says, "aren't we?" And then she laughs again, looking down at her hands, and the sound of her laughter fills him with an inexpressible joy.

"Alright," he says. "But tell me, what would be wrong with my seeing you again. What could be more simple than that?"

She looks around the yard, at the porch, the railing, the steps, the open toolbox, the empty china teacup and saucer lying near them on the ground. She touches the gilded edge of the cup.

"It's this," she finally says. "It's difficult because of this."

"Because of a teacup?"

"We don't have these."

"You don't have cups?"

"Not these kinds of cups."

"Why would that matter?"

"We don't have anything like them."

"It doesn't matter," he says. "It doesn't matter to me."

"But do you understand it makes things more difficult?"

"No. I don't understand that at all."

She looks up at him again and, for a moment, he thinks he sees a trace of anger in her eyes. Then she leans across the canvas between them, and she kisses him. Her mouth is warm on his.

"Please don't go," he says quietly as she draws away.

"You know I'm not going to stay." Her eyes are smooth and she touches the side of his face. Then she stands up and offers him her hand. She pulls him to his feet. As she walks down the driveway, he walks with her. She picks up her bicycle.

"Will you come back?" he asks. "Please."

"I think so," she says, and again she smiles, that warm shy smile that he loves.

"When?"

"In a while."

"A long while or a short while?"

She laughs. "One or the other."

"Do you promise you'll come?"

"Yes."

And he watches her from the end of the driveway as she pedals down West Beach Road. At the turn, she looks over her shoulder and waves to him. He waves back and she passes out of view.

The oil on his shirt has begun to seep through and he can feel it, heavy on his skin. He is thirsty. His throat burns. On his way up to the house for a glass of water he pauses by the empty teacup and saucer on the ground. He doesn't mean to do it, he has no mental thought before he does, but he raises his foot and brings it down firmly. He feels the china splinter under his boot, and he leaves it there, in pieces on the ground.

Cora

Twice that fall, when Cora and Luce were alone in the kitchen, Luce dug some money out of his pocket, pushed it at her, and said gruffly, "There, Ma, go and buy yourself something fine."

But there was nothing that she wanted. Nothing she would need. She kept the money, though, in an empty hatbox on the upper shelf of her closet where she kept a few other necessary things.

She can feel the rupture between her father and her son—the stilted, tenuous peace. They had never fit together well—she knows this—never easily, but the rift is deeper now.

On certain days, in the late afternoon, when she has finished her laundry, when the shirts are starched, ironed, folded, tagged, and she is down in the cellar wrapping them up in sheets of brown paper, cutting an even edge with a pair of scissors off the roll, she is aware of her body, wrung from the work of the day, her mind so light, as if she is drifting at the end of a very long string, brushing into the rafters, the ceiling dust, the creases in the beams where some rogue bird has found its way in, has built its nest of mud and straw.

She digs the pointed end of the scissors into her palm. She digs it in hard, to draw herself back down.

There is a certain kind of grief, she knows, that has no color. That has no smell or sound. Loneliness is not an empty feeling. It has a weight, a texture, like water in the lungs.

She can hear them above her through the cracks in the floor—Bridge and Luce—they are upstairs in the kitchen. They keep their talking low. Luce is griping about Honey Lyons, about how he is cheating them—Luce and Johnny Clyde—how they do all the work, duck all the danger, bring in the load, but he is the one who makes the trade, and what should be a good-size payoff, he will claim comes in short, and he pays them only a third of that. A third they have to split between them.

Cora goes on wrapping the clothes. She folds down the edges of the stiff brown paper. She squares off the ends. She picks through their words, choosing to attach herself to some, enough to make out their sense. She is drawn to her son's voice.

He has always been, still is, a falling star in her darkness. He came out of her upside down, his face bruised, the nose squished to the left. He was a blue baby, cord wrapped twice around his neck. He came in winter, hatched like an egg from the snow. As a mite still suckling on her, he would have her breast in his mouth, one huge eye staring up at her. If her hair was loose, he would take a thick strand of it, wind it tight around his fat baby fingers until the flesh buckled and turned white. It was how he clung to her that made her heart give in. He has always been the one that she loved most.

She knows what he does, and she considers it a sour business. She has noticed too that it does not bring the flush and easy dollars they all talk about. For so much trouble, so much risk, it might bring enough to eat a little better, to buy a little more, but it does not bring so much.

She sends him luck. She washes blessings here and there into his clothes. She will sit sometimes in the early morning when the house is still, and she will finger the soiled clothes he has left for her in a pile by the stairs outside his room. She will see into the dark low places of his thoughts, and she will put those clothes to soak in the hottest water. She will boil them two minutes longer than she would boil a sheet. She will try to scald the bad thoughts out of them. She will battle them into the wash, until the water is full of those thoughts, her hands, her mind, full of them. Then she will rinse in something pure. She will touch the edge of his sleeve, a trouser cuff. She will tuck something good into a pocket, a hem, a seam.

She hears the scrape of a chair on the floor above her, steps across the kitchen, the clatter of dishes in the sink. They go out. The door shuts behind them. Cora goes upstairs. Through the window, she can see them walking down the drive in the direction of the road. She can see the weak glow of the lamp in the shop. Her father passes across the open door and out of view.

She slips out of the house and walks north. She cuts around the garden and crosses the wagon path onto the land next door owned by Owen Wales. She walks through the woods down to the lower cornfield, its dead stalks plowed, seeded already with winter rye. It is almost dusk. The cows from the lower pastures have been herded up to the barn for their night milking. A few heifers left, they watch her from the other side of the split-rail fence. Down below is the river.

She walks in circles around the field. She keeps to the perimeter, her thoughts pushing her on, her thoughts of her children, Luce and Bridge, her other child, the lost Rose, other thoughts of how she had loved the river once. Long back, at one point when she was a young girl, she had prayed every night to the fields and the trees and the stones. Once, long back, water was many things to her, the river many things. It was freedom, redemption, the washing away of grief and violence and sin. An easy source of joy. And then it was lost in the shuffling of marriage, pregnancies, birth, swaddling clothes, the shuffle of long winters, fires, stews, baking breads, making beds, making do, swollen breasts, sore legs, chilblained hands, the shuffle of linens and overalls, tubs of wash, tubs of bluing, tubs of the rinse, the shuffle of days and deaths and years. Her feet quicken as she walks, they skim the uneven ground. She has never been able to keep her thoughts settled—they run like wild horses through her brain. She notices from a distance how her awareness shifts through the different stages of the circle—the soft wind strikes her face, then it is behind her, the light half of the sky by her shoulder, her head cocked slightly to one side, waiting, listening for the sounds under the earth, the burrowing of rabbits and moles, the slow push of water returning to its source deep beneath the soil. She counts the loops she makes until she loses count, until her awareness drops away and she has the sense that she is standing in the middle of the field, and the horses in her mind are at the end of a long tether, and she is holding them, she is taming them, they still run the loop around the edge, while she stands out of her body in the center. Through the soles of her feet, she can feel the distant thunder of their hooves.

Owen Wales watches her from the hill. He knows who she is, walking the loop around his field. He has seen her do this before, on an occasional night. She walks always the same way, around the edge of the field, her head bent to the side as if it is cut at the neck, tending to her shoulder. He sits on the cow fence, the split-rail closest to the barn. The post next to where he sits has a crack. It will bust soon, and he makes a mental note to see it is repaired. He takes out his pipe, a match, lights it. A bluish cloud of smoke works through his beard.

She leaves the field abruptly and walks down to the river. She pulls her dress over her head and leaves it folded on a stone. She lets her hair down from its pins. She is a beautiful woman, her body smooth. He can see her shape, dark as wire, through her underclothes. She wades into the river and the cotton shift billows out around her.

The sun has dropped and the sky is filled with color, the dusk is all around her, it spills through the river, the sky deep through everywhere, the clouds and the brutal autumn smells of honeysuckle, drowned marsh, earth, rose mallow, pine. She floats through the cool water—still with a hint of summer in it—the current pulling at the small of her back, a smooth light rush between her shoulder blades, and she imagines her son, Luce, floating this same way, she imagines his mind growing more gentle and more tender, softening into darkness, her hands are loose, they work through the water, sculling out the still and unkempt restless surface of his dreams.

Luce

It was a broken trip. One turn of bad luck after another. It had started out well enough. A dark night. A flat sea. They were going out for a prepaid pickup. Luce had his torn half of a playing card in his left trouser pocket. A seven of spades.

Johnny Clyde had pushed them off at six from the Point Wharf, and a Coast Guard patrol, docked at the river mouth, sighted them, then pushed off on their tail. Luce was used to the dance by now. The picket boat would shadow them a ways, then turn back and head in toward shore to regroup with the rest of the blockade.

Except on that night, for some reason, she didn't. It grew dark, and still she followed them, out past the Inner Mayo Ledge, out past the Sow and Pigs. Ten, twelve, fourteen miles out. This was not what they had expected, not what they wanted. Luce knew he couldn't lead her any farther on.

He was tired already. He had worked four out of the past five nights. The night before he had worked until dawn. He had slept through the early afternoon in his bed at home, but his sleep had been rough and fitful.

He had a handful of coffee beans in his coat pocket. He pulled a few out and gnawed on them to keep himself sharp as he tooled back and forth in the fringe of deeper water off a shoal, trying to decide what course to take. He kept his lights on. He made it easy for the patrol boat to keep him in sight. He even had Johnny Clyde throw out two trolling lines to pretend they were trying the fishing. Johnny's hands shook, and he fouled up one of the lines. He smoked one cigarette after another. He drew in deep on them, and they burned fast down to his fingers. He set the fishing poles into metal clasp holders, then leaned against the side of the wheelhouse, still smoking. The fishing lines trailed after them through the rip, skinny threads, long and taut and silver when they caught the light.

The sea had begun to build. Gentle swells running a good three or four feet. Luce headed out again, but off his intended course, away from the location of the rum-ship. He headed west-southwest. He picked up speed, and at one point he thought he had lost the patrol, but as he gained the crest of a swell, he looked back and glimpsed the top of her pilothouse, several troughs behind, before she folded back down again into the sea.

He made a wide circle then, slow and leisurely. He cut back over his own wake and veered in, heading north, back toward shore.

"Where you going, Luce?" Johnny asked. "What're you doing?"

Luce didn't answer. He gave the engine more gas. As Johnny went to light another cigarette, the nose of the boat struck a wave. Water splashed over the foredeck, and Johnny stumbled, nearly losing his balance. He grasped for the side of the wheelhouse, the match flailed on his shirt, and he beat it out. "Whoa, man, easy there, almost set myself afire."

"Keep it out," Luce said. "Don't light up." He didn't look back, but he knew the picket boat was still on their heels, and coming closer now. With the rougher sea, she did not want to lose them.

The wind was at his back, and he could hear her engines running. He steered around the shoal. He kept tight against the ledge in the calmer water, hugging the reef, and then he cut east-northeast, but still setting an apparent course toward shore. The ledge ended, and they moved out again into deeper water and the high, steep running swells outside the shoal. Again, at the top of a crest, Luce glanced back over his shoulder, and he could see the cutter's lights and the square cut shape of her wheelhouse. He kept his eye on her as she climbed, then dipped down and disappeared, and when she was gone, when he could not see her and when he knew she could not see him, he cut off his lights. He swerved south. He counted under his breath, then estimating he was well beyond her, he cut off his engine. They went still in the water, drifting up over the black and rolling swells.

"What?" said Johnny Clyde. "What are you doing?"

"Shhh," hissed Luce. "Nothing. Say nothing. Not one sound." And they hung there, the soles of their feet locked to the floor of the boat, in that cold dark silence, rocking over the waves. The cutter passed north of them, and Luce could not hear her engines. He kept his eye on her running lights, bobbing up and down. She threw a searchlight, harsh and white and sudden. The light in bright narrow circles at first, and then broader, picking up nothing, skimming out across the dark and empty sea. Luce waited. Five minutes. Ten minutes. He waited until she gave up and the light went out and there was no sign of her.

He started up the engine and kept her on low. He veered around and ran back along the ledge, headed seaward. Twice looking back, he thought he had a glimpse of the cutter, a distant running light, far, far north of them. She seemed to be edging slowly west.

He set a straight course out, south-southeast. He ran the boat without lights, climbing the waves, sledding down their backsides. He let Johnny Clyde light up a cigarette. He even took one himself, but the smoke dulled his mind. He stubbed it out.

———

They meet up with the ship—an old whaling bark, the *Alexandra*. She is scarred, an archaic hull, her sails patched. They come on her sooner than they expect to. She is not in safe waters. She has anchored just inside the limit, and Luce warns the first mate.

"Someone must've made a mistake," Luce says lightly.

The mate shoots him a dark look. "Your mistake."

"Fine then," Luce says and shrugs. He hands the mate his half of the seven of spades, and the mate matches it with the captain's half of the same torn card. Three men of the crew are sent down into the hold to drag up their order—sixty cases of Scotch and ten of champagne.

Luce is edgy the whole time they are on board. He stays close to the rail, leaning against it. He keeps checking the sea, but there is no sign of another boat. No sign of a light. No sign of any other living moving shape. He casts an eye across the *Alexandra*—her deck, her cargo, her crew. She is shabby and ill-kept, but he spies the long bony shadows of submachine guns, hidden in the furled sails.

They load up and push off. He has the engine on low, and as he turns her around to head toward shore, the wind strikes the back of his neck and he has the faint sick sense of something altered, something wrong. At first he cannot say what it is—nothing he hears, nothing he sees—but then he smells the slight reek of gasoline on the clean, salt wind.

He cuts off his running lights, and he can see her then—the cutter patrol. Right away he recognizes her by her lines: her sleek lean profile, low in the water. She is nearly on them.

The sound rips open the darkness—the sharp shrill blow of the Klaxon horn—ordering him to heave to. A moment later, the cutter throws her searchlight. Luce swerves hard, out of the light's path, but it nicks his stern. He hears the shout. He shifts into reverse, swings right, pulls around, then gives both engines the gun. He speeds straight through the line of the searchlight, his head down. The light strikes the wheelhouse, then the side of his face. White. Blinding. He looks away, and they fall back into the darkness. He hears the shouts of the Coast Guard men behind him. He heads straight for the *Alexandra*. Her crew is in motion now, alert to the danger, men shuffling on her deck, hauling anchor, hoisting sail, pulling out their guns. He can hear the groan of the chain through the hawse pipe. He speeds toward her, the cutter's searchlight still tailing him, groping through the churned sea of his wake. He has almost reached the *Alexandra*'s stern when the patrol boat fires a burst of warning shots. They have aimed ahead of him, but his speed takes him through the blaze of machine-gun fire. Bullets rake the wheelhouse, and he feels the shift in air as one passes close to his ear, the sound intimate, deafening. His heart stops for a moment.

"Down!" he shouts to Johnny Clyde. "Flat on the deck. Down. Now." He veers hard and fast around the *Alexandra* to make a shield between himself and the patrol. He knows that he is not the big fish they are after. He was the bait and they trailed him out. They must have known ahead of time she would be off position. Someone must have set her up. It was his dumb luck to be caught in the middle of it.

He turns again to the right and guns both engines, he heads straight out, toward nothing, running without lights as hard and fast as the boat will take him into the great black rolls of the sea.

It is not until they have passed out of sight and Luce begins to circle around again toward shore that he realizes they are taking on water. He can feel a new weight in the foredeck, a strange and fluid changing weight. He sends Johnny belowdecks into the hold, and Johnny finds the bullet holes, four feet off the bow just below the waterline, the sea gushing in.

Luce knows that if he cuts back on their speed, they will sink.

His first thought is to throw the entire cargo overboard, but even then, the boat by its own weight might still take on too much water for them to make it back in.

"Dump half of it," he shouts. "Move the rest aft. Do you understand, move it aft!"

Johnny does what Luce tells him to do. They keep the boat running unmanned, plowing through the darkness, and they throw more than half of the load overboard. They move the rest to the stern. They stack the cases to weigh down the rear of the boat. They throw tarps over them and tie them off with lines to keep the crates in place, and slowly, very slowly, the bow begins to rise.

Luce comes back to the wheel, checks his sights, and sets them back on course. He sends Johnny below to bail out what he can of the water, and then he puts the engine out to full. The bow rises inches more. He runs them in.

Luce guesses that the cutter will have radioed in. There will be craft waiting for him at the mouth. As he passes Half-mile Rock, he looks toward the Knubble, and just beyond it, he can make out the shapes of two patrols. His instinct tells him not to try to land at the causeway, and so he brings the boat in to the midpoint of the beach, west of the seasonal restaurant, by the bathhouses. The wind is in their favor and they come in on the rising tide. They throw anchor in the shallows.

They unload the crates onto the beach, and Luce sends Johnny Clyde across the bridge to the Point Wharf for the truck. While he is gone, Luce works on the busted plank. He resets it as best as he can. He cuts squares of canvas off one of the tarps and patches the holes below the waterline from the outside and the inside. He tacks the edges with copper brads, then smears it all over with grease.

Half an hour later, Johnny comes back with the truck. He drives over the small dune, across the beach, and down to the harder sand.

He tells Luce that Jeb Gifford, the constable, and a handful of officers were hanging around outside Blackwood's store, and so he had come back the long way around.

They begin to load the liquor crates onto the bed of the truck. They work in silence. Once, when Johnny Clyde's hand catches on a smashed bottle, the broken glass drives a deep black cut through his palm. He stops and looks down. He touches the wound. There is new dark blood on his fingertips.

Luce lifts another crate onto the edge of the truck bed and slides it back against the others. He takes off his cap and wipes the sweat from his brow.

"You think it's worth it?" he asks.

Johnny looks up at him.

"Just asking," Luce says. "I already have my own answer."

Even in the night darkness, he can see Johnny's face, the pain from the cut and then that other trace element—a low, smooth anger.

"They peppered us out there," Johnny says.

"Yup."

"Could've shot us up."

Luce nods. He picks at a spot of dried mud on the tail of the truck. "I know he's your family," he says slowly. "I know he's your blood."

"He's an asshole," Johnny says under his breath.

"But you'd never cross him."

"He'd kill me."

"If he caught you."

Johnny stares at him, then looks away. He tears a strip of cloth off the hem of his shirt, wraps it around his hand and bends to pick up the next crate.

By the time they are through and the truck is loaded, there is less than an hour and a half until dawn. To the southeast out over the water are fringes of false light.

Johnny climbs into the truck and starts the engine. Luce will take the boat, and they will meet up the West Branch opposite Judy Island. Luce waves him off. The truck heads up the beach through the soft sand toward the dune, and Luce turns and begins to walk back toward the water. He has just reached the wrack-line when behind him he hears a wheezing sound as the truck's wheels sink into a patch of soft sand. He turns and starts to run, shouting, but he is too late, Johnny does the unthinkable, he gives it more gas. The tires spin, the engine grinds, a throaty futile sound. The truck's wheels sink up to the axle, locked in.

Johnny gets out of the truck. "Jesus!" he says. "What the Christ are we going to do? Soon as light, they'll spot the boat, find us. We have to leave it."

"We're not going to leave it."

"There's nothing else. They'll be looking. They already are."

"Shut up," Luce says sharply. "Let me think." And Johnny is quiet, his breathing ragged. He takes a few steps away, fishes out his cigarettes, and lights up a smoke.

"You're going to take the boat," Luce says finally. "You're going to take it in to the wharf, and you're going to call Lyons from wherever you can call him and you're going to get another truck."

"Me? You want me to take the boat? Why me? I don't drive the boat."

"There's nothing on her. She's empty. Even if they stop you, they can't do nothing to you if she's empty. You'll come in limping. Some water in your hold and a caulked hole in the bow, but not a trace of booze on you."

And Johnny sees it then, he sees what Luce is saying. They take the peg locks off two of the bathhouse doors and haul the crates of liquor from the truck and up the beach. They load them into the bathhouses, stacking them floor to ceiling.

Luce goes down to the boat with Johnny. Her hull is still low in the water, still leaking. Luce gets her out of the shallows, past the wave break, then he slips over the side. He is up to his waist in the water.

"Stay close to shore," he tells Johnny. "Tide's high, you can take her on the backside of Cory's Island. If the patch on the hole breaks—it shouldn't, but if it does and she starts taking on water—just let her go and swim in."

"I can't swim."

"You'll swim." Luce pushes him off and wades back to shore. He walks up the beach to the bathhouses, sits down on the floor of one, next to the cases. He puts his head down on his knees and sleeps.

Daybreak. The light wakes him. Johnny is still not back. Luce finds a few leftover coffee beans in his pocket. He gnaws on them. The drug sparks his nerves.

He steps outside onto the deck, and as he does, he spies a deer on the shade side of a shed, grazing through a patch of grass. It is a doe. She senses him watching. She lifts her head and her eyes are pure and soft and dark. She is beautiful. He winces, and she bolts. Her hindquarters flash white as she kicks over a low hedge and vanishes into the scrub.

Luce walks out onto the beach. The truck is settled in the sand, a crippled shape, its rear wheels sunk up to the axle. The sunlight reflects off the passenger side window, blinding. He takes another step out into the open, lured by the water. It is green and smooth, a morning sea, and the surface is flat with light sheaves of mist across it. The waves break low.

He hears the shriek of gulls. He looks and sees a small flock of them farther down the beach, flying toward him out of the west. They skim the water, trailing something along the shore. He squints, and it comes into view, a darker, oily moving surface—a school of baitfish chased by bigger fish, blues. The water boils as their tails slap up. The blues are working the baitfish, pushing them into the shallow water, trapping them against the shore. On the wind, he can smell the strong ripe scent of fish meat and blood. As they come nearer, he can see the baitfish flipping up, bits of silver flashing, the sheen of the oil, the strewn pieces of the dead. The gulls move in. They dive and swoop, picking off the baitfish that the blues have herded in against the shore.

The gulls are scavengers. He knows this. Sea-rats. This is how they work. This is how they survive. No sense of loyalty, no judgment or morals. No seesaw of conscience, good versus evil, right against wrong. As he watches them now, working the space, working their prey, moving in by turn to take their feed, he can sense a power in the world around him—a sheer, indifferent power like a tremendous pair of hands shuffling through the sky, the light, the slow calm water of the bay—and still, he watches the gulls. He cannot take his eyes off them. The idea comes to him then.

Later that morning when the work is done, Luce drops Johnny off at his house and drives over to the Peirce and Kilburn Shipyard in Fairhaven. He tells them he is looking to buy a work boat, a small fishing boat for the river, but with as strong an engine as a boat that size can carry, so if he would have the desire, he could take her out to fish off Cuttyhunk or even as far as the Devil's Bridge.

The man he talks to first takes him in to see another man who is working in a shop, turning dory boats. The smells of the shop—the sawdust, resin, linseed oil, and pine tar—remind Luce of Noel. Gritted dry air in his throat, on his lips. There is not a man working in that yard who recognizes him. There is not a man there he knows. When they ask his name, he gives a false one. He tells them that he sailed as a boat-steerer on the *Wanderer* before she was wrecked, and now he has a wife and kid, lives on Water Street in downtown New

Bedford, and he is hoping to make an honest living for himself in a new trade.

They take him around the yard, show him a few boats that might suit his purpose, and he chooses one. He knows she is what he wants the moment he lays eyes on her—twenty foot, flat bottom—a simple design, the kind of design his grandfather might have built. He estimates that even oiled up with thirty cases, she will draw less than two feet of water. He will be able to run her in the shallows, among the rocks, and all the way up through Crooked Creek. He will be able to run her right up onto the beach. She is the kind of boat they used in the early bootleg years. No one would even think to use such a small and simple boat these days.

He has her fitted with a one-lunger engine so she will have the speed he needs. They tell him to come back for her the following week.

The boat is cheap and he pays cash. He has Johnny Clyde drive him over to the shipyard and drop him off there. Then he takes the boat and runs her west-southwest from Fairhaven out Buzzards Bay back to Westport.

He takes her into the river and ties her up against the marsh in the hidden pool at the end of Crooked Creek. In the boat, he keeps a quahog rake, a gaff, and a pail. He wades across the marsh through the damp suck of mud, the cordgrass and the cattails, to the higher ground behind the town dump. There is an old, unused wagon path that runs through the scrub. When he takes the boat out, he leaves the truck parked there, hidden in the brush at the end of the dirt road.

He starts with small acts of piracy, small acts of mooncussing. He breaks into barns, icehouses, haylofts, cellars, sheds. He salvages drops made by other crews. He hijacks loads of liquor from gangs that run out of Fall River. Then he drives the crates and cases twenty miles overland to downtown New Bedford, and sells them piece-meal, to rival gangs.

He knows enough to pull it off. He has a feel for the rhythms, the tics of the work, and he is careful. He chooses his jobs, picks his nights. He doesn't use Honey Lyons's truck. He borrows Johnny's smaller pickup. He never pirates a load of liquor too close to home. He doesn't mess with Swampy Davoll and his Point gang. He doesn't steal too much at a single given time. He picks off a few cases here, a few crates there. Several times a month, he takes the small boat, the new boat, offshore to meet with a barge or a steamer manned by a crew he has never worked with before. He pays cash for the liquor—his own cash—and he runs it in. He has done out the math. He can bring in one-quarter of an average-size load, split the profit with Johnny Clyde, and each of them will still make more than they would on a job for Honey Lyons.

He knows he is grazing trouble. The key, he understands, is to split himself—to work in a way that runs against reason, that runs against what is possible. He keeps up appearances. He and Johnny go on doing jobs for Lyons, working Lyons's boat out of the slip on the Point Wharf, and on the side they make their money, the real money—so much that Luce stops counting. He is smart enough to know not to spend it. He buys only poor-boy things, an occasional luxury, but nothing extravagant. He saves the rest. He gives some to Cora for safekeeping and buries the bulk of it under a ruined stone hearth in the woods.

Bridge

Within a week, she felt the shift in Luce. She knew he was sneaking around, and it didn't take much for her to knock a few pieces together and figure it out.

She watches him carefully but says nothing until one warm day in the midafternoon when they have rowed Noel's skiff to one of the islands downriver. It is a brilliant day, the first week of October. The sun is warm and it bakes them as they lie outstretched on the top of a massive rock, their arms bare against its cool uneven surface. She points out shapes for him in the clouds—a lizard, a Viking sword, the face of a bear.

"So tell me," she says, "about what you're up to now." She closes her eyes against the sun's glare. She does not turn toward him.

And he tells her. He tells her because he needs her. She is another pair of hands. She is smart and fast and good with a gun, and he can trust her.

He takes her with him to the old pesthouse, up the road on Pine Hill, back in the woods. It is the shell of a building, gutted by fire. He brings her up a wrecked staircase to the second floor, and she sits with him there, among the rot and cobwebs, as he builds a blind attic in the narrow crawl space above the ceiling. He cuts a hole in the top of a dressing closet. Bridge helps him load hard pine planks into a pull cart, and in the dark, they haul it through the woods to the pesthouse. Luce climbs up into the rafters, and she passes him the boards through the ceiling hole. He lays them down across the beams to make a strong rough floor.

It will be a resting place, he tells her, for loads between runs when they have brought in too much to sell it all at once or when the heat is on them. They will bring the bottles and the cases in at night and store them here.

Toward the end of the month, Luce hears news of a ship coming up from the West Indies. She will be anchored for one night off Browns Ledge.

Bridge drives the truck that night. It is a full-of-the-moon night, and they go out late, after the moon has begun to set, its heavy yellow eye growing larger as it falls. Bridge drops Luce and Johnny Clyde at the entrance of the trail that leads into Crooked Creek. She keeps watch as they walk across the marsh to the boat. From the road, she can see them working through the turns toward the river. She watches until they have disappeared. She waits an hour. Then she drives over the bridge, through the village at the Point, and up Main Road. She turns left down Cornell Road and drives around the West Branch past Gray's Gristmill and into Adamsville. At the phone-box, she places a call to the police—a tip—some men sighted in what she thinks might have been rum-boats on the beach at Richmond Pond near Brayton Point, the other side of town. They ask her name. She hangs up and drives back into Westport.

She meets Luce and Johnny at the landing on East Beach Road. She backs the truck right down to the water, and they load as many cases as the pickup bed will hold. They leave the rest with the boat in the shallows and drive a quarter of a mile to a summer house that has been boarded up for winter. They back the truck down the drive until the tail end comes right up against the rolling cellar door. They will unload here, then go back to get the rest of the cases off the beach. Later, in stages, they will shift the entire load to the pesthouse.

Johnny Clyde waits in the cab while Bridge and Luce go around to the side of the house. Luce pries back the batterboard from one of the windows and jimmies up the sash. He pushes Bridge through first, then crawls in after her. They walk through the rooms toward the kitchen, the hollow sound of their steps on the floor. Sheets have been drawn across the furniture. The tables and chairs glow like hunched white elephants in the darkness.

Bridge pauses at a doorway. "Come here," she whispers to Luce. He is ahead of her, halfway down the hall. He comes back. It is a library, every wall lined with books, two deep hulking chairs set together facing a dark fireplace, a small table set between them.

"When we're done, we'll come back for a smoke," he says and squeezes her arm.

She follows him to the back of the house. They go down the steps to the cellar and pull back the bolt on the door. Johnny Clyde gets out of the truck, and they begin to unload. They work silently, quickly. They have stacked almost all of it when they hear the peal of sirens from farther up the road coming toward them. Luce walks quickly to the cab of the truck, pulls his .22 rifle from behind the seat. He draws it out by the barrel and, as he does, the trigger catches on a spring. The gun fires. The bullet rips past his wrist and shoots into Bridge. She can feel a searing pain through her side, and the shock of the impact, the shock of the blast, sends her back against the cellar wall. She strikes her head on the concrete and her mind goes black.

Luce watches in horror—it all seems to unfold in slow motion—
each second drawn out, unbearable—she bends at the knees and the
earth catches her, she wavers for a moment and her weight seems to
settle as if she is poised in an uncertain prayer. She falls forward.
Her face strikes the ground.

Henry

It is the sirens that wake him. They sweep through the night out of his sleep. Vague lights pass through the east-facing window. Then the sound veers away and begins to fade as the police trucks turn up John Reed Road, heading north.

He lies in the darkness. The shapes of the bedroom slowly advance into focus. The desk against one wall. The ivy plant. The low bookshelf. The sheen of the framed mirror hanging between the windows. The sky outside. Black. Black.

He is dozing off again when he hears the knock, a soft rap on his consciousness, so indistinct that at first he mistakes it for a ghoul in the brain, some old cruel thought seeking entrance. Then it comes again, the knocking louder, more insistent. He hears hushed voices and realizes that they are standing, someone is standing, on the porch below.

He throws on a robe and goes downstairs. He opens the door.

Through the screen, he sees Luce Weld. There is a boy behind him, carrying a third person.

"What is it?" Henry asks. "What do you want?"

"I need a doctor," says Luce.

Henry hesitates.

Luce twists the knob on the screen. He twists it again hard, but the door is locked. The knob won't give. "We need a doctor," he says. His eyes are wild.

"I'm not a doctor anymore. It's been years—"

"Fuck years," Luce says. He presses his face up to the screen. "I need you to be a doctor tonight. Right now. I need you to unlock this goddamn door."

Behind him, the person in the boy's arms stirs, a low sound, a dark stirring out of sleep, the cap shifts on the face and Henry can see that it is Bridge. He unlocks the screen, opens the door, and leads them into the kitchen. He clears off the heavy oak table and throws down a cotton tablecloth and several towels.

"Lay her down there. Carefully. Watch her arm. Keep her spine straight." He checks her pulse, puts his cheek against her mouth. Her breath is slow and light, but even. He has time. He straightens and turns to Luce. "What happened?"

"She was shot."

"Where?"

"Down the road."

"I mean where on her."

Luce shakes his head. "Dunno. The gut, I think. Or her side. She hit her head."

"On what?"

"A wall."

Henry reaches for the chain on the electric light above the table, but Luce grips his arm. "No light," he says.

Henry looks at him. "If you want me to help her, I am going to have to work with light, and you are going to have to leave."

Luce shakes his head. "I won't leave her."

"I can't do a thing for her without light."

"I won't leave."

"You will leave."

The boy who carried her stands off to the side by the stove. He clears his throat. "Hey, Luce," he says, his voice jittery. "Maybe we should go finish up. I mean, I don't think we should just leave the—"

"Shut the hell up," Luce says. The boy nods his head several times and is quiet.

Luce looks down at his sister. Then abruptly, he turns away. "I'll be back," he says and, in one swift motion, he is out the door and down the hall, the boy behind him. Henry hears them leave. The low sound of the screen latch as it slips into place.

He turns on the light. She stirs. He finds the swelling on the back of her skull where her head struck the wall. He touches her body carefully, through her clothes, until he locates the hole in her side. He pulls up her shirt. She moans, waking. Her eyes open, staring unfocused. They close again. He rolls her body up, off the table, and locates the exit wound. It was a clean shot. A flesh wound. The bullet is already out of her. He lays her back down.

He takes the belt off his dressing gown and digs out a rope from a drawer in the pantry. He ties her down on the table so she won't roll off. Then he goes through the house and gathers the supplies he will need. Astringent from the medicine shelf in the upstairs bathroom. A bottle of rubbing alcohol. A tincture of laudanum. Morphine. Gauze. Two fresh washcloths. More towels. Vinegar. Wax. Thread. He pulls his doctor's bag from his dressing room closet. He has not opened it for over six years. He changes out of his nightclothes into an undershirt and trousers. He goes back downstairs.

She is waking, her eyes flicking open, then closed. She sees him, confused for a moment, the pupils dilate, she does not know where she is. She opens her mouth to speak and the pain hits her then, her eyes grow startled, huge. He puts his hand to her mouth and shakes his head. "Shhh," he says. "Lie still. Don't move." He takes a syringe out of his bag, sterilizes it, fills it to the lowest mark, taps it, then wraps her arm tightly until her vein rises. He pushes the needle in.

Within seconds, she can feel her mind begin to drain. The pain drops and is gone. Her eyes roll from side to side as she watches him move through the room around her. He is filling a pot with water from the sink, dragging a stool to the table. He sets the pot of water down onto it and there is steam rising, the room begins to swim. Another chair pulled over, a leather bag on it, open, he is rummaging through, locating something inside, and as she watches, she has the sensation that her body is floating inches off the table and there is water rushing underneath her, she is floating on the sea that has broken through into the room, and she can feel the cool flush of water on her skin and the heat of the drug through her veins, and the sea is a deep and distant roar, like a sound she has heard before with her ear pressed tight against a shell.

He cleanses both sides of the wound with water and a sponge. He swabs it with astringent, and then again runs water through it. The water drains off her into the washtub he has set on the floor. It fills with pink water and clots of her blood. The entrance hole of the wound is clean and round and small, but the exit hole is ragged, and again, he turns her onto her side. With scissors, he cuts away the ragged edges until the wound is wider but smooth. Then he holds the two sides together, and using a common needle and double waxed thread, he passes it into her skin. One at a time, he makes the stitches down the wound. He draws them tight and close and straight, leaving the threads loose until he comes to the end. Then he ties the tails of each thread, drawing them tight into hard double knots. He swabs the closed wound with alcohol, then lays her back down and dresses the opposite side.

She is sleeping again, he notices, as he rinses the needle in the tub on the stool. The water has cooled, and he watches his hands pass through it, dark traces of her blood around his nails. She is sleeping, and it is after two in the morning, and he realizes then that his hands had not shaken, not once, not at all. He picks her coat up off the chair to fold it, and as he does, a small piece of metal clatters to the floor. He bends and picks it up. It is the bullet, the head soft, mushroom-shaped. He washes it off and tucks it into his trouser pocket. She is still sleeping. He watches her sleep.

Luce comes back for her before dawn. Henry brings him into the front room. Bridge is lying on the daybed by the window, her eyes closed. Henry explains the wound to Luce, its dressing and care. Keep both sides clean. Keep her still. He hands Luce a bottle of pills. Give her these. One with water for the pain. No more than two. They'll help her sleep it off. Luce nods, looking down at her. He does not look up, even after Henry has stopped speaking. He is unable to take his eyes off her. He starts suddenly. "Let me pay you," he says, drawing out a pack of bills from his coat pocket.

Henry shakes his head. "No."

"Take it."

"No."

"It'll be bad luck if you don't take it."

"I'm not a doctor. I don't do this work anymore."

Luce looks at him, bewildered. "Will she be alright?" he asks, and Henry is struck by the sudden change in his face.

"Yes. She's going to feel it for a while, but she'll be fine."

Luce nods. He looks down at her again, unconvinced.

"It's a flesh wound," Henry says. "Keep it clean. Keep it dressed. The stitches can be cut out in two weeks."

Luce nods again. His sister's face is quiet, still, in the early light.

"She never sleeps this deep," Luce says.

"I've given her something. A tincture. The same substance as what's in the pills. It's making her sleep."

Luce shakes his head.

"She'll be fine," Henry says again. "But she needs to rest. She can rest here if you like."

Luce looks at him for a moment. "No, I'll take her home. She needs to go home." He bends down, slides his arms carefully underneath her as if he has done this a thousand times, as if he knows her weight and how much strength her body will demand, and he lifts her as if he is lifting the world.

After they are gone, Henry cleans up the kitchen. He wraps the towels in the tablecloth, empties the washtub and puts his doctor's bag away. He makes a pot of tea. A slice of toast. He goes to the writing desk by the window and draws out a heavy leather-bound notebook. He takes out a pen, wipes dried ink off the nib. He turns to the end of the notebook, flips back several pages until he comes to a blank page. He enters the date.

October 27, 1928 . . .

And he writes. He wants to write about her, but he can't. What he writes is awkward. He can find only poor words for it.

That morning he goes, as he has gone every morning, to his work at the mill. But everything is changed. He hears the men talking in the cotton bins as they take their lunch. They talk in low tones about the strike. They talk about the different kinds of soup given out—the maggoty scrap bone, boiled until it sheds to broth— and how the best stuff comes from the Workingman's Club—peas and barley, chunks of real meat.

They break off when they see him coming, their eyes cast down or toward the window, glassy, vacant, staring straight ahead. And he finds that this morning, for the first time, he cannot tell himself what he has always told himself before: that it is a natural gap, the gap between the handful of bosses and the workers at the mill. They are continents apart. He can feel this, and he cannot tell himself it does not matter.

He leaves the mill early that day, and on his way home, he drives through the strike zones, through the north and south ends of the city, and he sees what he has put off seeing, what he has not wanted to see—all types of children, thin, Saxon-faced, dark-eyed Portuguese, children in good boots and decent coats, others with shoes out at the toes. Outside the Workingman's Club, they stand with their soup pails waiting on lines wrapped twice around the block. He sees the small crowds gathered at the Labor Temple, the scabbed ears of the mill workers, and the police barricades, the billy clubs. His car nudges through the wasted city streets, the windows of the empty tenements plastered with old newspapers, and superimposed over it all, over everything he sees, is an image of her body laid out on the heavy oak table—knife scars in the wood and her bare flesh soaked with yellow light, the bruised eye of the wound in her side where the bullet passed through.

Midafternoon, he drives back to the beach. He sits on the porch at the cottage for the rest of the day, deep into the evening.

A red sky at dusk—clouds like blood-stricken birds. And still he stays sitting there as the wind settles down and the hard night chill moves in. His body is stiff as shadow in the porch chair. The salt air soaks his face, his hair, and when he closes his eyes, there are birds exploding in his head. Their wings burst up, and her body is drifting in that nether space, falling slowly through their wings.

Noel

Luce tells him she fell sick with a fever, and he knows it for a lie. He knows it when he sees her lying there, still, the sheets pulled up high and tucked around her chest.

"She's cool," Noel says, touching her forehead.

"Fever can make you cold."

"Was it a fever ship you went to meet last night?"

"She didn't go out to the ship, old man. We stopped in at a restaurant before. It must have been the beef."

"You ate beef?"

Luce starts to nod, then catches himself. He shakes his head. "I had chips."

"Just chips?"

"A cut of chicken."

"Don't you have things to do?" Noel asks.

But Luce won't leave. He sticks around her bed-side, folds back the edge of the sheet again and tucks it, smoothed, under her hand.

"I brought her to a doctor," he says. "Doctor said keep her still a day or so, let the fever pass. She'll be up and about. I'll look after her. Doctor said to give her these too." He nods at a bottle of pills on the night table. "Twice or so a day."

"Why don't you let me sit with her for a spell."

"She might wake up, need something."

"I'll get what she needs."

"I'll stay with her."

"Don't you have things to do?" Noel asks again.

"I got nothing to do," Luce answers.

Noel shrugs. "Alright then." He leaves the room. But an hour later, when Luce goes outside to use the privy, Noel comes back upstairs. He peels the sheet down and finds the wound in her side. The gauze has begun to leak through, a pale yellow stain. A wound, he knows, is like any other creature. It has its own life. It crawls and creeps and spits, a dust-bellied thing. It takes its own walk through the body. Heals in its own time.

Her face is gray. Thin violet shadows circle her closed eyes. He can tell by the dressing that at least Luce had had enough sense to get her well cared for. And she would heal, she would be herself again with no trace of what had happened—whatever it was that had happened—apart from a scar in her side the size of a fifty-cent piece.

But as he stands there, looking down at her, he feels the sudden pulsing shock of his own rage. It sweeps through him, rogue and buckling. Wave after wave of it.

He is waiting for Luce at the top of the stairs. As Luce takes the last step, Noel moves into the stairwell, blocking his way.

"You know what I see?"

Luce looks up at him.

"What I see is you like the bulk of a whale. You've been stuck, ironed, drawn in. They've hoisted you and started the cutting in, and that flesh of yours is spiraling right off the bone. Nothing left to you when it's all said and done. You'll be in a barrel or in the box, or maybe you'll wash up on the neck some sweet morning in the fall with the rest of the muck, and they'll find you there, or I'll find you there, a slug in the skull and crabs rooting their way through your ribs."

"Dirk McAllister crossed the wrong man," Luce mutters, looking down at the stairs.

"And who told you that? The wrong man himself tell you that?"

"He got what he had coming."

"You'll get what you have coming."

Luce takes the last step to the top of the stairs, and they are on even ground then. He is barely taller than Noel, and they stand that way together, toe to toe, nearly eye to eye. Luce's body is tight, his fist hard down by his side.

"Like I told you before, Luce, you haven't got the head for this work. But over my grave, I won't see you take Bridge down with you."

And it might be her name that does it, but Noel can see the briefest flash through Luce's eyes, silver and quick, and then, like some old blind has been raised, Noel can see deep into him, fathoms deep, through the hardness and the callused shell that has thickened around him over the years. It is like looking down into a well, looking through his grandson's eyes that are wide and beautiful and skinless, young the way they were once, the way they must have been when he was still a boy.

Luce looks away. He is against the wall. "You think I wanted this for her?"

Noel doesn't answer.

"It was you," Luce says bitterly as he turns and starts back down the stairs. "It was you, old man, who took that job and put us in this place to start."

He disappears at the bottom of the stairwell. Noel hears the back door slam.

He does not think long on Luce's words. They stick in him for a moment, little blades, but he lays them aside. He sits with Bridge through the afternoon, and when Cora comes upstairs in the evening, he leaves Bridge with her.

There is no sign of Luce in the house or in the yard. The truck is gone. Noel goes outside to the shop and does a bit of nothing. He drags out the panbone a foot from the wall, slides his hand into the pocket behind the jaw, and gropes out the roll of cash. He counts it. $1,128. He counts it again. Then he puts $1,100 in his trouser pocket and slides the panbone back. He digs through the half-cask in the corner until he finds a good tooth. He sands it down, and with a bottle of India ink and a scrimp needle, he goes back into the house. In the kitchen, he stabs down a block of ice, crushes the cubes, and mixes up a pitcher of switchel. He goes back upstairs.

He scrimps into the tooth and sits beside Bridge as the night moves in. When she stirs, he gives her sips of the water mixed with molasses and vinegar. The ice cubes crack as they melt.

It is dark. Through the window, he can see the black hulking shapes of the outbuildings, the barn and the privy, the henhouse and the shed. He can see the long-stretched empty clothesline with the cock-eyed wooden pins split on the string. He can see the bony shadows of the garden down below—the wooden stakes with the tangled skinny vines gone by, and the cabbages—their tousled heads, slick with the moonlight running over them.

It is everything familiar. It is everything he has built with the work of his hands. And it seems so meager now. Such a meager offering that he could give her.

He falls asleep in the chair by her bed. Just past midnight, he hears the sound of a branch scratching on the window glass. The wick of the kerosene lamp has burned down into the bowl. A soft glow washes over the room, the floor, the walls, and in that bare light, through half-opened eyes, he thinks he can see six white spiders crawling on his granddaughter's face. One of them walks with long white legs along her lip. It slips into her mouth and disappears. One by one, they vanish down her throat.

He knows that the soul can be winded, scuttled, stolen. It can rise up out of the body like a fire or the moon. It can be gray or many-colored. It can change its size. It can take the shape of an animal or an insect, a blade of grass, a drop of water or a stone. He knows that when the body is cut, it is the soul that suffers, and he wants to wake her. He wants to shake out the wound and what it stands for—his own weakness, his own greed, what he has done, what he did not see, what he did not want to see.

He had known when he took that job for Honey Lyons a year ago that it was the wrong work to take. He had known even then that he was wading into water too deep for a handline. He had known it in his gut, and he had recognized the feeling. It was the same feeling he had had that day years back on ship, that day in the Arctic when he was posted as lookout, the day he spied the walrus pod.

They were so far in the distance, the sows culling off the sheet ice with their pups, and he knew that no other man of the crew would have the eyes to sight them. Within minutes, the herd would be away, over the drop of the horizon and under the floes. He knew he had a choice. And he chose. Even now, so many years later, he does not know why he did it. But he did it. He made the shout. And the men set after them. Slaughtered them.

Henry

When he stops by the house the next morning, a woman comes to the door. Henry recognizes her as the woman he saw sitting next to Bridge at the Grange. She has her daughter's coloring, dark hair, deep blue eyes. She is gorgeous in a distant sort of way.

She stands in the doorway, her arm across the frame. "There's nobody home right now. You'll have to come back."

He takes off his hat. "I'm looking for Bridge."

"My father will be in this afternoon. You can come back then."

"I just want to know how she is."

"I don't know what you mean."

"Her brother brought her to me two nights ago. I dressed her wound."

"We don't want any trouble here," she says quietly.

"Can I see her?"

"No."

"Please."

"Did the police send you?"

"No. Is she alright?"

"She seems to be."

"It would mean a great deal to me if I could see her."

"She's sleeping."

"Please."

Cora pauses, her arm still barring the doorway. The man stands on the middle step, looking up at her, and there is something in his eyes, something in his voice as he asks about her daughter, that wrings her heart. She remembers him from the Grange. She remembers the look she observed passing between him and Bridge. It is not a doctor's concern that has brought him by her house this morning. She steps away from the door. "Come with me."

He follows her. He takes the two steps into the house and rounds the corner of the front entrance. He has to stop for a moment to let his eyes adjust to the dimness of the light. She leads him through a small parlor, past the dining room and the kitchen. There is a simplicity about the house and its contents that shocks him. The furnishings are clean but worn, the rooms stark. He pauses in the doorway to the kitchen. The floor is old, pine. The places where the knots have fallen out have been patched with flattened tin cans tacked around the edges. And as he pauses there, staring at the kitchen floor, he feels in a strange way that he has wronged Bridge. He has fallen in love with her, and in so doing, he has intruded on her life without recognizing or accepting what he realizes now she has always felt: that he is an outsider to her world. He thinks he finally understands why she has kept him at arm's length. He understands her resistance, her occasional resentment. He understands about the teacup, and he wants to smash every piece of china in his house and lay the pieces at her feet, but even wanting that, he knows, even wanting her the way he does, is not enough to change the way she sees it, the way she sees him. He feels ashamed. He feels the farce of his own life.

"Are you coming up then?" asks Cora.

He nods. She leads him up the stairs, down a short hall. She stops before a door and gently pushes it open. The room is small, with one window, a dresser, a lamp, old wallpaper with pink roses faded out by the sun. Bridge is asleep on the bed. Her face rests against the pillow, her mouth slightly open as she sleeps. She is beautiful, and his body aches, but he does not go to her. He stands on the threshold. He counts her breaths as her chest rises and falls. He listens for the sound, still and deep and even. Then he closes the door. "She's going to be fine," he says to her mother as they descend the stairs. "Change the dressing twice a day. Wipe the wound with a clean cloth and iodine. The stitches can be removed in two weeks with a sterile blade."

She leads him to the door. "Thank you," she says.

"Will you tell her I came by?"

"I will."

He nods, puts on his hat, and turns to go. She catches his arm.

"Her brother didn't mean to do it, you know. He loves her. It was an accident." Her eyes are focused intensely on his face.

"Of course it was," he replies, and he walks slowly down the steps across the yard to his car.

Cora watches him from the doorway. She watches him walk away, and she can feel the sorrow all around him. For hours afterward, she will feel it spread like a blanket of fine snow across the yard and through the hall upstairs and in the doorway of her daughter's room where he had stood. She will feel his sorrow everywhere in her house. He had come to her door with his beautiful desperation and he had left with that unbearable sorrow. She will feel it for the rest of the day—as she does her wash and her mending, as she fixes supper for her father and eats with him in silence. She will feel it as she sits beside her daughter's bed later that same evening and changes the dressing on the wound, "we are wind and water moving," she whispers as she soaks a cloth in iodine and wipes the wound clean.

Bridge

She drifts through the next few days, night col-
lapsing into night, pain and painlessness, a darkness
lapping up against her thoughts, her everyday mind
smashed.

Cora helps her with the bedpan. She fixes Bridge
trays of food, glasses of water with molasses and
crushed ice. Noel sits with her in the early evenings.
He feeds her warm broth from a bowl, spoonfuls of
jelly, and softened pieces of salt pork, minced fine.

For most of the day, Bridge is aware she is alone.
She is aware that some part of her has been broken.
She does not try to find the place. There is a kind of
solace, she finds, in the not-knowing. A kind of solace in the brokenness itself and lying still. The
room around her is a comfort—it is what she knows,
the room she has slept in since she was a child—the
paint-chipped dresser, the nickel-plated lamp, the
soft-brushed plaster of the ceiling, and how the eaves
slant down. The shadows change through the room
as the light shifts. They move like huge dark hands
across the clothes that her mother has laid out on
the chair. The day winds on, grinds down into dark-

ness, and in the coolness of the night air that moves into the room, she thinks of Henry. She imagines she can feel him near her. She remembers small details of the night she was shot. They leak back to her slowly: the hardness of the table against her head, the brightness of the room, how when she opened her eyes the light knifed into them. She had climbed out of herself—she remembers this—drifting up into one corner of the kitchen, and she had watched him from there as he moved over her, his sleeves rolled up; he found the wound in her side, cleansed it with the sponge, then stitched the edges of it neatly closed. She does not remember feeling any pain. She remembers the coolness of his fingers on her skin.

One night, she wakes to the sound of someone crying softly near her. It is her brother, Luce. He kneels by her bed, his head bowed. She moves her hand and touches his hair. He does not look up. He goes on crying, and she can feel his body shivering. The sound rattles in him like stones rolling on the ocean floor. She can feel his sadness on her face and in her hands. It spreads over them like water. There are threads of moonlight in his hair. He smells of sweat. Of salt. He smells of the sea. After a while, he falls asleep, his head on the bed next to her. She touches the side of his face gently, her fingers in the hollow of the bone. She closes her eyes, and she is down at the river. It is late afternoon, midsummer, years ago, and her father is alive. They have come to dig quahogs on the mudflats below Gunning Island. They ground the skiff and climb out: Bridge, her father, Luce, and Noel. They unload the wire baskets and three quahog rakes. Her father has brought a potato fork for her to use. She is young, still a child, and he does not expect her to keep at the work for long. The potato fork is old, and the tines are thick with rust. She rakes it through mud, and as she thrusts it down and draws it out, the rust begins to strip off. The tines grow silver again, brighter, glittering. As she digs, she stays close to Noel. He has a feel for where the clams are. His shoulders settle into the steady rhythm of the work. He rakes slowly, methodically. He does not leave a patch of ground unturned. He loads the quahogs into his pockets as he pulls them up, until his trousers bulge. Then he wades over to the wire basket he has left higher up on the flat and drops them in.

A great blue heron skims toward her across the still water. Its wings beat the air, sending ripples through the surface.

She notices that her father and Luce have drifted farther away. They work a distance apart from one another. She looks across the flat toward the riverbank. There is a cowpath leading off an old stone pier. It winds through pastureland and up into the hills. The sun has begun to settle in the west, and the light empties down across the river. It soaks the marsh, the path, the fields, the trees.

Her father is calling her. He has raked something up in the mud, and he calls her. It is something he wants her to see.

"Go on, then," Noel says.

She nods, but she looks back once toward the shore. The light has shifted. Tall shadows fall across the hills, and for a moment, she is afraid. Her feet feel cold in the water. She grips the potato fork tightly and begins to run across the flat toward her father. Her bare legs splash through the shallows.

Her father is kneeling in the mud, unearthing something with his hands. He looks up and sees her running toward him, and he smiles, his wide dark face opening to her, his hands buried in the water and the mud as he kneels in the silver light.

When she wakes, it is morning and Luce is gone. Her face is wet with tears. Her head aches. She can feel a dull stiffness in her side. She moves, and the pain is sharp. It shoots through her and leaves her gasping. She lets her head fall back onto the pillow. The morning air is still, a jagged rim of frost around the window glass. She can see the blacker shadows of the trees, pale handfuls of fog strung through their branches.

Sounds drift up through the metal grate in the floor: her mother loading wood into the stove, the scuff of her slippers across the kitchen, a cupboard door opening, the soft clatter of bowls. The smell of coffee, the smell of the fire.

Outside, the light has begun to rise. It catches in the frost along the lower edge of the windowpane and trembles there, a strange thin glow. She listens to the fragile sound of the skim ice cracking as it thaws.

She turns in her bed away from the window and the sun rising into it.

Noel

For three weeks, Noel walks around with the pack of folded cash in his trouser pocket. After the first frost, he picks up a ride from the Head of Westport to the trolley stop at Lincoln Park. He walks the rest of the way along Lake Noquochoke down Reed Road.

It has been a few years since he came by Rui's house. He notes the red trim paint around the windows and the front door. On the side porch in the shade, dressed skins hang to dry from the beams.

He finds Rui out back, six muskrats just dead, laid on the worktable. He is skinning them out. He takes the brains and works them through the hides to make the fur glossy, the skin pliable. He sprinkles them with powdered alum and saltpeter to preserve them from insects. Then he folds them lengthwise, flesh-side in, and sets them off, dressed, to the side.

"Nice, aren't they, Christmas?" Rui says as Noel walks up to him. "One damaged here in the leg. And this one's a kit. But the rest are fine. It'll be a good season."

"How you been then, Rui? Haven't seen you since Asa's."

Rui smiles. He points to the largest muskrat. "I might get three and a half dollars for this one."

Noel picks up one of the long knives. He fingers the inlay on the handle. "How many traps you have out now?"

"A dozen or so in the cedar swamp."

"You aren't setting in water?"

"You didn't come here to ask me about my traps now, did you, Christmas?"

"You're bringing in a good dollar with it then?"

Rui takes one of the midsize muskrats and, with the long knife, opens it to the gut. "For a side show, it's enough."

"You got something else going on?"

"You know smack well what I've got going on." He sprinkles the hide with alum, then folds it lengthwise and sets it with the others. He looks up at Noel. "What is it you want then?"

"Can you buy a few shares for me?"

Rui smiles and sets back to his work. "I hear talk about that boat you built. Quite a boat, I hear."

"Quite on her way to being busted up."

Rui laughs. "They say she fights shy. Fast and light. No patrol can beat her."

"I don't know anything about it, Rui."

"I hear talk about your Luce, too. He leaves no slick. They all know he's up to something, but they can't catch him at it."

Noel doesn't answer.

"He's been messing around with a girl from the cove. I know her old man. He'll get himself into some trouble with her if he keeps it up."

"I try not to keep track of my grandson," Noel says flatly.

"Okay then," Rui says. "Let me guess why you first took the job to build that sweet boat."

"You don't have to."

"You took it because you still miss the salt junk. Isn't that it?"

Noel nods.

Rui laughs. "Same Christmas as you ever were." He goes on working the knife through the last muskrat, gutting it out. With his fingers, he finds the midpart of the scalp, turns it throat-side facing up, and opens into the skull. He dips two fingers in and scoops out the brains. "These are the best there is to gloss up a hide, but only because they're brains just killed. They still have a little mind left in them." He slides the last dressed skin into the pile. "Help me string them, will you? Then stay for a mug up."

"Sure."

"Some fry fish?"

"Only if you scrub your hands real good."

Noel leans in the open doorway as Rui cooks. He lights his pipe, chews on the stem, but he doesn't smoke and the tobacco goes out. He lights it again. The doorstone has a narrow garden plot on either side where Rui keeps nasturtium and kale, sweet peas and herbs. The ground is dormant now. Noel can smell the fresh garlic and oil bristling in the pan. Rui rolls the fish whole in flour, and when the oil spits, he sets the fish in and lets it cook through on one side until the crust is dark brown.

They eat outside on the doorstone off tin plates, picking the flesh with their fingers.

"I'll tell you a thing or so about this stock thing," Rui says. "It's all common sense. You put your money in what you know. Solid names. Housekeep names. Radio. General Motors. U.S. Steel. Some talk about how it's emotion, the coaster ride of it, and that could be true—same as anything—if you stay on a bad ride too long, you'll get burned. But if you keep a level head, remember that your piece is your piece, your lay is your lay, if you don't greed after more than that, you'll do okay. Play it simple. Get in. Make a good dollar. Get out. And while you're in, do nothing. Just wait. No matter what kind of itch in your pants you get, all you want to do is sit back, listen to the boxing fights, the ball games, and do nothing. Is that your taste?"

And Noel can see that in Rui's eyes, in the deep shopworn crease between the brows, there is more than a question. He knows that in five strokes with a light ax, Rui can work a piece of square wood out of a round log. Rui is the fine thread that has always been there, working alongside Noel through the dark, uncounted years, the belly of his life.

"So how much have you got then, Christmas?"

Noel sets his plate on the ground, takes the roll of cash from his trouser pocket. He holds it out. Rui goes on eating.

"How much?" he says.

"Eleven hundred."

"Not so much. But not bad."

"Can you make it more?"

"Let me take a guess where you got it."

"You don't have to."

"That's what you made for that job last year, building that shy fast boat. You've been hiding it ever since. Let me guess where."

"Forget it, Rui."

"In the crook of that panbone."

Noel holds the money out to him, but Rui still doesn't take it. He scrapes the last of the fish off his plate. The oil shines smooth on his lips.

"Can you do something with it?" Noel asks.

"What do you want done?"

"What can you do?"

"You want me to double it?"

Noel nods slowly, skeptical.

"Fine. You don't believe me." Rui grins. "I'll triple it."

"No joke, Rui. I can't lose this. I need to get things right this rising."

"Not much time left?"

"I just need to get things right."

Rui sets down his plate. "Season's good now, Christmas. I can turn that little roll of cash into a field for you."

"This little roll of cash is all I've got."

Rui brushes his hands off on his trousers. He smiles, his black eyes cunning, bright. "Not for long." He plucks the wad of cash out of Noel's hand.

Part III

*The Season of
Open Water*

Bridge

A wild December. The surf is huge, ragged swells, the tide running high. In the middle of the month there is a five-day muckraker gale, fierce winds out of the southeast followed by a spell of kinder weather. On the twenty-first, the wind shifts into the northwest, rakes the river bottom, and the flood tide hurls bushels of scallops up onto the marsh. They lie there, glistening windrows, spread along the edge of the Let for three-quarters of a mile. The men go down, Noel among them, with pails and buckets and crates lined with rockweed, stacked end to end on the wagon beds.

He takes Bridge with him. They drive the wagon down onto the landing. She sits on the plank seat wrapped in a horse blanket, a scarf around her head, as he walks among the windrows of scallops with his pail, stooping to pick up the closed and pure carved shells.

On their way home, she asks him to take a ride down the causeway. As they pass Henry Vonniker's cottage, she noticed that the car is gone, the shutters closed.

"I haven't seen him around," Noel says. "Must've gone out of town."

She nods.

She is walking again, slowly. The wound still aches when she sits and stands. She stays close to Noel, hangs around the kitchen while he cooks. He shucks out the scallops and chops potatoes to make a stew. Luce brings them a fresh cut of beef for Christmas and two small hams.

The river thaws in the spell of warmer air, then begins to freeze again when the weather snaps back to its proper season. The tide pushes up against the weak skin of ice in the shallows of the marsh. A band of snow geese come into the river. One day as they are riding down to the causeway, Noel points them out to Bridge across the Let from the narrow part of East Beach Road. The flock gathers in the frozen reeds near Taber Point.

She sits in the shop as he works. He gives her small tasks to keep her hands from growing restless, and he tells her stories the way he used to, without looking for her to answer. He talks to her the way he did when she was a child wading through the shavings of wood as he worked, nosing through his tools, testing her small fingers against the serrated blade of the saw.

It is deep winter. They keep the woodstove stoked, full of burning, and one afternoon, as he is working to repair a busted gunwale, fitting new rivets and caulking the old holes, she notices a change in him, the way his weight leans more heavily into his tools, his shoulders hooking toward the floor. He seems smaller, more fragile, his balance uncertain. When he takes a sleep on the couch, she marks how he seems to sink deeper into the cushion folds, and there is a shift she notices in how he tells the stories. Certain moments stand out in relief. He takes his time with those, draws them out long, like the sun going down on a summer evening. Then suddenly, abruptly, as if he is snagged on some unfinished edge, he will push forward, covering years of his life in one stride, and then again, he will stray. He will linger over a detail. His voice will slow as if he is unwinding himself through the telling. The orange light sinks green shadows through his face.

One morning, as he is planing down a thick piece of oak, he tells her about the shapes in light that he remembers from his boyhood on Nomans Land. The shapes would come only in east weather, on an ash breeze: reflections of the other islands levered up into the northern skies above the clouds. He saw them once when he was out swordfishing with his father just off Old Man's Ledge. His father ruddered, and Noel was braced as lookout in the bow, and as they came around the tip of the island, in the distance he saw the reflection of the mainland city, wrenched upside down above the sea and floating there, wholly free—the millstacks and the warehouse buildings, whaleships lashed against the wharves, the spoke of one tall cathedral inverted in the light.

And as she listens, Bridge finds that for the first time in her life she questions what he tells her—not the truth of it—but why. He told her once, long back, that the stories that crave the daylight most are the ones that don't get told. She remembers this now, and she begins to listen differently. She does not crawl into the familiar lull of his voice and curl herself to sleep there. She thumbs through what he says. She holds the stories at arm's length, lifts up their edges and peers around. She studies the whale's teeth he has scrimped. She studies the panbone, the cycle of etchings of his life behind him, to mark any clue he has left in the carving, any tick or tail of ink that might open into the vast and shadowed halls of what he has left buried, of what he leaves unsaid.

When he talks to her about Kauai, about his life there with Hannah, she can see an old passion work through his eyes. His stories of that particular place have always had a bite of strangeness, an other-world aliveness. There is a sheen to his voice that she savors. Once, in late February, she asks him why he did not go back, and he looks at her for a moment, his eyes opening deep, she can feel herself pulled to some brink inside them. Then he looks away and serves her up an answer, so measly and glib she knows it for a lie, and she feels ashamed—ashamed for him and ashamed of herself for asking. She does not press him, but she wonders about it from time to time. She wonders why he made the choice to set himself here, so far from open water, in woods and cattails, with a house and several outsheds for ballast, close to the river but at the tail end of it where the current runs narrow and thin.

Even when her wound is healed and she is strong enough to work, she stays near the house. Soft chores. She cooks and sweeps and cleans. She draws water from the well, mucks out the barn and the hayloft. She feeds the hens and prepares the seeds for the spring planting. From time to time, she helps her mother with the laundry.

Luce moves out of the house late that winter. He takes an apartment with Johnny Clyde on Forge Road, up by Westport Factory, north of the Head. He stops by the house every few days, but Bridge bothers little with him and the work he does. There is a certain comfort in doing the simple tasks she's always done. She notices that she is more settled, Noel more settled, and their life, apart from Luce's occasional comings and goings, is almost back to how it used to be.

Noel's shares begin to climb. He reads about it in the papers, in the block letters of the headlines. He makes out what he can, and he has Bridge dig around through the finer print and read the rest aloud to him. There are a few rocky months early in the year. The Great Bull Market appears to be stumbling. Then it gives a snort, a mighty hoof and a roar, and takes up its run again. Noel settles in for the ride.

One day, late that April of 1929, Owen Wales comes by the house looking for Cora. He has brought two dress shirts that need to be whitened and pressed, and would she have the chance to get to them by Tuesday next?

She smiles at him, and he looks down at the hat in his hands.

"I'll drop them by your house when they're done," she says. "I'll just leave them by the door."

"No, no," he answers quickly. "I can stop back around for them. It's right on my way. I'd be happy to." He pauses. "If that's alright?" He looks up at her, and his eyes are unsteady, filled with sunlight and the question and wanting her somehow.

"That would be alright," she says slowly.

"Are you sure?"

"Yes, I'm sure."

He smiles at her. "So it's settled." And then he leaves and she thinks about him through the afternoon. The following morning, when she is flipping through the spring Sears catalogue, she spots an advertisement for a new-style swimming suit. Later that day, she takes the mail truck to the trolley stop up by Lincoln Park, and then the trolley into New Bedford. Downtown, at a secondhand store, she buys a bathing costume—not the exact one she saw in the catalogue, but close, a slightly older style.

She brings it home, takes it into her bedroom, and folds it away in the bottom dresser drawer. She wears it under her clothes—not every night, but some nights. On the first week of May, she wears it down to the river below the field at dusk. She wades in. There is an icy chill to the water, electric on her skin, and she floats on her back and watches the crows and the great blue herons with their heavy wings, their eerie calls. The shadows of the birds pass across the clouds and she floats through the new spring smells of thaw and wild orchid. The fabric of the swimming costume is tight against her body. It wraps her waist, her breasts, the tops of her thighs. It holds her, touches her as she floats through the colors of the sky turning toward darkness. The river is cold through her scalp, and her hair streams out like long dark grass.

That year, a fluke snowstorm strikes in May followed by a three-day frost that blackens the grass and the green bean pods. The hens set their eggs too early, and they are painfully small, the shells soft, nearly translucent. Even the asparagus are weakened. Their stalks shrivel and curl down toward the ground. Noel goes out with Bridge into the garden to pare back the dead harvest.

In June, the weather turns. The summer bursts open and it is glorious. They call it "the golden summer." The summer of wealth.

Luce buys a new car. A 1929 fancy soft top with chrome head-lamps and a full backseat. He drives it off the lot, and before he goes anywhere else he brings it by Honey Lyons's house. He has thought this out. He does what a young man would do. He comes by and shows it off to him.

"Took me awhile to save for it," he says smoothly as they are standing by the car, "with the cut you pay me, but I've done okay, I guess, saving. She's a beauty, don't you think?"

Lyons takes a walk around the car, stops once and wipes a smudge off the fresh paint on her back fender. He offers a soft compliment, then says casually, "Like you said, you sure have been saving, Luce." He pauses. "Haven't you?"

"Sure have." Luce nods, and flashes an easy grin. "But the other truth is, of course, I got a good deal on her, and my ma, she gave me a bit to help out."

"Of course," says Lyons, nodding. "Just to say, Luce, I'm glad you know it's always a smart idea to let me in on that other truth." Luce can see that Lyons does not quite believe him. He can see that Lyons is ticking up dollars in his head, the dollars that he himself has already counted. He knows that the number Lyons comes up with will be a stretch to what it must have cost Luce for the car, but it *could* have happened. And that is what matters. They both know this. Luce could be lying, but he could be telling the truth.

After he leaves Lyons, Luce brings the car by the house on Pine Hill Road. His sister walks out of the shop, carrying a crate of lead deadeyes, paint on her face. Her eyes spark when she sees the new car, the sleek curves of the sides. She touches the hood. She can feel the heat from the engine burning.

"Come on," Luce says, "get in." And she gets in and they drive fast down the swift, hilled turns of Pine Hill Road, and he is happy, for the first time in so long it seems, he is happy, she is with him and she is laughing, her dark hair flying off her shoulders. He takes a hard twist in the road, he takes it fast, and she shrieks and the sunlight swerves and breaks down across the windshield, its soft warmth on their faces with the cool fast wind.

"You've made a lot, haven't you?" she asks him once when they slow at South Westport Corner. "This isn't even the half of it, is it?"

He doesn't look at her. His right hand is on the wheel, his arm taut, his body coiled tight as loaded springs. "Don't ask me," he says. He lays his foot down hard on the gas, and they drive.

The summer continues. Day after day of dry, undaunted sunshine. The stock market is giddy, full of strident joy. Prices soar, shares split, and prices soar again.

The fine weather washes the summer people in. The town explodes, seems to double overnight. By the beginning of July, there has been just enough rainfall to turn their lawns a brilliant green. It is a summer of long steamy days and clear cool nights for surf-bathing, boat trips, angling off the angler stands, picnics on the sandflats, and they are all in a capital mood by the time Lady Judith Martin decides that the rather humdrum clambake the Bordens threw on the Fourth was simply not enough. Another celebration was in order. They would have to dig up a new occasion. Such a summer—a most successful summer, the kind of summer they would look back on and not remember where it had begun—certainly warranted more. So she sends out a round of invitations to a spur-of-the-moment party on the Fourteenth of July, le Quatorze Juillet. A night to commemorate the storming of the Bastille.

One afternoon when Luce stops by the house, he finds Bridge on the back steps shelling peas. He sits down with her, picks through the basket, takes out a handful, nibbles on them.

"How can you eat the shells raw like that?" she says.

"I like 'em raw. You making supper tonight?"

"Thinking I might. You staying?"

"Thinking I might."

She smiles. "How's your car?"

"Oh, she's fine."

"You give her a name yet?"

"Thinking I might call her after you."

"Aw no," she says. "Call her Betty. Or Polly."

He laughs. "Something sweet."

"Yeah. How's your place?"

"Good enough. We've been thinking about getting electric."

"The bee lady just got it."

"No joke?"

"Yeah. I rode by the other night on my bike. Her house was all electricked up. Too much light, I'd say, for such a cranky witch."

Luce laughs. He takes another few peas from the basket as Bridge goes on shelling. He chews on one, and then he tells her about Lady Judith's Bastille party.

"Where is it?"

"Down the beach, this Saturday coming."

"You going?"

"Might as well, I suppose. Swing in. Make a show. Have a feed."

She doesn't break from her work. "I'll go with you," she says.

"What?"

"I said, I'll go with you."

"Why?"

"Why not?"

"Last year, I couldn't have dragged you to one of their flings."

"Well, I can't stay home every night."

"No, I suppose." The steps are worn. He runs his hand into the smooth concave tread of one. He picks at a needle-shaped piece of wood that has come loose. He pries it up, revealing the lighter wood untouched beneath. He snaps it off.

"So are you staying for supper or not?" Bridge asks.

"You need something to wear?"

"What?"

"To the fling. If you like, I can buy you a dress."

She shakes her head and laughs. "I'm not that far overboard," she says. "I'll scare up something."

Henry

He arrives late and immediately regrets that he has
come. It is not even ten and most of them are well
on their way to being tight. Alyssia Borden comes
up to him as soon as he steps into the hall. She leads
him into the dining room. The long table is spread
with canapés, biscuits and cheese, smoked meats,
Limoges china, half a dozen crystal punch bowls.
Alyssia points to one of them. "Gin lemonade," she
whispers. "I would recommend it." Her breath is
sweet and warm and dusky, close to his ear. Around
the table, damask napkins have been folded into stiff
triangles. Pale flowers embroidered through the hem
of the tablesheet match the border on the window-
cloth. Will Borden comes up to them, and the three
of them talk for a while, shouting from time to time
over the music off the gramophone. Dick Wheeler
is fiddling with the volume knob, turning it up and
down, higher and lower and higher again. He tinkers with the records and sings alone, loud and off-
key, until someone smartly cuffs him and makes him
turn the music down.

The guests mill through the room, dancing,

drinking—champagne, punch, whiskey, single malt Scotch—the glasses shimmer in the white and glistening light thrown off the chandelier. Alyssia has her hand on Henry's sleeve, and as she talks to him, she keeps her grip on his arm, gentle but firm, her fingers on his wrist. Once, when she turns to have a word with Lady Judith, Henry murmurs an excuse, slips his arm loose, and melts back through the crowd. He goes to the fireplace at the edge of the room. He sets his drink down on the mantelshelf, wipes his face with a handkerchief, and rehearses a few lines in his head that will buy him an early departure. When he looks up again, Bridge Weld is standing in the doorway. She has come in with her brother, Luce. Her eyes play over the room—a slow and democratic gaze—almost disinterested, almost bored. She sees him. Her eyes still for a moment, then pass on. Henry reaches for his drink. The glass is cool and smooth and wet and he can hear the sound of the ice shifting as it melts, and he realizes then that she is the reason he came. He has been waiting for her—without expecting that she would arrive, without expecting he would see her on this night or any other night. Still he has been waiting. He is suddenly aware of his body, the tight shirt collar, the bow tie, the scrape of linen against his thigh. He is about to take a step toward her, a step toward crossing the room. He stops abruptly, catches himself, and in the same moment, Luce takes his sister's arm and steers her along the fringes of the crowd toward the French doors flung open onto the back terrace. As Henry watches, they step outside and her slim body is cut to shadow in the loose red light flickering off the paper lanterns. They move deeper out into the night and disappear.

He follows them. Without thinking, he does it. He leaves his drink and crosses the room, weaving through conversations, suits, cigar smoke, elbows, scattered greetings. He reaches the doors. Luce is at one end of the terrace, turned toward the rail, in an intent conversation with Albert Devereaux. And Bridge, where is she? Henry scans the terrace, the steps, the yard, and he sees her then, down

below. She is walking across the dance floor toward the soft sand
and the long folding table where they have set out the fireworks.

She has never seen so many. She imagines the explosion they could
make. She imagines lighting them, not slowly, not one at a time, the
way they will be lit, but all at once—a ferocious, volcanic sound,
sparks, shoots of light bursting out of the black night as if the sky itself had split and it was the blood of the stars that was falling.

She wants Henry to come out after her. He had seen her inside.
She was sure of it. He had looked at her from across the room, and
she had almost smiled—it wasn't that she didn't want to—she had
almost raised her hand. But she didn't. Why? Because of Luce? Of
what he would have thought? Of the scowl that might have crossed
his face? Why should that matter? Perhaps it wasn't Luce at all,
but rather something unbrave in her. Either way, she had let Luce
steer her through the room and out onto the terrace. There, he had
stopped to have a word with someone and Bridge had wandered
away, down onto the sand, trying to collect her thoughts. What was
it about Henry Vonniker that made such a shambles of her thoughts?

Laid out on the table are boxes of red Roman candles, sparklers,
cannon crackers, ladyfingers, pinwheels. She stops at a box covered
in blue silk and lifts the lid. Inside it are the skyrockets. They lie
wrapped in white tissue, braided wick to wick.

A short distance away from the table, a man in a black waiter's
suit is kneeling in the sand. She knows him by face but not by name.
He lives next to the Poor Farm on Drift Road. He is a mason, and
they have hired him for this. He has shoveled out a short trench
and now he is digging a deeper spot in the belly of it to set a small
launching pad. He lays blocks of wood and stone in a square around
the hole, and places a small stand inside to hold the rockets, their
wicks straight, angled out to sea and up toward the sky.

She feels someone behind her and she turns. It is Henry. He says,

"Hello," and she finds she cannot think of anything to say. She can feel the current pass between them, again. Her heart is wild, and they stand there, close together, their feet sinking into the soft sand.

"So tell me more about your life," she says.

He laughs. "More?"

"Tell me something."

"I am afraid when it comes to life, if you haven't yet noticed, I am a bit of a passerby."

She doesn't answer. Her eyes are steady on his face, but they feel cool and it makes him nervous.

"I came by your house last fall," he says. "To see you. To make sure you were alright."

"My mother told me."

They stand for a moment, an awkward silence.

"You went away this winter?" she asks.

"I did. For business."

She nods.

"Did you notice I was gone?"

"I did."

"Did you miss me?"

She smiles. "I might have."

He doesn't know what to say. He feels that he should offer her something. Some explanation, confession, apology. He remembers the day she came by his house at the beach, the day of the box wrench and the teacup. He remembers her mouth on his. He wants to tell her that he remembers that moment as if it happened yesterday.

"Any run-ins lately with an oil pan?" she asks lightly.

He shakes his head.

"Not once?"

"No. I brought the car to the garage."

"The garage?" Her voice bends, and he is uncertain if the slant in her voice, the slant in her eyes, is intended to include him. "You give up easily," she says.

"I think you know that's not true."

She is still looking at him with those cool and empty eyes, eyes dark and blue, currents at their surface, rippling light, and down below that, swift dark running water.

He rights himself, clears his throat. "Have you eaten?"

"No."

"They have food inside. Quite a spread. Some sort of fish. You do eat fish, don't you?" He is blundering now. Flustered. "Are you hungry?"

"Sure."

"Will you go in with me?"

She pauses for a moment, still looking at him, then she nods and takes his arm, and they begin to walk back across the dance floor through the soft red light of the paper lanterns, and for the first time that night he feels that things are good, they are more than good. He is with her and she is holding his arm, and they are walking together toward the steps and the terrace, toward the clink of glasses, the clatter of silver and china, the shimmering waves of light and jazz and voices, barely contained by the thin-shingled walls.

Bridge sees the woman coming toward them before Henry does. They are on the first landing, and she is above them on the terrace, her tight blond curls and long white arms. She has noticed them. Bridge recognizes her as Alyssia Borden from Horseneck Road. The woman who was talking to Shorrock that day Bridge saw Henry at the store. She is with her husband. She calls out Henry's name. Her voice is strong and she is gorgeous, walking toward them as they step onto the terrace. She wears a white sheath dress and stockings. Her mouth is painted red.

She reaches them and puts her hand on Henry's other arm. "We need you, Henry. I must steal you, for just a moment." She does not look at Bridge.

Will Borden comes up behind her, smiling broadly. "She seems rather desperate over it, Henry." Henry feels a twinge of disgust toward Will, his friend, for being so blind and, at the same time, disgust toward himself for the old betrayal.

"This is Bridge Weld," he says curtly. "Bridge, Alyssia Borden and her husband, Will."

Alyssia's gaze plays over Bridge. She gives her a stony nod, then looks back at Henry. "We do need you, Henry. Please. For a moment."

"Actually, we were on our way in to find something to eat."

"Fish," Bridge adds. Henry smiles.

Alyssia looks at her coolly. "You must be Luce Weld's little sister."

"Yes."

"Well isn't that just grand."

"It has its moments."

"Come on, Alyssia," Will says. "Leave them. We'll catch up with Henry later."

Alyssia glances at Bridge, then back at Henry, a sly look in her eyes, and he can see that she is about to add a remark, and he knows it will be cruel.

"Later," he says quickly, with a subtle but definitive intent, a warning or a promise depending on how she chooses to read it.

Alyssia bites her lip. "I will hold you to 'later,' " she says, and she shoots him a winning smile, then takes her husband's arm. They walk back toward the other end of the terrace that looks out onto the sea.

"I've heard she keeps jasmine flowers," Bridge says, looking after them.

"She does."

"Have you seen them?" She does not look at him. Her voice is measured, even, and he knows what she is asking.

"Yes," he replies after a pause. "A few years ago. I've had no interest in them since."

They fall into silence. Notes of a new jazz music strike up from the gramophone. Bridge looks toward the doors. Her eyes sweep the room inside. She spots her brother in a corner, leaning against the wall. He is talking to a woman in a slim black dress. His glass is filled with a ruddy whiskey. He drinks it off and picks up another from the end table next to him.

"Do you want to go in now?" Henry asks her.

She smiles. She doesn't look at him. The lights from the room inside play across her face. "I did miss you," she says. Her voice is still and soft and deep, complicit. He cannot take his eyes off her. He cannot see any other thing, has no desire for any other thing except her face—the thin arch of her brow, the delicate line of her jaw. She turns and looks at him, and he feels that he is falling toward a place inside her that has no floor.

"Are you still hungry?" he asks slowly.

"No."

"They're going to have dancing later. A band outside. Fireworks."

"Where's your car?" she says.

"Next door."

"Let's go."

He does not ask where. They go outside into the night, through the narrow alley between the houses, across the yard to the second drive.

"Give me the keys," she says. He looks at her for a moment, then hands them to her. She slips behind the wheel.

They don't speak. She drives along East Beach then north up Horseneck, past Bald Hill and the Glen. She kills the lights as they make the second left-hand turn. She cuts off the engine and lets the wheels roll on their own down the lane.

He knows now where she is taking him. He can see her face in the darkness beside him, the lean angles of her profile against the window glass, the eerie reflected glow off her skin, and he wants this moment to go on, this suspended pause as they coast down through the darkness toward the bottom of the hill.

Ahead and to the left, he can see the glass roof of Alyssia Borden's greenhouse set in off the drive. Bridge lets the car roll past it. She twists the wheel slightly and steers across the lane into a turnoff by the brook. She lets the front hood of the car push into the brush. The wheels come to a halt.

They walk back twenty yards to the drive. They walk in silence, slightly apart, this last, carefully maintained distance between them. They reach the door. Bridge presses down on the latch with her thumb. The bar lifts. The door swings open on its hinges with no sound.

He follows her through the rows of plants, the peat pots, the galvanized buckets, the watering pails, past trays of seedlings set on stepped shelves. She leads him through the steam, the warmth, the soft-brushed scented light until they come to a cluster of jasmine plants.

She stops and points to the flowers on one—five-starred and open. She points to the buds, slight pale bulbs on long-stemmed necks among the leaves.

"You can't touch them, you know," she says. "They won't open if you do." She takes his hand then and places it on her neck, his fingers at the edge of her throat. His mouth grows dry. His hands feel awkward on her skin, and he wants to explain it. He wants to explain that for years he has let his hands grow numb, unable to feel.

"No," she says quietly, as if she is reading his thoughts. She puts her finger to his mouth. She touches the side of his face, and in that gesture, so simple and complete, he can feel his body begin to thaw. It is painful—so much more painful than he could have imagined—those first few moments of returning—the blood winding back in a slow and knifelike rush.

He slips the strap of her dress off her shoulder, and she takes his coat and lays it on the floor. She pulls him down with her. She is warm. Her body is so warm. Her skin tastes of salt and he can smell the jasmine. There is sweat in the curves behind her knees, and he is holding her tightly. She cries out.

Afterward, as they lie together on his coat on the cool dark floor split by circles of thin light, he tells her that he wants this. He wants her. It matters. She looks at him, but she does not answer. Her face is inscrutable in the soft, warm darkness.

"I need this," he says quietly. "You. I want you to need me."

"That might not be a practical thing to want."

"Come home with me."

"No."

"Tonight."

"No."

"Please."

She kisses the side of his neck, then presses her mouth into his shoulder. "Do you see the moon?" she says. He turns his head toward the window with the ring of yellow light through the beveled glass.

It has been cut. The space between them. She has cut it easily.

"Your life is your life," she says gently, her mouth still against his shoulder. "My life is mine. What you're looking for, what you need, has nothing to do with me."

She starts to roll away from him, to push herself up, but he grasps her wrist and pulls her back. "What I need," he says, "has everything to do with you."

She stares at him for a moment, then shakes her head. "No. That's not true. What time is it?"

"It is true."

"What time is it?"

He looks at his watch. "Ten past one."

She smiles. "We've been gone for two hours."

"Come home with me."

She shakes her head. "Come on. Let's go." She stands and straightens her dress. She rakes one hand through her hair, then turns toward the small pots of jasmine on the table. She picks over a few, finds one she likes, and she takes it. They walk through the rows of plants to the door.

Outside, they walk in silence to Henry's car. Bridge puts the jasmine on the floor of the passenger seat. Then she comes around to the driver's side and steps up onto the running board.

"Let me drive you the rest of the way home," he says.

"It's an easy walk," she replies, and she leans through the window and presses her mouth on his. "Go," she says, stepping away. "Go."

Bridge

Luce is waiting for her, half stewed, at South Westport Corner. He peels out of the darkness and steps in alongside her as she walks.

"Whoring, were you?"

She doesn't answer.

"Weren't you?"

"Get yourself gone, Luce."

He takes a step ahead, then turns sharply so he is standing in front of her. She stops.

"I saw you leave with him."

"You're loaded."

"He's got a wife."

She doesn't answer.

"Didn't know that, did you? He don't see her, I guess. Don't live with her. But a wife's a wife."

"Who cares, Luce? This has nothing to do with him."

"Oh yes, I think it does."

He pulls a cigar out of his vest pocket, bites off the tip and spits it on the ground. He strikes a match. The light rakes his face. He inhales, bluish smoke leaks out of his mouth.

"He's not the kind you should go with."

"I will do what I want. I'm tired now. I want to go home."

He takes a step toward her. She takes a step back. He looks at her for a moment, then laughs.

"These here are fine cigars. Cost me something, you know."

She doesn't answer.

"Maybe now, though, they're not fine enough for you." And as he moves in again toward her, she can see that this time is different, she can sense a vague incoherent threat as he reaches for her arm. She slips away and begins to run. Her heart is pounding in her chest, and she can hear him, for a good half mile up the road, calling her name through the broken dark behind her.

At the house, she comes into the kitchen and lights the woodstove. She blows up the fire, pumps a pot of water and sets it on the heat. She drags out the tub. She stands by the stove and watches the bubbles as they sprout in small crowds. They scurry together and grip the floor of the pot. They thicken and rise. The water comes to a boil. She pours it into the tub. The steam is wet on her face. She strips off her clothes, turns down the lamp, and climbs into the tub, and she lies there, her body still, her ears below the surface, as the fire settles in the woodstove. She listens to the underwater sound of her heart. She watches the skinny shadows spar on the walls, and she lets her mind drift back over the night: Henry, the soft red light off the Japanese lanterns, the first time his hand touched her arm, the greenhouse and its cool hard floor, his skin warm, the scent of him, her body underneath him—she feels it all now. She wants to see him again. She smiles to herself quietly. He was right, wasn't he? It was true. What she felt, what she wanted—it did perhaps have everything to do with him.

Henry

He wakes soaked, an oily film of sweat on his skin, his mind in dreams—dreams of having her, loving her, losing her—dreams of black rivers, corridors, dead ends. He feels too much. He wants too much. He tries to remind himself that he has lived thirty-four years of a life without a trace of her—a stock of over three decades when she was not even a foot-print in his brain. He tries to be rational, to remember the laws—the theorems, pithy axioms and their proofs—*life tends toward chaos, sunlight kills the plague.* In the past they have steadied him. In the past they have always been enough to calm his nerves. He tries to be rational, to balance himself between clear values of true and false. Practicalities. Probabilities. He tries to ground himself in reason. It has been three days since he was with her—three days since that night in the greenhouse. He has eaten one half of an apple since then, and in the sweat that soaks the bedsheets, that soaks his nightclothes and his hair, he can smell that telling ammonia reek, the sign that his own body has begun to consume itself.

In the months after he returned from France he

woke this same way, with this same stench, this same sense of dread, his thoughts in havoc, as if someone had come and doused his mind with kerosene and set the lot of it on fire.

The sweat has pooled in the cavity under his ribs. He gets out of bed. He washes and shaves. He dumps out the basin of soiled water in the bathroom sink. The soap foam collects around the drain, strung through with bits of his scruff. He turns on the tap and rinses the basin down.

It is half past five in the evening.

He goes downstairs to the front room, rifles through the bookshelves until he finds his volume of Epicurus. Epicurus, that great and ancient philosopher of the garden who did not believe in Providence or fate and claimed at best a lazy God.

Henry sits at one end of the sofa and reads. He skims the text until he finds what he is looking for—the three possibilities of a body in motion—and there, that third declination—the occasional, free and inexplicable swerve of an atom off its normal path.

She has said she is not on his path. She has stated it clearly. More than once. His life was his life, and hers was— He doesn't want to think about it. He slams the book closed, puts it back roughly on the shelf, not where it belongs, but somewhere else. He goes back upstairs, pulls on his clothes and leaves the house.

He gets into his car and drives. He drives to forget her. He reminds himself again of the reasons. There are so many reasons. They are too different, a universe apart. He is, technically, married. She is just a girl. He is almost twice her age.

The sun is low in the sky on the hills across the river.

He drives north. He will drive to the store at South Westport Corner. He will buy some food. He will take the long way home, down Drift Road, through the Point, across the bridge, back to the beach by John Reed Road. He will cut a few vegetables, cook a light supper. He maps it all out in his mind.

There is a crick in his neck, a tightness in his shoulder. He shifts his hand on the wheel, cracks his head to the side to stretch out the muscle, to loosen the ache. It is a crick from sleeping wrong, he thinks, from sleeping too much, from living too long in a box and twisting himself in order to fit inside it.

But that is not about her. No. She was right. She must have been right. His life has nothing to do with her.

The grass heaves off the side of the road as he takes the curve just past the farm. There is a fallen branch on the road ahead of him. He swerves around it. He draws up a list of groceries in his head. He won't think about her. He won't even think about not thinking about her. He will make a stew for supper.

He remembers the pale dusty light on the floor of the greenhouse, how it nicked the edge of her hair as she moved underneath him in the dark. It had surprised him, how easily she opened herself to him, and how when she came, her body tensed to the hardness of wood.

But there was no reason to remember that. There was every reason not to.

A beef stew. Carrots, potatoes, beans. Spices if they carry them. A jar of bay leaves. Would they be likely to sell bay leaves?

He presses his foot down on the gas, takes the Model T up to forty, forty-five. The needle on the speedometer quivers at the speed, the car rattling as if the frame will shake loose off the axle.

It will not be difficult to forget her. He tells himself this. There is no bend in the road beyond this. No path at all. He will take a blade to what he feels. He will cut it down and pack the pieces away in the back of a dark, locked room.

After supper, perhaps a banana. A banana would be fine.

That should be enough. That should be all he needs.

He passes the second farm, its fields sloping down toward the river, squares of land patched out by stone walls, some ancient and some new, long black shadows, the ruffled scalps of trees.

The road dips, then curves into the trees. Splinters of indirect light. Cool, evening light. The road rises again, the land on either side dropping down into the fields, and he sees a figure on a bicycle pedaling toward him on the opposite side of the road. He lifts his foot off the gas to slow the car as he passes by. It is her. He can see that it is her.

His foot lands heavy on the brake—the car lurches—he eases it onto the shoulder. He can see her in the rearview. She looks back once, then continues on.

"Turn," he murmurs. "Turn around." He keeps his eyes fixed on her. But she keeps pedaling south, away from him. She disappears around the bend.

He puts his head in his hands against the steering wheel. This is the way it is, he thinks to himself. This is the way it is supposed to be, a searing pain behind his eyes. They live in the same town, a small town, and he might see her, from time to time, around. That is just the way it will be.

He continues driving down the road, and for the first time in a long while, longer than he can remember, he feels a little free. There was a choice and she made it. It was not the choice he would have wanted. But it was the choice that she had made. And it was done.

He takes the left turn onto Hix Bridge Road at the corner. He passes the post office and pulls up in front of the store just as Maddox Tripp is latching the windows to close for the night. Henry parks the Model T behind the mail truck and takes the three steps onto the front porch.

"You've got five minutes," Maddox says. "You know what you're looking for?"

"A few vegetables, coffee."

"Coffee's second aisle on the right. Vegetables are in the back."

"Do you have fresh peas?"

"Sold out."

"Oh."

"Got the peas in the cans though, that aisle there, by the California lima beans."

"What about bananas? Do you have any bananas?"

Maddox takes him in with a glance, then looks away and goes on wiping down the counter. "Have to go to the Point for them. Not even sure he's got 'em now—now being the early part of the week, and if he did, they'd be over-ripe from last week." Maddox refolds the rag and starts again on the counter, using the clean side. "Bananas come in on Thursday," he goes on. "In time for the out-of-towners."

"Oh right," Henry says, and he can feel the flush spread across his face.

"Closing in three minutes," Maddox says.

"You mentioned that."

"So get what you need."

"What I need—" Henry starts to say, then stops himself. He steps into the second aisle, takes a tin of coffee off the shelf and a can of stewed peaches in their juice. He is standing there, debating whether or not it will be worth it after all to make a stew, when he hears the door open. He turns, and she is standing there, the last raw light of the day balanced on her shoulders. She steps inside.

"We're closed here, Bridge," Maddox says, annoyed.

"Not quite, it seems," she answers, looking at Henry.

"Two minutes." Maddox's voice is gruff. "Two minutes, I'll be turning the lock on that door."

Bridge nods. She steps into the aisle next to Henry. She is very close to him. She turns away and picks a jar of black olives off the shelf.

"I saw your car on the road," she says, examining the olives. "Wasn't that you? I saw your brake lights go on. Did you stop?"

Henry just stares at her.

"Was there something you wanted to ask me?" she says.

"Are you buying those olives, Bridge?" Maddox says.

"Yes," Henry answers.

"No," says Bridge. She sets the jar back on the shelf.

Henry walks around her to the counter, lays down the coffee and the can of peaches and a loaf of bread. She follows him.

"Is that it?" Maddox says.

Henry nods.

"No peas?"

Henry shakes his head.

"So what was it then?" Bridge asks, leaning into the counter.

Henry rifles through his left trouser pocket for a bill.

"What was it?" she asks again. She is standing close to him, and he can smell the faint reek of salt wind off her skin.

"What about you?" he asks, turning on her. "Was there something you wanted?"

"Me?"

"You were going the other way, weren't you? And now you're here."

She shrugs. "I forgot the newspaper."

"The newspaper?"

"Yes."

"That's all? The newspaper?"

"That's all."

"So you want a paper?" Maddox says. "Is that what you want, Bridge?"

"Yes. Evening, if you've got it."

"I don't."

"Alright then, I'll take what you've got."

"That'll be fifty cents," Maddox says to Henry. Henry nods, hands him a dollar. "And a nickel for you, Bridge."

"I'll get it," says Henry.

"No, that's fine." She sets a nickel on the counter and picks up the paper. "See you then." She walks out.

She is waiting for him outside. Her bicycle lies in the grass by his car. As he comes out of the store, she picks up the bike, dusts off the seat, and fiddles with one of the gears. She walks it to the road around his car and, as she passes the driver's side, she tosses the newspaper in through the open window. It lands on the seat. She glances back at him over her shoulder. She smiles.

"I'll see you there," she says lightly and sets off pedaling down Hix Bridge toward the turn onto Horseneck Road. His house.

It is dark by the time she meets him at the cottage. A black sky in the east. In the west, a few last traces of steep blue. They eat outside on the porch. He lights the mosquito torches, and they eat the bread and the peaches from the can. He opens a bottle of wine that has been cellared for years, and she drinks it slowly. The wine loosens her tongue. He can see how it softens her, makes her a little careless. She tells him about her life, about her grandfather Noel, his boat shop, his ship tales, his garden, how the tomatoes he grows are brutally sweet, unlike any other tomatoes she has tasted. She will bring him a few someday. She promises this. Her voice is like music, and he finds himself staggered, speechless. At moments he can feel his eyes burn over her, wanting her, and he hopes she will not notice. At one point while she is talking about her grandfather, he realizes suddenly that the man she is describing is the same tough, battered creature he has seen on the beach mucking up the weed. He wants to tell her this. He wants to explain how their lives have already crossed, have been crossed for years this way. He is on the verge of telling her, but then he stops, afraid that if he speaks, somehow he might disrupt the magic and the wonder in her voice. So he lets her go on. He sits near her, listening. She tells him about her grandmother. Dead now, she says, but they had been so in love. They had fallen into one another in such an unlikely, incredible way. There are tears in her eyes as she talks—he can see this— strange, faraway tears. She does not seem to notice, but there is water on her cheeks, and he wants to touch it, to touch that smooth and glistening surface of her face. His hand moves. He pulls it back, sharply. He fingers the stem of his wineglass instead. She stops talking then and looks at him, and he can see, for the first time, her age. He can see that as young as she is, there are years on her, years that have only just begun to settle into thin light lines around her eyes, and again he wants to reach out and touch her, but he does not, and they sit together that way on the steps of the porch, the torches blazing in throes of jagged light around them. He feels the wind on his face.

They move inside and put the food and wine away, and she leads him up the stairs to the bedroom. She lights the lamp and turns the flame low. She takes off her clothes, and it is like they have always done this. It is like they have already grown old together and their bodies know the script of this night. It is everything familiar, being with her, and at the same time, it is everything new.

Bridge

It is afterward and they are lying in bed.

"Are you sleeping?" she asks.

He smiles. "Just closing my eyes. It feels good to have them closed."

She lies still. Through the open window, she can hear the sound of the waves against the shore.

It is black in the room, not quite a wash. There are the deeper shadows of a bureau, a bookshelf, a chair; muffled, unfamiliar shapes; the musty smell of wood eaten down by salt air.

He is lying on his back. She can barely see his face. There is an ivy plant hanging in the window. She finds the shape of a heron at the edge of the plant, the ivy leaves like the folded wings of the paper birds Noel taught her how to make when she was young; their bodies in hard, creased triangles, wings bent up once, then pressed down, pulled away at an angle to mimic flight.

She hears Henry's breathing shift, and she listens for it, that deepening toward sleep. She pushes into his chest, her shoulder into the side of his rib. He is like clay in the darkness—what she knows of him, of who he is, of where he comes from, what she knows of his life apart from her, all of it is drowned out in this darkness, and they are alone, floating on this bed that is a continent, this bed that is a speck of light.

She says his name quietly. There is no answer.

Again, she looks to the ivy plant hanging in the window, and she remembers a story Noel told her once about a woman who took out her heart so a bullet shot into her chest would not kill her. She fingers her own wound in the dark, the rip in the skin, the snarl of new tough flesh around the scar.

She has always been able to divide her body from her heart. She has always been able to let her thoughts drain and pool and splash, never solid or constant, never resting for too long, never getting too settled on any one person or thing.

She wakes close to dawn. She slips out of the bed. Through the window that faces east, she can see out past the tip of Gooseberry. Fine streaks have begun to gnaw at the edges of the dark. She pulls on her underclothes and her shirt. In the corner by the window is an old-fashioned mahogany shaving stand—a washbasin, a flat razor, a green glass bottle of cologne. She glances over her shoulder at the man on the bed. He is still sleeping, his face turned away from her. Quietly, she unscrews the cap off the cologne, tilts the bottle and takes a few drops onto her fingers. She sniffs it, rubs it into her wrist, her neck, below her ear. She sets the bottle down again and looks around the room. Below the window is a crate of old lamps—squat vessels of thick glass, looped handles, two on stalks, one nickel-plated with a milk-shade glass. There is a tiger-maple dresser and, above it on the wall, a mirror, a skim coat of dust on its surface. She runs one finger through the dust, along the edge where the glass seams into the wood.

On top of the low bookshelf opposite the bed, she finds six 100-

franc notes and a handful of coins. She picks up one of the coins. It is a foreign coin, a French coin. She smiles to herself. Puddle jumper's money.

A sound comes from the bed, a sort of sigh. Without turning around, without moving her arm, she slips one of the 100-franc notes into her hand, closes her fingers around it. Then slowly, casually, she glances over her shoulder. He is facing her now, his eyes still closed. The soft light cuts across his face. He is still sleeping. She swallows. The base of her throat is dry. She glances at the alarm clock on the bedside table. Half past five.

She folds the 100-franc note into the pocket of her shirt and leaves the room. She walks down the hall past the water closet and takes the short flight of stairs down to the kitchen. It is a modern kitchen—a small plug-in icebox, a sunken counter with a sink, running water faucets, a cookstove. Set back on the counter is one of the new pop-up toasters. She pushes down the lever on the toaster and holds her hand above the slats to feel the heat. The inside walls turn bright orange, and she can hear the hiss of the electric coils as they warm.

She opens the icebox. The shelves are empty except for a jar of brewed iced tea, an unopened bottle of coffee milk, a can of fancy Hawaiian pineapple. She takes out the pineapple, tilts the lid, and picks out a chunk with her fingers. She examines the iced tea. The leaves have settled at the bottom of the jar. She draws out the coffee milk instead, unscrews the cap, and takes a deep drink from the bottle. As she is setting the bottle down on the counter, she notices the photograph on the window ledge above the sink. It is a picture of a group of people standing in a garden. There is a light film of dust on the glass. She doesn't move it, doesn't touch it, but she leans across the counter to see it more closely. She finds Henry, a younger version of him. A woman stands beside him. She is slight, dark-haired, in an evening dress, her hair set in the fashion of a few years back. His arm is around her. Bridge can just make out the edge of his hand coming around her waist. It is his wife. She knows this. And there is something about knowing it, about seeing it, that sets a quease in her gut, the kind of feeling she has had before when she has shot a creature, then found it not quite dead.

She lifts the bottle of coffee milk to take another drink, but the smell seems too sweet to her now. She put it back in the icebox. She will go upstairs, get her trousers and boots. She will leave before he wakes up. She will not come back. She is turning away toward the stairs when across the room she notices the jasmine, set on a child's chair against the wall. She walks over to it. He has replanted it in a glazed pot, and the earth is dark and fresh and loose. She finds one flower on it and three more that have gone by.

There is a daybed underneath the picture window, a writing desk, and beside that, an unfinished wooden sea chest. The original hinges have been replaced by shiny brass, but the box itself is beaten, gorgeous. A rough crack runs halfway across the lid. She lifts it slowly. Inside is a notebook, heavy, leather-bound. She lifts it out, sits down on the daybed, and turns back the front cover.

Walking the meadows of the risen earth, the children shall find in the grass the golden chessboards on which the gods played out their games.

The passage is alone on the first page. It had been cut out of another book and pasted in, its lines perfectly crisp as if he had used a straightedge and a blade to do it. She turns to the next page.

How shall my heart be unsealed unless it be broken?

She continues turning the pages. She finds an essay on pisciculture written in 1881, and one from a 1919 medical journal about the use

of common magnets to extract bullets from the brain. She begins to
flip more quickly. She passes black-and-white etchings, abstract de-
signs, stamps from Africa, Asia, rough watercolors of pomegran-
ates, grapes, sunflowers. She runs her fingers over them. The pages
around them have wilted, shrunken as the paint dried. She comes to
one passage cut like the others but in a different type and framed
out with black ink.

each Swallow followed
those that had gone before it as though guided
by the marks of wing beats in the air.

She finds ticket stubs and flowers pressed and dried, orchids, lilies,
postcards from France, Amsterdam, Spain; a yellowed photograph
of two men and a woman in fine clothes standing on the front porch
of Shorrock's store. She keeps flipping the pages, more quickly now,
looking for a handwritten entry, a passage not lifted, cut, or taken
from somewhere else, looking for words that were his alone, that he
had written directly onto the page.

Finally, at the end of the book, she finds it, after a long section of
blank pages. A fluid script. Legible. Not what she would have imagined. It begins on the last page.

October 27, 1928

*How has it begun to tick in me again? Gears. Wheels. Cogs.
Rusted out from lack of use. Why this new stirring? Why
this desire?*
Some things are not meant to be seen.
Some things not meant to be wanted.
I should know this.
Was it Millay who wrote:

"No place to dream, but a place to die,—
The bottom of the sea once more."

Wasn't it Millay?

Bridge looks up from the page to the small writing desk against the wall. Black iron legs and a thin cherry top. She wonders if he wrote the words there, or if he wrote them early one morning, sitting outside on the porch steps. Maybe he wrote them somewhere else entirely. But she suddenly finds that she needs to know, not what the words mean, but where he wrote them, what he was looking for as he wrote them, what he wanted, and why would he start from the wrong end of the book as if he were trying to write himself back toward the cut-and-paste collage that was the rest of his life.

She stands up, walks over to the writing desk. She cracks the long drawer and rummages through it for a pen. She opens the notebook and turns to one of the blank middle pages.

Henry.

No. She crosses it out. She will not use his name. Her hand freezes then, above the page in midair, her skin suddenly cold. She puts down the pen and begins to flip back through the book, slowly at first, calm, then more quickly, but with control. She flips past the pressed flowers, the postcards, and the etchings until she comes to the photograph. The two men and the woman standing outside the Head store. They are well dressed. Strangers. She does not recognize them. Judging by the style of their clothes, the photograph was taken awhile ago—perhaps fifteen years back—and there in the corner, sitting off to the side on the steps—what she must have glimpsed the first time through, what must have been sidling through her brain—there is a child—a girl—barefoot, in simple clothes, a pair of battered shoes on the steps beside her.

He couldn't have known. Even now, if he looked at it, he would have no idea. She does not remember being there. She does not remember when that photograph was taken, but she has the sudden awful sense that someone, something, has been stalking her, watching her all morning. And it is suddenly, desperately wrong. Not just what she has done, rummaging through his things, but all of it. Her being here. With him. There is a line she has crossed, a world she has walked into where she has no business being.

All around it was a mistake. A mistake. She knows this now.

She folds the notebook closed and puts it back in the chest. She walks quietly up the stairs into the bedroom. He is still sleeping. She finds her trousers on the floor, her boots under the chair. She looks back once at the man lying on the bed, his arm across the empty space where she had been. The new pale yellow light streams across the sheet and washes over his chest.

She leaves the room, drawing the door closed behind her. She still has her fingers on the knob when she remembers the 100-franc note in her pocket, and it nags her. For some reason, it nags her. She tries to twist the knob and close the door, but that note in her pocket, that note she took, even though it is foreign money, useless money, even though she had stolen a thousand things before and he probably wouldn't notice it missing, wouldn't care if it was, but knowing that he might notice and that it might matter, not that it was gone, but that she had taken it, that she had taken it from him, for some reason, some stupid, blasted-up reason, it just didn't seem right.

Quietly, she lets the door swing open. She crosses the room and puts the bill back on the bookshelf where she found it. She hears a movement behind her, the rustle of sheets.

She swings around.

His eyes are open, his head is on the pillow. He smiles, and she can see that he is happy, looking at her. She can tell by his face that he did not notice what she took. He did not see her put it back.

"You're leaving," he says.

She nods.

"I don't want you to go."

And it is simply this—what he says and how he says it. His eyes wash through hers and every other thought is swept out of her mind. She goes to him, without knowing why, but knowing it is the one thing, the only thing, that she is meant to do.

Henry

They show up the next morning. Two black cats. Scuffed fur. Young. From the same litter, he thinks. He leaves food for them, and they take up informal residence under a corner of the garden shed. He leaves them scraps at first, and then on a whim, he bakes a small whole chicken, and places it outside in an exposed part of the yard so he can watch them feed. They come slowly at first, testing the limits of the shade. They cling together at the edge of the brush, then split apart, each approaching from one side. He watches them from the front porch, and he can see how the nose of the smaller one stiffens to the air, the smell of the cooked meat drifting downwind.

Bridge comes again that Saturday, and as they lie together in the crisp blue summer light filtering through the window blinds, he thinks of those two cats, and it occurs to him that she is not unlike them. She has that same wariness, her eyes that same detached and cool stealth way of prowling the space around.

She lies on her belly, her mouth slightly open, her

breathing light, but even though she sleeps, he has the sense that she can hear him, feel him.

He turns her body over in his hands. He rolls her onto her side against him. Her skin is damp, like dark wood, and smells of shade. He spoons himself around her, gathering her arms in his arms, and as they lie there together, her slight warm naked curves against him, he remembers what someone told him once, about how men are fuel, how they burn to be consumed, how they are fire and heat and ash.

"I have not lived like that," he says softly.

Bridge shifts, her weight against his arm.

"Not at all like that." His mouth is on her hair, and she stirs, her face turning toward him. He breaks off. Her eyes shift under the lids. They do not open. He does not want to wake her, but he touches the side of her cheek gently, and she smiles, and he wants to tell her that when he is with her, he walks so close to his heart, he can feel his bones crack, and this hunger, this need he has for her, it is the most beautiful thing he has ever felt, the most beautiful thing he could feel, and at the same time, it is the sky weeping. It drives a deep trench inside him, dread rising up out of it like smoke.

She comes to him that following Tuesday, then the Friday after that, then the next dark of the moon. He marks the summer out by her comings and goings. He measures each day by how many days it has been since he last saw her, how many days it will be before she comes again. She brings him early tomatoes from her grandfather's garden. They eat them together in the late afternoon sunlight. They sit on the grass by the porch steps, and he watches her hands with the knife as she cuts the tomatoes in half. They fall on the cool green grass—seed, sunlight, skin, a devastated red. She slices the halves into quarters, then splits them again, and they chew the pieces slowly, and the taste is fresh and sweet, as she had promised, an almost unbearable sweetness, juice shooting through his mouth.

Luce

They have been making good money. All through
the spring and the summer, they have made good
money, doing their jobs for Honey Lyons, and then
the other things, the occasional picking off, the
stealing. They have been careful, not too greedy.
They have picked their jobs well. They have not
been caught.

That night on the last weekend of July is a free
night—a Saturday night. There is no job to do, no
liquor to run or pirate, scavenge, or unload. When it
is still light, the sky that steep thick blue, they go to
the Portuguese diner up by the Narrows for sand-
wiches, and then to the Castle Theater downtown
to see the new Laurel and Hardy.

They sneak in a bottle of whiskey and drink it off
in swigs, passing it back and forth across the empty
seat between them. They sit through the movie,
cracking up, laughing, hooting at the uprooted trees,
the smashed windows and busted doors, the pair of
crazy twins, one skinny, one fat, falling prey to disaster after disaster. They holler when the piano is
rolled out and hacked up. They slide down in their

seats, doubled over, laughing and drinking, and by the time the last match is thrown into the leaking tank of gasoline, they are both tight and the bottle is empty, rolling around on the floor under their seats.

They step outside into the warm clear night. The moon is full. They trip down the block, looking for Luce's car on the buckled side streets, trying to remember where they had parked it. When they do finally find it and slide in, Luce starts up the engine and gives Johnny a choice of where they will go next—a dance, a fight, a game of cards? What'll it be? And when Johnny can't choose, can't make up his mind, which is so much like him, Luce announces that they will hit all three—first, the fight, to get them gunned up, and then the dance. But they get to the dance, and the band is no good, and there are no good-looking girls, so they don't stay. At the card game, Luce wins big at a five-card draw, and they pick up another bottle of whiskey, climb back into the car, and they drive and drink, passing the bottle back and forth, the darkness howling with the speed through the open windows.

"Let's swing by the cove," Johnny suggests.

"Forget it," Luce answers.

"You still seeing that girl?"

"That girl is nothing."

The stars are sharp and glittering, fine and smart as diamonds poked out through the thin black sky. They are laughing and it is good. They talk about the money they have already made and boast about the money they will make. They drive fast down the roads through Dartmouth. A rum hook on the floor behind them rattles from side to side as they slide around the curves, and Luce tells Johnny Clyde to reach back and throw that thing on the seat. They speed into the village at the Head. It is after midnight and the town is quiet. They pass the gas pumps and fishtail around the corner onto Drift Road, heading south. The car gathers speed. The road heaves and falls underneath them, the black night skimming by.

They pass Widow Kirby's house, and the road twists and begins to rise. They drive faster. At the top of the hill, Luce slams his foot down on the gas, the pedal to the floor. They tear past the orchard, past the farm, toward the S curve at the bottom. Luce takes the curve hard, he takes it fast, too fast, the tires spin out into the soft shoulder of dirt, and they are running off the road toward a stone wall. He jerks the wheel left to swerve back, but the tie rod snaps, and the car plows head-on into the wall. There is the sound of metal folding, glass shattering. Stones explode. Luce's head snaps forward, striking the wheel, then snaps back hard against the seat, his knee jammed up against the steering column, and there is glass everywhere—in their hair, down their shirts, on their pants, the light crinkling sound of glass raining down like hail. The front end of the car is smashed, stones busted through the radiator, puncturing it, a cloud of steam rises over the hood, through the open space where the windshield had been. Luce looks through it. He tries to see through it, the fog softening. They are at the edge of a shallow ditch, one wheel sunk, the front hood mangled. One headlight points straight ahead into the field on the other side of the ditch, the other headlight cocked at a wild angle up into the trees. Luce can feel a warm crawl down the side of his face. He realizes his head has been cut. He wipes at it with his hand. There is blood on his fingers, wet and sticky.

"Shit, Johnny, we got to get out of here," he says. He thinks he says this. It is his voice, but distant and small and vague. He is not sure the words have made it out of his mouth aloud. He reaches to turn the key. His knee aches, a sharp stab, but he stretches his leg against the pain and pumps the gas. The pedal is cold and he realizes he has lost his shoe. His foot is soaked and he has turned the key. He is turning the key and nothing has happened. The engine is dead, and the bottle of whiskey has busted open on the floor, and his foot is soaked in it. The reek of the whiskey and the stink of the radiator steam fill the car. Luce turns in his seat toward Johnny.

Rough bits of glass fall down the back of his shirt, glass crunching on the seat underneath him.

"Johnny," he says, his voice louder now, maybe too loud. His ears are ringing. "You alright?"

Johnny grunts, a low strained sound.

Luce blinks. What the hell was he seeing? Nothing. No, there is nothing. Only Johnny's hands clasped together on his lap. They are smooth and white as bone in the queer light.

"My neck's sore as hell, Luce," Johnny murmurs.

"I know, I know. We got to get out of here." Luce yanks at the handle of the door. Jammed. He pushes his shoulder against it, then slams harder into it, but it won't give. He remembers the rum hook—he can use it to pry the door open—and he turns and reaches behind him. He sees it then: the metal rod straight and thin and black, it seems to float in the dark space behind the passenger seat, the claws of the rum hook are caught in the upholstery and the butt end of it is dug into the base of Johnny's skull.

"Christ," he whispers.

Johnny grunts again.

Luce looks at him, then looks away, straight ahead out the open space of the windshield. The earth is tipped, the sky, the edge of the road, the ditch, all of it tipped, and the field extends out ahead of them, stark and luminous, washed over by one headlight and the moon.

Johnny reaches out and touches the sleeve of Luce's coat. His fingers are cold, and once more, Luce pushes his shoulder hard against the door, throwing all of his weight into it, and the thing gives. It swings open, creaking, twisted on its hinges.

"You can't leave me here, Luce," Johnny says. His voice is quiet. His grip on Luce's sleeve is tight and hard.

"I can't move you, Johnny. I'm going to get someone."

"Get who?"

"Someone. Some help. I'll be back."

"You can't leave me. We got to get out of here, the two of us together. We got to get the cases out of the trunk. What if they come by? What if Lyons comes by? We got to get those cases out, get 'em to the pesthouse."

Luce sits back in his seat. He leaves the door swinging open. Johnny is still gripping his arm, and the grip is a vise.

"There's no cases in the trunk, Johnny," Luce says.

"I can smell it. I can smell whiskey."

"The bottle broke. That's all."

"Don't mess with me. I put those cases in there myself."

"There are no cases in the trunk."

"He's gonna find them, Luce. He's gonna find us and he's gonna know we've been around behind his back. He's gonna know what we've been doing. I heard him talking a few days back to my dad, asking around where I've been, asking if I might be doing something else, some other work. He smells it, Luce. He's onto us. And if he comes by tonight, if he drives by—"

"Shut up," Luce says.

But Johnny blazes on, talking gibberish, there is sweat pouring down his face. Luce looks over his shoulder at the rum hook. At the point where it enters Johnny's neck a thick dark rim of blood has begun to soak onto the seat.

"He's going to kill us," Johnny says. "We're going to be dead when he finds out."

"He's not going to find out."

"He will. You watch. Just my luck, he'll come around now, find those cases we took off him. He'll find the truck, the boat, he'll find it all." And he goes on, and Luce just sits there, half listening, Johnny's voice smashing around like pieces of busted tin, smacking up against the roof of the car, shrill, then low again, a whisper. Luce can smell the blood now, his own blood. He can taste it on his mouth. It makes his stomach turn.

"You got to shut up, Johnny, you can't keep talking on like this."

But Johnny doesn't listen or doesn't hear him. He just goes on about Honey Lyons catching them and the cases in the trunk, and Luce realizes that someone will come. At some point, some late night driver or a cop will pass by and stop for them, and Johnny will be sitting there on the passenger seat, with the butt end of a rum hook through the back of his head, babbling up a storm, and that will be no good. Then they will be caught—Johnny, if he makes it at all. Luce tries to think it through, how to get them out of this, how to get himself out of this. He tries to think through the haze of steam and the smells, the soft and beautiful night now turned so wrecked, everything that he has worked for, everything that he has wanted, on the verge of being thrown.

He can feel a restless tremor in his hands, the strength of his hands, and he imagines it. It is unthinkable, but he imagines it as if it were happening, as if he were moving across the seat, reaching over, and he can feel Johnny's throat in his hands. He is kneeling on the seat, and it is happening, he is kneeling over Johnny, his knees ground into bits of glass, and he is straddling him, Johnny's throat in his hands, the words twisting off, not talking anything now, he can feel the sensation of blood pushing under his hands, blood pounding as his fingers squeeze, digging in to meet the bone.

The thought is awful, the possibility of it, the necessity of it so awful that it takes him a moment to realize the car is silent. There is no sound except the occasional snap of the engine as the block cools and the soft wind outside working through the trees. He turns to look. Johnny is asleep, or more than asleep. There is no sound off him, no breath. His eyes are open. Luce gets out of the car, glass rattling off him as he stands. He starts walking south down Drift Road. He calls the police from the Poor Farm. His voice is shaking. He does not have to pretend. They come. They look over the junked car and the scene and Johnny Clyde, and Luce overhears one of them say to another in a low voice that wasn't it damn lucky for that poor boy to have been so drunk. He wouldn't have felt a thing.

———

Later, when it was all settled and done and a towing truck had come for the car, Luce got a fellow to give him a ride down to the Point Wharf. From there, he walked across the bridge down John Reed Road. It was three in the morning, still dark.

Just past the old dump, he cuts onto the dirt path and takes the deer run across the marsh to the pool at the end of Crooked Creek.

He takes the small boat up the river. He throws anchor in the shallows off the flats below Indian Hill. He can't quite bring himself to leave the boat and walk up to the house. So he sleeps on the floor, drifting on the still water. The moon rocks the sky.

He wakes after sunrise, sore as hell. His entire body aches. He washes himself in the river. He strips to his underclothes and wades in up to his waist, his feet sink into the mud. He flushes the grit from a cut on his shoulder, peels back the piece of loose skin, and holds the wound open. He can see the slight tint of blood as it washes clean.

Farther down, the sandy beach gives way to the cattails. Ahead of him, a snapping turtle slips off a rock, and he can see its small hooked eyes above the surface, black glittering stones. It watches him, then sinks down and disappears.

He swims out into the deeper water of the channel. The surface is smooth, but the current runs strong underneath, and he dives toward the bottom, his hands outstretched, weblike in front of him, the ends of his hair green in the clear underwater light. He hangs there, his body suspended above the ridged sand floor, holding his breath, the sound of the river in his ears. He tucks his knees under him, looks up, and he can see the surface, the sky behind it, white and brilliant, back-lit by the sun, and for a moment, it is as if he is looking through to heaven. He pushes off toward it, his body through the clear cool water, the river rushing over his open eyes. He breaks through and swims back in toward the shore. He is sick in the shallows. He sits down afterward, gasping, his body weak, his head light. The marsh grass is thick and green, and the luster of it, the richness of it, softens him, the beauty of the world so simple and, for the moment, so forgiving.

Cora

The house is empty. Her father—gone up the road to Lincoln Park for a smoke and a talk with Rui. Bridge—gone on her bicycle midafternoon, to wherever it is she goes. Gone more and more often these days.

Cora is up in the bedroom when she hears voices outside in the yard. She comes downstairs into the kitchen. They are arguing—her son, Luce, and Honey Lyons. She hears the crinkle of ice in a glass, the strike of a match, the smell of tobacco paper burning. They are arguing about a cut, money, a go-through man, someone got not enough, someone else too much.

"I don't want that job, Lyons," Cora hears Luce say.

Late sunlight spiked with shade. A wash of yellow dusk. Through the open window, she can smell the swift sharp reek of pine. The sky has grown taut, a fragile skin with soft dark ribs. New weather pulling in.

She sits down in a chair with some mending, a few socks to be darned, a skirt hem unraveled, a shirtsleeve hopelessly torn. Patching a tear in the elbow of her father's coat, she pricks her finger by mistake. She sets the sewing down in her lap and holds up her hand to the light. She watches the blood squeeze out. One drop. She lets it congeal. A small red bug crouched on her fingertip.

When Owen Wales stopped by the other day to pick up some linens, she had asked him to stay and have a lemonade with her outside on the porch, and he had accepted so quickly, so eagerly, that it astonished her, it made her think he might have been waiting weeks for her to ask, and they had sat together on the porch in the shade and talked about this and that, goings-on around town, the clambake coming up at the Grange. She asked him once if he had heard talk about her son. She worried about him and the kind of trouble he might be knotted up in. And Owen Wales had looked at her, his eyes somber, and asked, wasn't working for Honey Lyons trouble enough? She had nodded. She did not answer. He had apologized for saying it. No, she said. I do know that.

Outside, the voices seize up, sharp. Silence. Then Honey Lyons says in an even voice, "I don't feel so good, you know, when I think about what happened to the kid. Freakish thing. Funny, too, I'd just had myself a good talk with him a week or so back."

And it is not what he says, which is what it is, but how his voice turns up at the end. He leaves a question, which might be an implication or a bluff or a threat, and it floats through the silence, loaded and cruel. Cora can feel her son. She can feel his sudden confusion.

"He was my friend," Luce mumbles. Through the window, Cora can see him looking down, his head bent. He spits in the dirt, then rubs it in with the toe of his boot.

"Well, take care of yourself then, Luce Weld," Lyons says. "Don't go turning down too many jobs. Someone might get to thinking you don't need the money."

Lyons crosses by the window. She hears the car door close, the engine started up, the crush of the tires over the marl.

Luce comes inside. He nods at her, opens the cabinet, and takes out a box of crackers. He unwraps a block of cheese, pares down an edge, sits at the table, and looks out into the yard, chewing slowly.

There are windows in her hands. Points in the hollow of the flesh where the lines cross that itch to open. When she unfolds her palms a certain way and turns them to the world, she can take in sounds, currents, temperature, light. She can take in the smell of the blossom off the apple tree. She can take in the intent under words. She can feel things that are not said. Now in the kitchen, she opens her hands slowly toward her son—a slight and unobtrusive gesture. She knows he will not notice. His mind is rattled, distracted, his face turned away, its sullen stubborn beauty, and through the windows in her palms, she can hear the grit between his thoughts. She can feel he is afraid.

She wants to tell him what she knows will be no use. He is her child, has always been her dearest child, her only son, and even now that she can feel the doom around him, she loves him still. So much. She will always love him.

She says his name and he looks up and she can see his fear. It has set wildfires inside him. She tries to hold his eyes in one place, but they are elusive, untenable, like sand.

"Are you hungry?" she asks gently.

He swallows hard, nods.

She fixes him a plate of food. Cornbread and a cut of ham. She watches his fingers with the knife moving back and forth between them, the long teeth of the fork with bits of flesh and meal.

When he has finished, she clears his place and puts the fork and plate in the sink.

"Are you tired?" she asks.

He nods.

"Go upstairs to your old bed and have a sleep."

He looks at her then, his eyes full, tears on the brink of them, and although he will not say it, he cannot say it, she can see that he is grateful. He tells her to wake him at nine, and she listens as his feet take the stairs, and then there is silence. All through the house, silence.

She finishes her mending, then goes outside. She sweeps down the hen yard, shoos the chickens into their shed and bolts them in. She mops the kitchen floor and sorts out her wash for the following day. She draws the curtains in the front room that face the road.

It is a beautiful night. A perfect swimming night. But she will not go down to the river. She will stay in the house with her son asleep in a room above her. There is a rightness in the house that she feels when he is in it.

She dims the light, sits in the kitchen, and unpins her hair. She runs the brush through. She peels the strands off the horse-bristles, winds them around her finger, and puts them in the shoe box that she keeps in a cupboard under the stairs. For ten years, she has saved her hair, these strands given up off the root. She has marked the color changing, the lightening from brown toward silver, as if with age it gains some value.

She waits until the clock strikes nine times, and when the striking is done, she waits a few minutes more. Then she wakes Luce, and he leaves. When the house is empty again, she walks with her aloneness through the rooms. She unpacks the blackest spaces, the closets, the corners, the long and untouched shadows under a bed, a bureau, a chair.

The darkness bleeds together. One shape is equal to the next. The design of the world, every hierarchy in it, leveled.

After ten, and still her father is not home yet. He does not see well in the night. It is unlike him to be gone so long past dark.

Noel

Every other Sunday through that summer, Noel and Rui meet at Lincoln Park on the bench in the pine grove between the carousel and the casino ballroom. They smoke and watch the children playing on the swings and chasing one another through the trees; men in suits, ties, straw hats, women in summer cotton dresses strolling by.

Sunday is the big day at the end-of-the-line park. It is the one day of the week the mills are closed and ten cents buys an all-day trolley pass. Rui and Noel sit on their bench through the late afternoon and into the evening. They toss scraps of bread to the pigeons and watch the ebb and flow of queue lines at the concession stand and the Japanese rolling games. They yarn about nothing in particular—old times, stocks, baseball. They listen to the tin music playing on the carousel. The late sun glints off the polished brass, the painted horses slipping by.

"The old carousel, the first one, had lions," Rui remarks one day. "Do you remember that, Christmas?"

"Never came back then."

"Never with Hannah?"

"Hannah didn't like parks."

Rui laughs. "A tough-to-chew woman you chose. I was never so fond of her."

"I remember."

"She might have liked those lions though."

It is early evening and the lamps are lit. Two girls pass by, their hands sticky from tearing at a warp of cotton candy. A younger boy straggles behind them. He scuffs his shoe through a tuft of wild grass.

Rui clears his throat.

"Bit of a cough?" Noel asks.

"Had it awhile."

"It's from those cigarettes you smoke. Get yourself a good pipe."

"Cough's nothing much."

"Didn't expect it was."

They fall to silence.

"But I've been thinking some lately, Christmas, about our shares."

"Thinking what?"

"I've been thinking things are looking a little slush these days."

"Are you off your socks?"

Rui shrugs. "Just a gut sense. It might be time to make a change."

"What would you sell?"

"Most all of it."

"What would you buy?"

"Don't think I would for a while."

"Would what?"

"I don't think I'd buy in on anything right now."

"You're saying you'd just cash out?"

"For a while."

"String it up with your rats? Are you nuts? I could lend you a safekeeping place in my panbone."

"I'm not messing with you, Christmas. Everything's looking scrap to me these days."

"You talk rot."

"No."

"It's rot to me. This is the first time in my life, Rui, I'm getting somewhere. I'm doing just what you told me to do. I have my money in and I sit back. I sit on this bench and watch that carousel turn. I'm doing nothing and I'm getting somewhere. The whole world's pouring in now. I see it. Hear about it. New money coming in from overseas. Everyone's hankering for a piece. Why the hell would I want to pull out now?"

Rui weaves his hands together, turns them back. His wrists crack. "Back in 1755, Christmas, time of my grandfather's grandfather, there was an earthquake that came in off the sea, hit Lisbon. Brought in a giant of a wave. Her trough came first, arrived at port, sucked all the water out the bay. The whole town came down to see it, crowding in, pushing over one another—don't you imagine it must have been a thing to see. All drowned, of course, when the crest struck."

"You're telling me to get out."

"I'm just saying watch yourself."

"I know what you're saying without saying, and I know you're saying to get out."

Rui shakes his head, his eyes fixed on two pigeons bickering in the dirt path. "I wouldn't be the one to tell you that."

"Are you getting out?"

Rui nods.

"You're selling all of it?"

"Might leave a buck or two in."

From the direction of the casino, there is the sound of an orchestra band striking up. The first few notes of the Charleston. A young girl steps out of the ballroom onto the terrace. A red dancing dress, her hair slicked back. She leans against the rail and lights a cigarette.

"Why would you get out now?" Noel says. "Everything's up. Breaching. Sky-bound. Bridge reads it to me out of the papers. I hear talk. They're calling it a perfect season. All new rules."

Rui shakes his head. "It's like the rum-work, Christmas. It's like whaling. Things are good early on, then the world gets in and wants a cut. Stocks are no different. I took the trolley the other day down to the wharves, stopped in to see Stinky Howard, still wearing his old slops, overalls and jumper, still selling rides in skiffs nobody wants to take out, so sprung with leaks and rot—so there was Stinky and he started in talking about how he'd just bought four hundred shares of some puddler company out of Illinois." Rui pauses and takes a long drag on his cigarette. He exhales. "The whole world's coming down from the town to see it."

Noel watches the girl on the terrace of the casino. Through the swinging door, he can see the gleam of the dance floor. A man in a lounge suit strolls outside. He comes toward the girl and leans against the railing near her. He draws a flask out of his pocket and offers her a drink. She turns her back on him.

"It's easy for you, Rui. You've made your money."

"Made some."

"You've made enough."

"What's enough? As I recall, you aren't the one best at knowing when enough's enough."

Noel doesn't answer.

"We've never had weather like this," Rui goes on. "And doesn't it make you dizzy? Such perfect sunshine day after day?" He follows Noel's gaze to the casino, the girl on the terrace. She tilts her head back and her throat is lit like smooth alabaster in the electric light. Rui leans in toward Noel's shoulder, his voice taut. "When you see a woman, Christmas, just that kind of woman, the most beautiful woman with baubles, a body, rich hair. You feel her in your blood, and that's when you know in your gut, don't you, she's the woman who'll dance you right down the drain."

There is a shriek from the giant coaster. The cars shake against the tracks as they climb. The front car reaches the top, slows, arcs over, and begins to dive. Noel can hear the screams off the cars hurtling down.

Rui stretches out his legs. "You want a frankfurt, Christmas? Let me spot you a frankfurt."

"No thanks."

"We'll walk down to Crawford's then for a duck sandwich."

"Not hungry."

"You sure?"

"Sure."

"Suit yourself then. I'm going to buy myself a frankfurt." He stands and ambles across the dirt path toward the concession stand. The pigeons skip ahead of him, then scatter.

Noel looks away into the pine grove. It is not quite dusk and there are a few children still at play on the swings. He can see their white shapes flitting through the trees. In a patch of clear air, he can see packs of gnats. They swarm up through the dying light—a sure sign the next morning will bring fair skies.

He takes his time going home that night. He strolls through the darkness down Reed Road, the soft loose shape of the summer wind bending through the trees.

He will not sell his shares. He told Rui as much. Not now. In nine months the value of what he put in has more than tripled. The paper he owns is almost thirty-five hundred dollars. He will let it go to four. He will take it out when it has reached an even four.

He knows that Rui is right in saying that at a certain point, the wealth won't keep coming. An age can't last forever. Every stretch of luck—wrong or good—has a finite time—and eventually it swings around to become the other.

But now, it is a summer darkness, a warm smooth wind, the deep smells of wild grape and honeysuckle, and he will keep his money in for just a while longer, he will hold his shares just a while longer through this season. As he walks through the night, he hears the call of a whippoorwill, and he feels something close to joy in his heart, something he has not felt perhaps since he lost Hannah. The stars are nimble in the sky, and he lets himself fall back into that smooth summer darkness, without trying to see too far ahead. He walks home through the night, and as he lies awake in bed, the damp air pressing through the open window, he feels her close to him, Hannah, close to him. The next day and in the days that follow, still he feels her. She moves like soft hushed light across his shoulders, over his hands. The summer draws out long through Labor Day and into September. He does not go to meet Rui. He works in the shop. He takes the skiff out on the river. He fishes, pulls crabs and eels, and digs quahogs on the flats. He stays close to what he loves, deep in what he loves, still with that sense of Hannah knitted everywhere around him, her voice like the sound of a distant sea in his ear, her hand on his shoulder as he tends the hens, mucks out the barn, tills over the garden, pulls what is ripe and lets the soil reseed. It is only Hannah, and she is loving him, forgiving him for what he has done, for what he did not do, for what he gave her, for what he could not give.

Mornings, he takes the wagon down to the beach. He rakes sea muck and gathers clams. He takes his walks through the dunes. He wanders off the road and up into the sand hills, along the paths through the dune grass and the scrub flowers, the dusty miller, the sea oat and the beach pea, the gnarled roots that hold fast and grow in such a harsh and unkind soil. He knows that in the fierce winds, the winter winds, these plants will break apart, shed their seed and sleep through the dead-time buried in the snow. It is the earth he loves most, this rugged sandy earth, the resilience of its creatures, its stubborn steadfast life. And above all, the salt rose. He loves it because it was her flower, Hannah's flower. He loves it for how it throws its bloom again and again and again, so even now, coming into fall, the scent of it fills the air, a last and rich and unexpected scent, reckless, in the lulls of softer weather after rain.

From time to time, on his way down East Beach Road, when he looks across the bay at the wind as it moves in gusts, pressing out in sheets across the sea, he will sense her there. He will see her in the swells, in how the water bends.

Through those weeks, he feels himself grow transparent, his body more and more transparent. He is water and light, the sounds and smells of the world passing through him. He lets his sight turn inward, and he finds himself more gentle, softened, even to Luce, gentle in the warmth of the long and Indian summer, the lushness of the trees still unwilling to turn, gentle in the sweet dank reek off the marsh, the halcyon days, the swallows and the line storms, the ebb and flow of the moon tides, the aching autumn light.

One day, when he is working in the shop with Bridge, he describes it to her this way:

There is a door at the end of his mind, and when he walks through it, he is with Hannah again. When he walks through it, he is back on the island. His old life unfolds slowly, floating on the vast belly of that other ocean. When he walks through that door at the end of his mind, he can pick up the coarse black lava rock, he can smell the plumeria, the gardenia, the sudden fresh reek of the air before a storm. He can smell the burning cane.

He pauses, and she can see that he has drifted away from her, far away from the room in the shop, and she knows that he is back somewhere on Kauai, somewhere with Hannah, in a lost place perhaps that he led her to through shade and tumbling sunlight, high in the mountains behind the cliffs, toward the sacred falls above the *heiaus*, cold clear water running off the streams, and he is with her there and their bodies are young and strong, brown skins turning through the sweet green fern.

"Papa," Bridge says softly, and she can see how he draws himself back in again, his eyes swing off the wall to her face—the one eye broken with the weather inside it, the white cataract fog. For as long as she can remember, this eye has been broken. It has always been the aspect of his face that she most loved.

Someday, he says, you will have a door like this in your mind.

It catches in her—not what he says, but how he says it—with intent, almost as if he is taking her shoulders in his hands and turning her gently and deliberately toward what he has left unsaid. She can sense that he is asking, without asking, for her to confide in him, to tell him about Henry and the stolen hours at the cottage, the ivy plant in the window, the shadows of its leaves like folded paper birds. She can sense that he is asking her to tell him where she goes, why she goes, what calls her.

And she hears too in the silence—she can see in his old eye—the ancient eye, the eye of sorrows, so beautifully worn like a conch by the sea—that he is telling her perhaps what she already knows—that this will be the season of her life that she looks back on—years from now—this will be the summer that she meets when she walks through that door at the end of her mind—this will be the time in her life—brief, endless, full of youth and love and hope and joy—that every future happiness will be weighed against.

That evening, she rides her bike down to the cottage. She and Henry sit out on the porch chairs. They smoke and watch the swallows in the dusk—a long country of hammering wings. They flood the sky. Henry lights another cigarette, and he tells her about a theory—beautiful and ancient, as old as Aristotle—of how swallows lived out the winter underwater. Bedded down among the reeds, they would sleep through the long cold months clustered together beneath the ice. It was a belief that lasted for centuries, he tells her, and there were tales to prove it: tales of fishermen hauling up the birds in their nets—clumps of swallows frozen, the wings of one folded into the wings of another—he braids his hand into hers as he says this—there were other tales too of how they could only be thawed, slowly, by fire, restored to a brief quickening life.

She smiles quietly in the chill darkness gathering around them. She knows that it is his own story he is telling her—he is a man waking up, and she is that fire. They are quiet together, wrapped in their coats. They watch the last light pass out of the sky. The night is cold, the sea drawn still, and they move inside.

Luce

On a late afternoon in October, Luce comes by the house on Pine Hill Road. Noel's wagon is gone, the shop door closed. The kitchen is empty. He calls up the stairs for his mother. No answer.

He feels shredded, unglued. She has always been the place he could return to at the end of a day when the world got wild.

He comes back into the kitchen and sits down in a chair, his head in his hands. He can hear the sound of his own breathing, shallow, as if his throat is half closed and he is holding air in his lungs. He presses his thumbs into his temples to ease the splitting ache in his head, and for the briefest moment, he wishes that he could empty himself here, in her kitchen, into this worn familiar room of comfort and warmth and smells.

He stands up and walks outside.

He finds Bridge down in the garden, throwing hay over the garlic.

"Hey you," she calls out as she sees him walking toward her down the hill. She shifts the basket onto her hip.

"Hey yourself," he replies, managing a smile. As he comes up to her, she takes him in detail by detail: his unshaven face, unkempt clothes, an odd feverish light in his eyes.

"Where is everybody?" he asks.

"Noel's up at the sawmill."

"Where's Ma?"

"Went to the store, I think. You feel alright?"

"Sure. Yeah. Why not?"

"You look like you're full of pins. Like you need a sleep."

He laughs. "Sleep's been a little rocky. You know . . . since Johnny." He looks down at the green shoots of garlic poking up through the hay. He pushes the toe of his boot against one of them. "They're tough rascals, aren't they? Setting in like they do right through winter?"

He digs into his pocket for his cigarettes, hits one out of the pack, swears as he drops it. He picks it up off the ground and strikes a match.

"You want one?" he asks.

"No thanks."

He inhales, a long deep breath. It seems to settle him.

"I came by the other night," he says. "You weren't around."

"No?"

"Where were you?"

"Out I guess. What night?"

"It might have been Sunday. Yeah. Sunday."

"I was out on Sunday."

He looks at her. The smoke blows soft out the corner of his mouth. He seems to expect her to continue. She doesn't. She reaches into the basket for another handful of hay and sprinkles it over the last row of garlic.

"You're seeing someone, aren't you?"

She glances up, surprised, not that he had guessed it, but by the gentle way he asked. She answers without thinking. "Yes."

"That's good, Bridge. I could tell, you know. You've been happy."
His voice is wistful. "I'm glad for you. I really am."

"What's eating you, Luce?"

He avoids her eyes, draws in on the cigarette, and looks across
the yard. "I'm getting out of the work."

"Did something happen?"

He shakes his head. "I can just feel it, chewing my insides right
down."

"You're really going to quit?"

He nods.

"Did you tell Ma?"

"Not yet."

From the corner of her eye, she sees a squirrel dart across the
yard. It disappears around one corner of the woodpile.

"I got something, Bridge." She hears the shift in his voice, a low
burning thrill. Her pulse quickens. She doesn't want what she
knows is coming.

"Tomorrow night," he says.

"You just told me you're done."

"Last one."

"I don't want to hear it."

"This one you do."

She starts to walk away. He catches her by the wrist. His face is
on fire.

"It's an easy job, Bridge."

She twists her arm loose. "No."

"You can't believe how easy."

"Don't tell me."

"No risk. No guns."

"Forget it, Luce."

"I need you."

"No," she says sharply. "You don't." She sees his face fall, the
sudden aloneness, the silence a vast field between them. He takes

one more drag on his cigarette, drops the butt, and grinds it out in the grass.

"Please," he says, and something in his voice slides through her. She remembers mornings when she was a child, standing at the end of the drive, watching Luce and her father walk away, down the road to work at the icehouse. Every few steps, Luce would turn around and wave. "We'll be home soon, Bridge," he'd call back to her, his voice buoyant, and she would stand there, with an unbearable sadness, watching until they had taken the bend and disappeared from view.

"Please, Bridge," he says again to her now. "I can't do this one on my own."

Even as he says it, she knows that with or without her he will try to pull it off. And with no help. He will end up caught or worse, end up like Asa. She hates him then, quietly, for bringing this to her and, even as she relents, she curses herself for letting her heart soften to his desperate reckless dream.

"This is the last time," she says finally. "I've never said it to you before, Luce, but I am saying it now. This is the end."

He smiles at her, his face coming alive again. "It'll be easy, Bridge. This one we could do in our sleep."

Bridge

That night, after supper, Bridge goes to Henry's house. He is reading in a chair by the window. He looks up, startled for a moment, as she walks through the back door. He smiles when he sees her.

"I didn't know you were coming," he says.

"I wasn't, I guess." She lays her coat down over the arm of the sofa.

"You couldn't help yourself," he teases her. "You're going all to pieces over me."

She laughs. "Not yet," she replies, but a shy smile plays over her mouth. "I just missed you."

He goes to her. Her hair is damp and windblown. Her face is cold. He kisses her forehead, her eyes.

"You missed me?" he says softly.

"I did." She slips her hands under his shirt.

They go upstairs and make love, and afterward, he lies close beside her. He runs his hand over the edge of her hip and asks her softly what she thinks—if there is a difference between fate and coincidence.

"Kind of like destiny or dumb luck?" she says, and he smiles because it is the kind of phrase that she would use.

He kisses her neck. "Do you think it was dumb luck," he asks, "that I saw you at Millie Sisson's house that night, and the very next morning, I forgot my cigarettes, walked into Shorrock's store and saw you there."

She laughs. "Of course it was."

"And do you think it was dumb luck your brother brought you to me that night you were shot?"

"That was common sense. Where else would he have gone?" She stretches her arm over her head, arching her back. He can feel the deep curve of her spine away from him, the cooler space left between his skin and hers.

She is turned away from him, and he touches her slowly, still tracing her hip, the ridge of the bone. He does not take his hand off her. "And do you think it was dumb luck that you walked away from me that night in the greenhouse, and told me to walk away and not to think about you. It was not practical, you said. That's how you put it. And I woke up a few days later with my brain on fire because I could not do what you asked, I could not stop thinking about you, and so I got into my car and drove up Horseneck Road, and I was almost there—do you know that?—I was almost free of you. Do you think it was dumb luck that, at that moment, I passed you on the road?"

She doesn't answer.

"Can you be so sure?" he whispers.

They have been together for four months, and sometimes when he is above her, making love to her, the light rests like a fine wax on his shoulders and the only pressure in the world she feels is the weight of his hands on her skin. He is so different from her—not only who he is and where he comes from, but how he watches her, touches her, needs her. The whole tone of his being is unlike anything that has crossed her life before—and the way he loves her—she can feel it changing her, and it is strange and beautiful. When she is with him this way, lying naked in a cool blue darkness, she has the sense that they are drifting together and at the same time, each alone. The darkness surrounds her like a shell, but at the edge of it, she imagines she can see the loose glow of a new world rolling open.

For a moment she thinks of Luce, and she feels a twinge of sadness. The sadness comes not just because she has outgrown their closeness, but rather because, in some deep and elemental way, they are still bound. Luce is a part of her. He has always been a part of her. Even if she were to cut him out of her life completely, she could not excise the part of her that he belongs to, the part of her that belongs to him.

She rolls over in Henry's arms. His cheek is against the pillow, and he is watching her. She touches his mouth, and he smiles. He does not take his eyes off her.

"Why do you watch me like that?" she asks. "Are you afraid I'll disappear?"

"Yes," he says. "That's exactly it."

She laughs softly. "You look like you are waiting for something. Like you are hungry and waiting for food."

"Yes. It is that too."

He touches the front of her belly and runs his hand between her legs. She is tired but she lets him. She wants to sink down, to close her eyes, not to think for a while, just to be still. He pulls her closer, gently pushing her legs apart, and she lets him. She will always let him. This is something that she knows.

"Are you asleep?" she asks.

"Just closing my eyes."

That night, he tells her he has begun to dream about the dead.

He tells her this when they are lying in a half-sleep after making love, wrapped around each other in the darkness. His voice is murky, low. He tells her stories of what he remembers from the war—the trenches, the free-running sewage, the blood transfusions performed vein to vein.

He tells her that sometimes when they cut a man, they would discover other things lodged inside him, bits of metal, stone, wood. Once in a while they would find a piece of bone that had belonged to another soldier.

She touches his hands—they are hands that have seen every-thing—fingers strong and deft.

He tells her about the woman brought in late one night to the trench hospital at the border, the first woman who died on him. She was a nurse, with a severe case of fever—chills, quick pulse, a sudden astonishing loss of strength. He wore a mask as he cleaned her. He turned her on the bed every three hours so her blood would not pool. He fed her water with a syringe and sat with her until her eyes turned black and her hands grew stiff, her insides rose up through her chest and soil came out her mouth.

He tells her these things, these people he has seen, their dying he still dreams. He tells her that in his dreams, he is always helpless. He tells her about his fear of an empty sky. And she wonders how it can happen, on this kind of night when they are so close, lying wrapped together in this same soft darkness, she wonders how he can slip away from her into these kinds of dreams.

The wind has picked up. She can hear the hollow burn of it flooding through the crawl space above their heads.

He is lying on his side, faced away from her. She looks past his shoulder to the window and the hanging ivy plant. She cannot see the birds. He must have turned it. Sometime in the past few days, in the span of time since she has been away, he must have turned it to even out the growing of the leaves.

"Are you asleep?" she asks again.

No answer.

She runs her hand between his shoulder blades and lightly down his back, along each vertebra, each disk of bone bound to the one before and the one that follows, the fluid space of softer tissue in between. Her fingers pause at the base of his spine, and she remembers then what he said to her that first night as they lay together on the hard, cool floor of Alyssia Borden's greenhouse—how he told her that he needed her and he wanted her to need him.

She listens for his breath, the slow rhythmic sound of it. She listens and realizes that if she were stealth enough, if she did not love him the way she has come to love him, she could steal it. She could pull his breath hand over hand up from his lungs until it is gone.

The wind howls through the walls. It is a new wind, and fierce. She can sense the cold edge of the coming winter on it.

The next morning, before Henry leaves for the mill, he makes her breakfast. She watches him from the chair across the room. He cuts a thin pat of butter off the quarter pound, sets it in the shallow tin eggcups.

She watches how he stays close to the stove, close to the pan, his fingers near the knob to adjust the flame as the upper rim of the cup begins to shake. He has a sensitivity to food, she has noticed this, a thoughtfulness, a mindful patience, his kindness, she has called it, and it occurs to her now, watching him, that the way he stays close to those small tin cups and the shuddering, broken eggs inside them is not unlike the way he might turn a dying woman over in her bed, the way he might strip the soiled sheets from her body and gently wash her with a cloth. Bridge has seen him do this—she realizes it now—she sees it even in this moment, as he is standing by the stove across the room, she sees how he will fold that woman's bladed hands and wipe away the uncertain color that has begun to leak out of her mouth, how he will close gently, with his fingertips, her dilated eyes.

She bites her lip and looks out the window toward the sea, a light-distressed surface. The jasmine is set on the writing desk. He has replanted it into a larger pot. He has dug new holes for the roots in the dark earth with the blunt end of a drawing pencil.

"The flowers are gone," she says.

He answers her without looking up from the stove. "I've noticed they don't seem to last more than a day."

"It's growing though," she says, and it might be something in her voice, a stumbling, a catch he has not heard before. He looks up.

"What's wrong?" he asks.

"Nothing."

"Something is."

"No."

But that morning as he is leaving, after they have eaten and he has drawn on his coat and they are standing together by the door, he holds her and it is suddenly unbearable. It is breaking her heart. Even though it is just like any other day, any other simple inconsequent leaving, she does not want him to go.

Her body stiffens, and he feels it. He holds her away from him at arm's length. He studies her face.

"What is it, Bridge?"

She shakes her head.

He touches her neck, her throat. He tilts her face up toward him. Her eyes are wet, and she looks away.

"You wanted this," she says quietly.

"I do want this. I would give up everything for you," he says.

"I don't ask you to."

"This is all I want."

"You'll be late," she says. "You have to go."

"I don't have to go."

"You do."

He puts his arms around her and holds her then, his face buried in her hair. He grips her tightly.

From the doorway she watches him crank the engine on the car. It stammers once, then turns over and starts. He climbs in, unrolls the window, and waves as he backs out of the drive. He heads off down the road. She stands in the doorway watching his car, and all the things she has not told him flood through her, incomplete thoughts, ragged and brief, nearly realized. She finds the words for them at last. They come to her now as she watches the old-style square black roof of the Model T pass between the trees and down the road away from her.

Just as he bears around the turn that will take him out of sight, she sees his arm come through the window, his hand closing, the fingers crimped, then opening again, as if he were releasing something to her on the air.

When he is gone, she steps back inside and closes the door. She looks around the room, and for the first time in the four months since she has been with him, she feels like she could stay here, in this house that is his. She could brew another pot of coffee, drink it, make the bed, sweep the kitchen, beat out the rugs, tend the plants and straighten the shelves. She could wait for him to come home.

She drinks off the rest of her coffee and collects her things. She writes Henry a short note. She leaves it folded by the jasmine.

She steps out the door. The day is warm. Dry air. Sharp light.

Halfway across the yard, she hears the sound of a wagon coming toward her down the road, the steady beat of hooves, the familiar creak of the wheels. She freezes. Above the boxhedge, she glimpses the top of his head, the set of the beaten sea-man's cap, unmistakably his.

He will see her. He is ten feet from the end of the hedge and he will see her. She slips into the shadow of the garden shed. Quietly. She presses herself against it. There are tears in her eyes and she bites her lip to stop them. Her mouth washes warm with the sweet light taste of blood. He passes by.

Noel

Once when he and Hannah were quarreling over something, Noel had dished out a remark so backhanded and vicious that, as soon as it was out of his mouth, he regretted having said it. Hannah had just looked at him. Her eyes filled, and she pushed her face into his shoulder.

"Be nice to me," she said quietly. "You'll only have me once."

He remembers this waking up. Perhaps he dreamed it. He tries to remember what else, if anything, she might have said, but his brain is tired. It cannot seem to hold all that it used to. He loads the wagon and heads down toward the beach. The day is unnaturally warm and there is a stillness to the road. Once in a while, a quick breeze wriggles through the grass.

He can smell wood smoke as he takes the turn past Ben Soule's house on the knoll onto East Beach Road. He can smell the dank reek of weed trapped under the sand.

He almost missed the carcass—nearly drove straight past it, and would have likely, if he had not heard the cry of the other one.

She crouches in the brush—a small black shape—a young cat, pink mouth, slight white teeth like baby knives. She eyes him warily, then takes up again with her crying. He looks and sees the dead one lying farther in some grass at the shoulder of the road. He can tell right away it has been hit. An easy read. On another day, he might have left it, he might have passed on. But something about the other one and her crying makes him stop. He climbs out. He takes his spade from the wagon and digs a shallow pit at the edge of a lawn. He has just finished digging when he notices that the other one, perhaps sensing his intent, has come and gripped the scruff of the dead one in her teeth and is dragging it by the neck back into the brush.

She licks its face to wake it up, and on another day, he might have let them be. But he goes toward her, and she being shy, not tame, skits away. He takes the carcass, drops it in the hole, and lays the dirt in until it is covered. He stamps the earth down hard. And still, he can hear her, crying in the brush. He looks in the direction of the sound, and he can see her pale eyes watching through the shadow of the leaves.

Henry

As he walks through the high-ceilinged rooms of the mill, he finds himself looking up at the time-clock, down at his watch, then toward the window, the blue dusty light streaming through, and he has the sense that she is out there, somewhere in that light, in that free sky. Again, he looks at the clock. The second hand has barely moved, is barely closer to the end-of-the-day bell, but still he cannot stop thinking of her. Through the drone of the machines, the soft talk of the workers standing by the bins, he thinks of her. His mind is filled only with her, and finally he walks into the office of one of the other bosses and explains that he is leaving, for the day at least, perhaps for the rest of the week. He gives no excuse, no explanation. He takes his coat, his hat, and walks outside. He gets into his car and drives.

He drives away from the city. The trees thicken along the road. The fields open out. He is barely aware of the wheel in his hands. The car twists, making the turns on its own, slow, hypnotic, his foot down on the gas, gaining speed. The last autumn leaves cling to their branches. The shade bends toward him, then away, a stealth, slow-moving wind, he can feel it through the open window, and the world is drenched with color, stunning fluid gorgeous, and he drives, thinking of her, his mind spinning with the trees, sky, leaves falling, the sun and the shade and her body, this thought of her, the tincture of every other thought infused by her. He takes the last hinge of the road. He climbs the hill toward the sudden drop of the fields down to the ocean. The sky is stark, blue and endless, colors, trees, stones, wheeling and alive, the fields gold and shimmering underneath him, laid out in the midafternoon sun, and it is so beautiful, so breathtaking, this first glimpse of the view from the top of the hill, that he stops. He pulls over and gets out of the car. He stands at the edge of the road watching the wind as it works through the tall thick bleached salt hay and, for the first time since the night he was with her in the greenhouse, he has a sense of peace. From where he stands at the top of the hill, he can see the fields stretching down to the sea, the low and gentle shelter of the sky. There is a soft ache to the light. This is the moment he has been traveling toward. He is standing on the brink of it now, on the brink of the rest of his life with her. He will be with her tonight. He will hold her tightly. He will hold her tomorrow and the day after that. He will not let her go.

They come then. Suddenly. A shocking blackness. Heavy pulsing wings. Crows. They burst out of the tall grass of the field. They shriek and rise. Four. No, five of them, six. They swoop and dive and rise again, chasing a smaller bird, a cowbird, out of the tall grass. They chase the cowbird high, higher, up into the unprotected sky. They form a loose circle around it to keep it contained, and then they begin to move in, a tightening knot. One swerves toward it, then another, beaks, claws slashing. The cowbird pauses once in midair, then darts suddenly, its wings swift, a small dark lightning, it skirts between two crows and it is out of the ring. The crows screech, scolding one another as the cowbird flies low to the ground across the field into the thickets. They chase it, still squawking among themselves. They hover around the thicket. Quietly they wait, but the cowbird is gone, deep in the brambles.

The field is silent. The wind rakes softly through the salt hay. Silent. The world, the sky, the stones, the sea, all of it silent. Henry climbs back into his car, shaken. He drives the rest of the way home.

She is not at the house. He finds the note she has left for him by the jasmine. *Tonight, after ten*, she has written. Just those words. He folds the note and puts it in his trouser pocket.

He fumbles in the kitchen. There are crows trapped in his chest. He can feel the furious hack of their wings. He cuts off a piece of bread from the hard loaf, but he cuts it too thick for the toaster slats, his hand rough with the knife. He tries to cut the edge of one slice down, fails. He tears off a piece and gnaws on it, but it is too dry. He leaves it and goes outside onto the porch.

The sun is settling into the sky. It moves deep, receding. It hangs low over the water tower on the far side of the harbor mouth. The light chaps the surface of the ocean. He sits on the porch steps—still with those wings in his chest—water, colors, light trembling, wild, uncertain.

A couple walking passes by. A girl and an older man. Her father. He has seen them before. They live at the Point. He does not know their names. The man walks with a stick. He pokes it into shells, a bit of driftwood, a dead horseshoe crab. The girl drifts behind him in a long wool coat, her body thin, feet like minnows. She glances up at Henry as they pass by. She smiles. She is shy.

Young gulls hover in a loose pack on the dry sand. The sanderlings have begun to flock up in their tribes. One rogue fish hawk, solitary, restless, casts long circles over the beach.

The waves scour in, then fall away. Henry watches as the light shifts down through tidal pools, skates' eggs, flat gray rocks and stones so white they seem to hold the moon inside them. The sky breaks down into a fire, and he looks west again. Far off, at the end of the beach, he can see the pair walking, the older man and the girl, still apart. They are close to the breakwater where the land hooks back into the dunes. Henry follows the girl with his eyes, cuts the details of her shape. She is as black as a doorway in the dying light.

He goes inside. He picks up the newspaper, opens to the sports page to read a few scores, but the numbers are a mess in his head. He throws it down again. He flips through his records, picks one out, and winds the phonograph. He sets the record on the turntable, draws the arm across and locks it in place. As the record starts to turn, he sets the needle into the groove. Music fills the room.

He lies down on the daybed. Through the long window, he watches the darkening sky. The wind has shifted. It brings the fog in.

Bridge

Before she leaves to meet Luce that night, she goes
into the shop, sits on the stool near the door and
cleans her gun. She works the bolt back and forth
and empties the unused shells into a pile on the
workbench. She slips out the bolt, takes the cleaning
rod, snaps in the wire brush and works it through
the barrel to take down the flakes of old powder.
Then she strings a strip of flannel rag into the rod,
dips it in alcohol, and runs it up and down the barrel. She does the same once more with a second
rag dipped in oil, and thinks of how when she was
a child Noel had taught her to shoot woodchucks
from the shadow of the backhouse door—she remembers the look of astonishment on his face when
he saw how easily she snapped them off as they
munched down the heads of his broccoli. Afterward
he would gather them from the garden rows. He
would find them among desecrated leaves, their small
chests blown open.

She rubs down the stock, smoothing the rag and
working it into the wood with the gentle attention
she has always used caring for her guns.

Luce had told her that tonight she wouldn't need it. "It's not that kind of job," he had said. "You're bringing yours," she had replied. "No reason for me not to bring mine." Although the truth of it was, it really didn't matter to her either way. Now all she wanted was for the night to be done, so she could get back to Henry. It makes her happy, thinking of him, his eyes on her face, his hands on her body—it fills her with a quiet joy. Sometimes when he looks at her, she feels like he is seeing all that she has seen and felt and grieved and wondered. Later tonight, when she meets him at the cottage, she will tell him this. She will tell him how she had felt that morning in his house, even after he had gone. She had felt that she belonged there. It had become familiar to her, almost home.

She works the bolt again back and forth to make sure it runs loose and free. She loads the bullets, puts out the lamp, and leaves the gun leaning in the shadow against the outside wall of the shop. She goes into the house. Noel is in the kitchen, pieces of the old can opener on his lap. With his pocketknife, he works at the screw in the handle, trying to tighten it up.

As she washes her hands in the sink, he glances up and notices how beautiful she looks. Her clothes are neat, her boots polished.

"Where are you off to tonight?" he asks.

She points to the can opener parts on his lap. "How many times are you going to fix that piece of junk?" she says with a smile. "Don't you think it's time to break down and splurge for a new one?"

"This one here's an old friend," he answers. "You watch, Bridge. I'll get it fixed right this time."

Before she leaves, she comes to the chair where he sits and bends to kiss him on the cheek, in her quick way, that constant way. Then she goes out, and the door settles onto its frame behind her, and Noel is left alone in the kerosene light.

———

He cuts wood later that night. He takes two axes down to the woodyard. He works with the heavy one first, and when his shoulders grow sore, he switches to the lighter one. He stacks the last cords into the pile. As he is passing back through the yard toward the house, he sees that Cora has left a shirt out on the clothesline. Its arms twist white as if there is a spirit trapped inside. Its chest fills with the wind.

The grass is wet with the stiff green smell of rain. The fog has cleared. The moon has begun to press through the clouds.

Henry

Half past nine, and there is no sign of her. After ten, he reminds himself. Her note had said, *After ten.* He tries to arm himself with this. He keeps the phonograph playing, and he reads by the kerosene light. When the lamp burns down to a beaten glow on the end of the wick, he takes the empty tin out to the woodshed and refills it from the drum.

At quarter past eleven, he puts down his book, goes over to the phonograph, and switches it off. The needle grinds to a halt. He lifts it, slides the record into its case, and closes the lid of the box. As he starts to walk back toward his chair, he sees a pool of wavering shadows from the lamplight on the floor. He stops, transfixed, staring at those strange elusive shapes. The smell of the jasmine spills through the room—that dusky, everywhere scent reminding him.

He hears gunfire. Shots out of the west. He goes up to the second floor, then takes the narrow flight of stairs into the attic. He goes to the window and looks west toward the end of the beach, the harbor mouth and Charlton Wharf. He can see the orange bursts of light, the lean bright slice of tracers through the dark, shadows scuffling on land by the pier, masses of craft on water—several smaller boats, the shape of draggers, sparring off the larger black hull of a Coast Guard cutter, its lights thrown on full beam. And as he is watching—it seems impossible at first—a trick of sound—but he hears another round of shots, fainter and more distant, from the east. He crosses the attic to the opposite window, the window that looks toward Little Beach. Again he sees orange flashes and masses of shadow on the sea. He is frozen, his hands pressed against the cold glass. He knows she is out there somewhere in that darkness, but he does not know where to find her. He is aware of the sound of his own breathing, and silence. He is surrounded by the heavy stiff black silence of the indoor night, every sound from the world outside muffled through the walls, the world outside moving so fast, her, somewhere out there in that darkness, in that danger. Somewhere in that night she is not safe.

He remembers what she told him once about decoys—how they are always in the shape of their own kind. She had described two ponds baited with wood-carved birds and a duck blind, her brother Luce's blind, set on the marsh between them, "he would always wait between them," she had said, and then smiled, the slow and melting smile that he loved, and her eyes had glanced away from him as if for a moment she were turning back toward that still water and the decoys placed in the reeds, the other flock, the live flock, moving in.

"My brother is a good thief, because he always works against what you'd expect, what you could imagine."

Slowly now, Henry turns toward the third window, the south window under the dormer that looks out onto the dark ocean, her words still in him: "He always finds the last place anyone would think to look, and so often, you know, it is the place that is most obvious, most exposed." And Henry looks out into the deep well of the dark moving ocean, toward the long slung arm of Gooseberry Neck that divides the bay.

Bridge

That night was a good sand night. The wind had kicked into the west just after sundown, and by ten it had driven the beach hard as new macadam. The tide was on the ebb. A dark sky. The moon slipping through the clouds.

They drive over the Point Bridge, down the beach road past the seasonal restaurant and over the low dune. They drive out onto the hard sand, then turn east and head toward Gooseberry along the water's edge with the headlamps out.

They park by the rocks below the causeway and walk across it to the island. They cut in on the old path, the one they had walked together so many times. Luce stamps down the overgrown places with his boots, and they wind through the middle of the neck past the inland pond. They cross out onto the beach that faces east. The boat is there. Luce had driven it over earlier in the day and left it anchored in the cove.

They wade into the shallows and wait, eels running over their feet.

———

He had laid it out for her as they drove. He had told her how it would all go down—and as they wait in the shallows, looking northeast toward Little Beach, it unfolds exactly as he said it would.

There was one rum-ship, a Canadian vessel, and two gangs. The gangs had split up the load, fifteen hundred cases, over a hundred thousand dollars' worth. It was a big operation, a Syndicate job. After unloading half her hold off Inner Mayo Ledge to Swampy Davoll's gang, who would then run it back into the Point, the rum-ship had come in past Hen and Chickens and anchored just offshore of Little Beach. There were dories waiting for her there.

"Isaac Bly's gang from Dartmouth," Luce whispers.

Bridge strains her eyes against the darkness, looking out across the black water toward the far-off paler strip of sand. She tries to match the faint slight movements she can see with what she knows they are doing—unloading the crates off the smuggler into the smaller boats, then running them in, carrying the stuff up the beach, filling trucks and cars; crates of liquor heaped in piles at the edge of the shore.

She does not ask, but she knows that Luce must have tipped off the Feds, because she can see it does not surprise him when they come, swarming out of the night from the land-side, trapping the rummies on the narrow strip of Little Beach, and it is mayhem— distant black shapes running, shouts, gunfire echoing over the bay, truck engines starting up, headlights backing fast around, more shots. The dories are abandoned in the shallows, half unpacked, some with their full load still on them. The Feds will be vastly outnumbered, she knows this, because they have been split between the site at Charlton Wharf and the site on Little Beach that she and Luce are watching now. Her brother would have waited to tip them. He would have waited until it was late in the evening, too late for them to call up an adequate reserve. There are men at the edge of the shore now—Feds—they are firing out at the rum-ship. She has already begun to nose around. She cuts off her lights and throws her throttle open, heading straight out toward the black and heavy sea.

Bridge watches with Luce. She is close to him, less than three feet away. This is how he said it would happen, and they would wait, watching from the hook in the shore of the neck. No one would see them. No one would think to look for them there. The Feds would round up what they could of the gang and bring them in, but in the end it would be a numbers game. There simply would not be enough of them to deal with all that liquor. They would have to leave it, at least a good part of it. They would have to leave and come back with more men, more trucks, to haul it away.

And that, she knew, was what they were waiting for, that rip in the night when the land would fall silent again, the rum-ship gone, the gang scattered, the beach empty with those crates of liquor piled on the sand and lying heavy in the dories in the shallows. The Feds might leave a man behind, two at the most, but they would post them at the top of the road. No one would expect a boat to come in off the sea.

"Just awhile longer," Luce whispers to her. "Not long at all now." The smuggler speeds past them, headed toward open water. She has just come level with the tip of the island when out of the darkness the patrol boats appear, two lean fast shadows, engines roaring. Bridge hears the call of the Klaxon horn. One patrol throws a searchlight, but the smuggler revs her engine and refuses to heave to. The gunfire begins.

The patrol fires one burst—a stream of orange tracers beating through the night—and then a second. Abruptly, inexplicably, the rum-runner swerves. She takes a hard turn, a hundred and eighty degrees, and guns it. She comes back fast, headed straight for the firing patrol as if she would ram it. The patrol darts left, just barely avoiding collision, and fires another pan of machine-gun bullets toward the runner's engine room. The smuggler slows, then stops. She lies still, dead in the water. No sound off her. No light.

A few hundred yards of black water separates her from the shoal at the tip of the island. There is a sudden explosion, the night shattered, a burst of flame—yellow, orange, red, blue. Fire roars off her deck, a huge ball of fire soaring up into the sky.

Bridge grips Luce's arm. "Did you do this?" she whispers. He shakes his head, staring, his face lit by sheets of rippling orange flame. She can see it all reflected in his face. He pulls her down to kneel in the shallows. They crouch behind the rocks. Her coat sleeves drag in the water, and she can feel the cold soaking through to her skin. Still they watch, as the wind blows strong out of the west and drafts the flames high. The fire arcs up like a demon, sparks shooting out and falling onto the deck of the patrol. The patrol backs away as the fire leaps out, then edges in again. There is the smell of burning. There are men screaming. Bridge can hear them—the rum-runner's crew, six or seven crowding against the deck rail. She can see their hands, their faces, their coats on fire, and they jump, first one and then another, then the rest at once. They jump off the starboard side, their arms like freakish orange birds, into the black water. The ship falls back into flames, the sound of timbers cracking as her hull caves in and she is consumed. She lists to one side, then begins to sink, her bow nodding up as her stern drops. Lower and lower in the water she goes. The flames thin down. The steam hisses off her, rising like a fog on the black surface where she disappears.

The two patrol boats come in from either side toward the men in the water. They pan their lights over the waves. They steer carefully through the wreckage and pick up the men from the smuggler's crew. The men are shrieking, some of them, crying from their burns, lost in the water, their arms flailing. But the patrols find them. They come alongside each man and hoist him up onto deck, and when the last man is found, they turn and speed off through the night heading east-northeast up the bay toward New Bedford harbor.

Bridge and Luce don't speak. Still they wait. They crouch behind the rock, watching. The darkness falls still. The sea quiet. The land quiet. Their boat is lying in the cove, still at anchor behind them. As the moon slips into the clouds, they crawl out from behind the rocks and look back toward Little Beach. The shore is empty. There is no sign of movement, of men. But they can see the cases, heaped in piles on the beach, and the dories still loaded full, aground at the edge of the sand.

Luce doesn't ask her if she still wants to go. He doesn't assume that her mind might have changed either way. He touches her arm and, without a word, begins to wade through the shallows toward the boat. She follows him. They climb in, over the side, and he draws up the anchor and coils the line. As he walks to the stern to push them off, by some uncanny instinct, some queer thrust of the moon, he glances up at the beach, toward the higher ground, and catches a glimpse of tweed in the brush. As he is reaching for his gun, tucked between the fishbox and the gunwale, he sights the arm. He follows it down to the wrist, the long pale fingers of the hand resting on the knee. He knows, as he raises the rifle to his shoulder, who it is. He squints and tracks his eye down the barrel. He knows there is no threat, but he is already aiming at the cloth, the inner part of the arm. He is already shifting the end of the barrel by the exact fraction that will equal the distance between the edge of a man and his center. The smooth wooden gunstock rests in his hand. He clicks the safety. He hears his sister turn behind him, the sharp gasp of her breath. The slightest cry. He fires.

Bridge

She sits in a chair in the bedroom, turned away
from the bed, facing the window with the lamp off.
It is almost three in the morning. The moon hangs
over the ocean, and the sea is still. She had told
Luce to get gone. Just to be gone. That was all she
wanted from him.

They had brought the body back to the house,
and it is lying on the huge oak table downstairs, a
blanket pulled over the face. She had done that. She
did not want to see his face.

The moon begins to set, and when the clock
strikes four, she lights the lamp. She goes down the
hall to the water closet, fills a pitcher of water from
the sink, and brings it back to the bedroom. She
takes the ivy plant down from the window and waters it, then turns it and hangs it again. She sets
the pitcher on the small table by the door. She
will bring it downstairs. She makes the bed, turning back the edge of the sheet, and smoothing it
over the blanket. She props the pillows against the
headboard and pulls the coverlet over them. His flannel shirt and pajama bottoms are on the floor. She

picks them up, folds them, and sets them, folded, on the chair. She turns off the lamp and leaves the room, closing the door behind her.

She will have to call them at some point, she thinks, as she walks down the stairs.

In the kitchen she does not look at him lying on the table. She keeps her back turned as she cleans out the icebox. She empties a bottle of milk, half a bottle of wine, and a jar of iced tea down the drain in the sink. There is an open can of cut pears and another of asparagus spears, two apples, and half a stick of butter. She throws everything into the trash and wipes down the empty shelves with a damp kitchen cloth. She rinses out the rag and leaves it hanging over the faucet.

She goes to the phone in the hall, turns the crank, and dials.

When she hangs up, she brings the water pitcher into the front room. Fine light streaks in the east have begun to break up the darkness. They will be here soon. She has half an hour at most. The thought frightens her suddenly. This is the last time she will be alone in this house. His house. She crosses the room to the jasmine. She tilts the pitcher and floods the dark earth. The water fills the dish under the pot, then spills out onto the floor. She wants to take the jasmine home with her, but she won't. This is the light that it knows. She sets the pitcher down on the desk and opens the long drawer. She picks through his pens, a deck of cards, a few stray keys. She closes it again and looks around the room, aware that she needs to find something, anything, something that matters that she can take with her. She looks through his papers, his records, his books. She lifts the lid on the sea chest and draws out the heavy leatherbound notebook. She opens it, then closes it. She puts it back into the chest.

Across the room, he lies on the table under the blanket she drew across him. She wants to go to him. She wants to lie down with him under that sheet. She puts her fist to her mouth.

She hears them coming toward her down the road—the low

sound of car engines. They grow louder, nearer. She turns toward the window. The sun has risen. The clouds are banked over the ocean, a long flung line, their tops sifting off into looser strands. The light spills through them. It spills over the causeway and across the water, sheets of silver light, so stark and free that for a moment, she forgets. A catboat threads its way from the mouth of the harbor toward the bell, then farther out into the bay.

Cars pull up in the drive outside. She looks down at her hands resting on the window ledge. She hears steps on the porch, a rapping at the door. She notices a small ashtray at the corner of the desk closest to the window—a folded sheet of paper inside it— the note she had written to him the day before—and then deeper in the shadow of the bowl, a small and odd-shaped piece of lead. She tips the ashtray, and it falls out into her hand. A .22-caliber slug, its head flattened over, mushroom-shaped. Her fingers close around it, its strange cool hardness digging into her palm, as she walks to the door to let them in.

Luce

The dawn comes fast. He dreads it. The light filling the room, illuminating every crack and hole and
brokenness. A single bird has begun to sing in the
woods outside, and he sits quietly, as he has sat
all night, in the large downstairs room at the pesthouse. There is moss on the walls, grass growing up
through the floor. He has not slept. He has not
closed his eyes. They ache now, from dryness, from
staring at the rubble of an old fireplace on the opposite side of the room.

Earlier, after he had left Bridge with the truck
at the cottage on the beach, he had run. Up the
road toward home, toward any solace, comfort, salve,
his feet pounding, mile after mile, and at last he
had reached the house on Pine Hill Road. He had
stopped at the edge of the yard. Noel's wagon was
parked in the drive, a few pieces of Cora's laundry
strung on the clothesline. Every window in the place
was dark. Luce had stood for an hour in the trees,
and by then he knew that no matter how long he
waited, the door would not open. He could not enter.

So he had come here. He had found this corner

and pushed himself against the wall, trying to find some meeting of hard surfaces that could hold him. He had picked one shadow apart from the next. It was the first night in months that he had had no fear. The night sounds, the night smells, were everywhere around him—a sort of wild reckoning—and at one point he had almost managed to convince himself the day would not come.

There is a pain in his head, a shooting pain, the two sides of his brain still split: the feverish side, the cool side, the side with passion, the side with none. The side that made him do what he did and aches for it now, the other side that can explain it—he did not know who it was, he did not aim to kill.

He knows what is lie. He knows what is truth. And as the morning light settles into the torn room, he cries for the wreck of every structure of his world.

Noel

That morning when Noel goes out, without knowing what has happened, how it happened, he can feel
the shift in wind. It is a winter wind, out of the northeast. It drives hard over the marsh, tearing through
the scrub. It is the kind of wind that will haul the
snow down from the north, and bring the Arctic
birds, the snow buntings and the buffleheads—the
kind of wind that will sweeten the turnips. It will
freeze the river, bring in the surf clams, and wash
the muck high up on the beach.

He sees the line of cars gathered by the third
cottage. The police truck. The undertaker's long
black car. A knot of men stand outside in the drive.
They look up at him, suspicious, as he comes around
the bend. One officer steps out into the road and
motions for him to stop.

"How are you then, Noel?"

"Fine, Joe."

"Do you know anything about it?"

Noel shakes his head. "What happened?"

"He was shot. She called us early this morning."

"Who was shot?"

"Henry Vonniker. But she won't tell us how it happened. She's with him there, inside." He jerks his head toward the house, and as Noel looks toward the doorway, Bridge appears. She sees him. Her face is sundered, unfamiliar, unlike anything he could have imagined.

She gives a slight nod, then steps back into the house and disappears from view.

They bring her home that afternoon. She does not speak about it. She tells Noel where to find Luce—at the old pesthouse in the woods, she says. And Noel goes and looks for him there, but she is wrong. The ruins are empty. Starlings fly toward the holes in the roof as he walks through the gutted rooms.

Five days later, the stock market crashes. The Dow Jones is cut in half, prices slaughtered in every direction, ten billion dollars lost in one day. By the time Noel sees the headlines in the paper the following morning, he knows it is too late. What he had bought, what he had held, all of it is smashed to flinders. He chucks the newspaper into the trash barrel outside Shorrock's store and takes Old County Road back toward Pine Hill.

As he is passing by the church, he sees Luce sitting on the wall out front. His face is haggard. Noel goes and sits down with him.

"You're waiting on them then, to come and find you?"

Luce nods.

"Which one you waiting on—Lyons or the constable?"

Luce shrugs and answers that either one would do. They fall to silence. It is a cool brisk wind, and it takes the oak leaves down. Noel sits with him on the wall until the police truck comes around, and when they have taken him and he is gone, Noel walks the rest of the way home alone.

The next afternoon, Rui stops by the house. Noel is down back, looking over the cabbages, debating whether to pull them or to let them ride out another week or two.

"Thought I'd see you by my place," Rui calls out, walking toward him.

"Don't know why you'd be thinking that," Noel answers. He finds a loose stake set at the edge of the garden. He pulls it out and throws it toward the pine wood. He will replace it in the spring.

"Thought you'd be curious to know how it all shook out," Rui says. "With the money, I mean."

Noel takes his pipe out of his pocket and puts it in his mouth, unlit. "I think I know it all shook out."

Rui laughs. "So you've been following the papers."

"Always do."

"I heard talk about some trouble your Luce got himself into."

Noel nods.

"How's Cora doing with it?"

"She'll be alright."

"Well, I brought this by for you," says Rui, "in case you might have a use for it." He tosses Noel a small sack, tied with a piece of thin rope at one end. Noel catches it midair. He loosens the slip knot. There is money inside, bills folded together and banded with clips.

"I don't need a handout, Rui." He reknots the rope and holds out the bag.

Rui shrugs. "No handout, Christmas. You know I'd be the last one to give away what's mine."

Noel looks at him. The sun is in his good eye, and the light is strong, and he can't see his friend's face clearly, but he can hear him chuckling.

"Come on up to your shop then," Rui says. "Pour me a mug of something good you have hidden in there. You owe me that much for looking after you and what's yours."

Noel understands then, and he is angry for a moment. "You son of a bitch—"

Rui laughs. "Son of a nothing. That temper of yours is no good, Christmas. It's never been good. What you have there in your hand isn't more than what you had to start. I did what you told me to do, so don't go bitching at me. That there is just a little pillow I pulled out for you in case."

Noel smiles. "You're a devil, Rui."

"And you're lucky to have a devil like me around."

Noel grips the sack tightly, and they walk together back up the hill.

The day before Bridge leaves, Noel watches her pack her things into a canvas bag. He tells her to take one of the trunks. Too big, she says. She takes only what she needs. A comb, a knife, a piece of scrimp he carved for her once. A few changes of clothes. She moves through the room, picking through her things, taking what she wants and leaving the rest.

There is so much, he knows, that he could tell her.

He says her name and she looks up and he can see the wounds in her face. He can see there is a part of her, a deep part of her, that is already gone, and the grief that has risen to fill the absent place has rendered every object in the world lighter and more silent.

He is aware that her leaving has already begun to work through his bones. He knows that this is only the tip of what he will feel. It is unworked ground—her leaving. It is not that he thought he could keep her, but he had never imagined it would come so suddenly.

He thinks of the black cat—not the one killed but the other. For months, he knows, it will spook around that spot in the road. It might stalk off a ways to hunt and feed, but it will come back, week after week, month after month, through the change of season. Even in dead winter, some sense more primitive than smell will draw that creature back to that same frozen shoulder of the road, and it will nose through the grass with the dim sense of a wrong solitude, without knowing what it knows.

He could tell her this.

He could tell her that a heart is just that way. It is made for losing. Even his old heart, he could tell her, after so many years, sometimes it still seems to be as raw and young and as easily broken as it ever was.

She goes to the dresser, opens the middle drawer, and lifts up some folded shirts. She pulls out the sack of money he gave to her, and she dumps it out on the bed. She does not look up at him as she counts out the bills. Her hands are ruthless, every softness in her gone. She makes three rolls and holds one out to him. He shakes his head.

"I don't want it."

"You'll need it."

"For what?"

"For living."

"No."

She smiles and drops the roll into a drawer on the night table. She takes the other two and puts one into each pocket of her coat.

She fastens the clips on the bag. The window is behind her, full of milky winter light. Her hair has grown out and she has tied it back and her face is beautiful and she reminds him of his Hannah—of all the years of loving her and all the years since she has been gone, and it seems impossible that he could be losing her this way, losing them both somehow, all over again. He cannot tell her this. He tells her instead that there are windows all around her. There are roads all around her. When he was her age, he had to travel halfway around the world and back to find what he was looking for, and what he was looking for was not at all what he had imagined.

She looks at him, and her eyes are gentle on his face. "I love you, Papa," she says, and he realizes then that he is only telling her what she already knows.

That night, Noel and Bridge and Cora eat together in the front room. Noel shaves and wears a starched shirt and clean trousers. He lets Cora flat-iron a crease down the front of the leg. He lets her set the cuffs.

The table is laid out by the time he comes in from the shop. Cora has cooked a roast. It sits on the table, uncarved. Their plates glisten in the silky yellow light, and they sit together, quiet as they eat, and after dinner Noel and Bridge go outside onto the back porch. They sit on the steps and watch the smoke as it slips from his pipe and sets across the yard, and tomorrow she will leave. Tomorrow she will leave.

Acknowledgments

A number of people shared their time, knowledge, wisdom, and memories with me as I was writing this novel. I am particularly grateful to Roger Reed Jr., Al Lees, Cukie Macomber, Patricia and Arnold Tripp, Jim and Ginger Pierce, Daniel Davis Tripp, Norma Judson, Carlton Lees, Claude Ledoux, William C. White, and Ab Palmer.

For helping me to locate old charts and maps: Richie Earle, Bill Wyatt, and Sharon L. Wypych. For building me a perfect place to write: Leo Chretien. For reading earlier drafts of this book and for offering invaluable insights and corrections: Al Lees, Kim Wiley, Alison Smith, Peggy Aulisio, Pamela Tripp, Rebecca Cushing, and William C. White.

I am indebted to Capt. John Borden, who read it twice and took the time to help me get the details right.

Inestimable thanks to the team at Random House for their support and commitment, and in particular to Robin Rolewicz, Frankie Jones, and Danielle Posen; to Vincent La Scala, for his expertise and

patience; and to my editor, Kate Medina, who found the essence of
the novel and understood how it had to unfold.

Deepest gratitude to Bill Clegg, for his vision and his faith in my
work; and to Jenny Lyn Bader, for her friendship.

Finally, to my son, Jack, and to my grandfather, Arthur Noel
Clifton, who have stretched a heart beyond its known forms.

Without my husband, Steven H. Tripp, this story, as every other,
would not have been told.

Texts

For descriptions of rum-running, of the vessels and characters in-
volved, and in particular, of the seizing of the *Star* off Little Beach,
I am in debt to *The Black Ships*, by Everett S. Allen. Two other texts
that were useful: *Rum War at Sea*, by Malcolm Willoughby, and
"Westport Rum Runners," in *Spinner: People and Culture in South-
eastern Massachusetts* (vol. V, 1996), by Davison Paull. For descriptions of the season of open water, and of whaling and walrusing in
the Arctic: *The Children of the Light*, by Everett S. Allen, and *Arctic
Dreams*, by Barry Lopez. For details of Henry's experiences in World
War I: *From a Surgeon's Journal* by Harvey Cushing. For descriptions of icing: *Turtle Rock Tales*, by J. T. Smith, and David Allen's
brilliant "Interview with Everrett Coggeshall," in *Spinner* (vol. IV,
1988). For details of the 1928 New Bedford mill strike: *The Strike of
'28*, by Daniel Georgianna with Roberta Hazen Aaronson. For descriptions of Lincoln Park in the 1920s: *Lincoln Park Remembered
1894–1987*.

Bertrand T. Wood's *Noman's Land Island* is an exceptional tribute
to that place.

Finally, I am indebted to Clifford W. Ashley's classic book *The
Yankee Whaler*, which is nothing less than a treasure of an age gone
by. In particular, Ashley's moving description of the last days of
whaling in New Bedford inspired the scene of Noel's return to that

city. Also, in the glossary of Ashley's book, I came across several whaling terms that I have not found elsewhere.

The brief passage on page 221 is paraphrased from Neil Philip's retelling of the Norse Ragnarok. The following single line that has been set apart is from *Sand and Foam* by Kahlil Gibran. On page 222, the passage about swallows is from *The Travels of Birds* by Frank M. Chapman.

ABOUT THE AUTHOR

Dawn Clifton Tripp lives in Massachusetts. She is the author of *Moon Tide*.

ABOUT THE TYPE

The text of this book was set in Janson, a misnamed typeface designed in about 1690 by Nicholas Kis, a Hungarian in Amsterdam. In 1919 the matrices became the property of the Stempel Foundry in Frankfurt. It is an old-style book face of excellent clarity and sharpness. Janson serifs are concave and splayed; the contrast between thick and thin strokes is marked.